THE HIDING PLACE

part one

MURDERS UNDER THE SUN
SEASON THREE; INTRO

MOLLY: Welcome to *Murders Under the Sun*, a podcast that explores a series of unusual crimes that have occurred in sunny Southern California.

I'm Molly Shure, your host. For the past five years I've worked as a journalist at a local news outlet. Stories of murder and mayhem come across my desk weekly, if not daily. However, one day last March, I noticed something startling.

There seemed to be a connection between several crimes that transpired over a five-year period—seven crimes to be precise. What connected them? Location for one. They all took place within a twenty-mile radius of each other, but that alone wasn't significant.

The thing that pinged in my brain was that many of the people at the center of these crimes knew each other. Not the criminals, which would be an obvious thread, but the victims. I know, I know, six degrees of separation. Didn't I already say the crimes took place in a twenty-mile radius? But we're not talking six degrees here. It's more like one degree.

You'll see if you stick with me for all seven seasons of the show, the crimes circle back around. The people you meet in the first season play a role in Season Seven's story.

Am I imagining things? Is the connection real? Is there one mastermind behind the crimes? Or are they linked by some kind of social, psychological or even spiritual force? I'm afraid that's something you'll have to decide for yourself.

Each season, I'll do a deep dive into just one

of these stories. You'll hear from the people who were victimized, and listen to transcripts of journal entries, memoirs, and letters from others who were involved—sometimes the criminals themselves--and behind-the-scenes information you can't get anywhere else.

So, get out your sunglasses. We're pulling back the curtains and letting the light shine on some of Orange County's darkest mysteries.

part two

MURDERS UNDER THE SUN
SEASON THREE; EPISODE ONE

MOLLY: It's hard to believe we've arrived at Season Three already. As I promised at the end of Season Two, we have a most unusual crime this time around. I've titled it *The Hiding Place*.

As our story opens, our heroine, Abby Travers—who we met at the end of last season—has locked herself in the swallow's nest exhibit at the San Juan Capistrano Mission. She's been there for weeks. Her plan is to stay hidden for 40 days in the small room she and her father constructed.

Why? It's a really weird thing to do, but she had a reason. Abby wanted to publish a book about medieval anchorites, a group of religious men and women from the Middle Ages who engaged in a strange practice. She believed this practice—or at least a version of it—has application for people today. That it would change our modern perspective, make us more in tune with nature, more thoughtful, less shallow and self-absorbed.

I'd never heard the term anchorite until I read about this story. I assume most of you have never heard it either, but rather than trying to explain it, I'll let the expert do it. Here's a quote from Abby's writing on the topic.

The medieval anchoress would often be laid on a funeral bier and given last rites before being carried to her anchorhold, a small cell built into a cathedral wall in which she'd be entombed for the rest of her days and sometimes beyond. Some anchorholds contained the anchoress's open grave as a *memento mori*, or reminder of death.

The ceremony represented her commitment to die to the world and live for Christ. No longer a participant in the affairs of men, she became an observer, viewing the world through a window in her cell wall. The symbolic death of self—one's desires, biases and agendas—may be the only path to true objectivity.

MOLLY: Abby was fascinated by anchorites, and what she believed could be a life-changing experience for people today. However, she felt she had to do what they did if she was going to write about it. She wouldn't hide away for the rest of her life, though. That would defeat the purpose of her thesis. Who cared if you were a better person if you never came out of your cell? Nope, she decided to lock herself up for the 40 days of Lent.

The other thing you need to understand before we get into the story is why she chose the mission for her experiment. Why not hide in her bedroom? The answer is because the anchorites were observers, as she stated in her manuscript. They watched the world go by through their windows. They were in the world but not of it.

Listeners from other locations may not realize that the California missions are historical landmarks today. Most are run like museums, with tourists able to wander the grounds and view the rooms the padres and natives once occupied.

The San Juan Capistrano Mission is called the jewel of the missions. It's a beautiful property with flower gardens dotting the grounds surrounding the ruins of an old stone church and other, better preserved buildings.

It's also owned by the state, so there's only one small chapel where religious services are still held. However, Abby felt the Great Stone Church ruins were as close to a cathedral as she was going to get in Southern California. When I interviewed her, she also admitted she hoped the stunt would help her get a publisher and spark publicity for the book.

I've done my best to write her story in a way that will bring her experience alive for you. Along with Abby's narrative, I'll be reading emails from a mystery woman. The emails were written by this woman—who we'll call The Wife—to her cousin. The Wife was deeply involved in the crimes. Understandably, her cousin asked that she remain anonymous, so I've redacted the greetings and signatures.

As in previous seasons of the podcast, you'll find out who the mystery woman is when Abby does and not before. To maintain The Wife's anonymity, I've also taken out the names of her family members. Her husband and son will be referred to by their relationship to her, not by name until her identity is revealed.

I think that's all you need to know before we begin. So, without further ado, here's Abby.

3.1.2

THE SNAP OF BRANCHES, a wet thud, and a strangled wheeze woke Abby. The sounds weren't loud, but she'd only been in a half-sleep. She slipped out of her bedroll, crossed the dirt floor to the squint her father had made for her and peered out.

Her view was limited. To the right, she could see as far as the public restrooms, to the left, the spot where the path that led to the cemetery and Father Serra Chapel disappeared around a bend. There was a grassy area directly in front of her on the other side of that same path, beyond that was a barrier of shrubbery, and finally, the concrete wall that separated the San Juan Capistrano Mission grounds from the city outside. This had been her only vista for the past twenty-one days.

As she stared into the night, she saw a pair of booted feet move through the bushes, followed by a pair of sneakers. "This is stupid," a hushed voice, young and male, said. His head and torso were invisible to Abby, hidden behind foliage.

"Shut up. Do as you're told." The older man had a deep voice and an accent she couldn't place.

There was more rustling of brush and the two men, the crescent of a body dangling between them, emerged from the bushes. Their faces were masked by shadows, but their builds were so similar she guessed they were father and son—the heavier man a preview of what the younger would become in time.

They side-stepped to the open area. A whine of air, like the exhalation of a balloon, came from the form as they laid it on the grass. Without another word, the men turned to the wall they'd just climbed. Before they disappeared into the shrubbery again, the younger of the two looked over his shoulder. For a brief moment half his face was illuminated by the moonlight. His dark eyes and high cheekbones wore an expression Abby couldn't read. It might as easily have been annoyance as regret. Then the men were gone.

The person, if it was a person—it could have been a large dog, she hadn't gotten a good look—lay unmoving where they'd left it. Her heart thudded in her chest. What should she do?

Abby couldn't leave her cell. Not without help. Her father had wanted to give her an escape hatch, but she'd said no. The experience had to be as realistic as possible. If she could come and go whenever she wanted, it would defeat the whole purpose. But she'd never imagined something like this would happen.

Guilt and anxiety itched like a hair shirt. What on earth had possessed her to take six weeks off work to lock herself in these four walls? She hadn't anticipated this feeling of helplessness. She'd only thought about the peace solitude can bring and her publishing goals, of course. She pushed herself off the stones, walked five steps to the other end of her enclosure, pivoted, and took five steps back. Repeat. Repeat.

It had to be a dog.

People wouldn't toss another human being over a wall like a pile of trash. A dog was bad. No, it was terrible. But a person...

She peered out of her tiny window at the black bundle on the grass. The moon was almost full, but the shape was blanketed in shadow, impossible to decipher. She didn't think it was breathing, couldn't detect any rise or fall. She'd heard that whine when the men laid it down, but didn't bodies emit gasses and noises after death? She was sure she'd read that somewhere.

The longer she stared, the more it looked like a dog. Maybe it was a trick of her eyes, but after a while she thought she saw its tail trailing out into the moonlight.

On the outside chance it was alive and might be comforted by her voice, she began to sing. She'd learned the old hymn, "Nearer My God to Thee" from her Lutheran grandmother. "Though like the wanderer, the sun gone down. Darkness be over me, my rest a stone. Yet in my—"

A wail, hollow and otherworldly, shattered the night.

Horror tripped up Abby's spine like an electric shock. She flew to the squint. The black form, now on its side, bore an unmistakably female shape. "God. God. God." The prayer escaped her lips. The woman outside, her voice pained and pleading, uttered words in a strange language. "I don't understand you. I'm so sorry, I don't understand." Despair flooded Abby's veins.

She ran to the one loose stone near the floor of her small cell and slid it from the wall. A soft breeze brushed her face. The opening was too small for her to squeeze through, but maybe she could enlarge it. She gripped the stone above the space and pulled with all her strength. It didn't budge. She planted her feet on either side of it, held on with both hands and put her legs and back into the effort. On the day she entered the anchorhold, her father had cemented this stone in place behind her. She knew she could fit through the opening if she could remove it.

She struggled and strained for long minutes. Nothing shifted.

She thought about digging her way out. The floor was dirt, but the dirt was packed down hard. It would take hours, more hours than she had before daylight. Besides, she had nothing to dig with.

She wiped at the sweat rolling down her forehead and looked frantically around her enclosure for a tool. Maybe she had something she could use as a crowbar to pry the stone loose with. Her bed was only a roll of foam laid on the floor with a few blankets on top. No help. A stump of a candle, a book, and a pack of matches lay on the floor next to it.

Her gaze flitted to the camp chair on the other wall. Its legs were aluminum—the only metal she'd brought with her. She tore off the canvas seat, placed one of the leg joints across her knee and leaned her body weight into it. She heard a satisfying pop, but all she'd managed to do was bend the leg at an odd angle.

Still, it might work. She dragged the chair to the wall and struck the cement with the misshapen leg. It bounced away with a hollow ping.

She struck it again and again, but only managed to chip away a tiny piece of concrete. This would take all night and half the next day. The woman would be found long before Abby managed to escape.

The woman.

She ran to the squint—a narrow rectangle of a window too small for much more than air to pass through—to check on her.

Labored pants filled her ears. Abby gripped her hair and squeezed her eyes shut. *Think. Think.* What could she do? She had no phone. It was the middle of the night, if she called out for help, no one would hear.

She threw herself against the iron bars of the squint in frustration. It was a useless gesture. Even if she could remove them, she'd never fit through the opening. "Please, I can't come out. I'm trying, but I can't." She heard the tears in her own voice.

Anguished moans were the only reply. The woman didn't understand Abby's words any more than Abby understood hers. Abby slid down the wall and sat on the cold dirt. She hugged herself with both arms and rocked as if she could comfort the stranger on the grass by proxy and began to pray.

As minutes became hours, her prayers for human help became prayers for the ease of pain. As the moans became less frequent and more hushed, she prayed for the woman's acceptance into God's loving arms.

Abby wanted to watch, to keep a vigil. It was the least she could do. The only thing she could do. But emotion had exhausted her, and she dozed.

When she woke, black night had turned to gray morning. She stood, her body stiff and aching. She knew she should look out, check on the woman, but she was afraid she'd be dead.

She dragged herself to the squint and peered through the bars. The form on the grass was young; a girl, not a woman. She was younger than Abby's twenty-eight years, but her face had been aged by illness, or neglect, or both. Her eyes were red hollows. Despite the bloodless pallor of her skin, Abby could tell her complexion had once been olive.

She was slight, thin to the point of emaciation. Knots of elbows and bony forearms protruded from the tattered sleeves of a threadbare blouse. The only thing of beauty Abby saw was what she'd assumed to be a dog's tail the night before. A ponytail of shining black hair spread out behind the young woman, hinting at what she'd looked like in health.

There was no breath. No movement. And something in the way the body lay, told Abby it was empty. As if to prove the point, a squirrel scurried over and sniffed an outstretched hand. Moments later a scrub jay landed only feet away and searched the grass for its morning meal, unruffled by any human presence. The girl was gone. Abby sank to the floor of her cell and let grief wash over her.

3.1.3

SEVERAL HOURS LATER, Abby heard footsteps on the concrete path. It was too early for the Mission to be open, so it must be an employee or volunteer. She didn't have a clock in her cell but gauged the time by the passage of the sun. It was amazing how quickly the rhythms of life became second nature. Most people were oblivious to the nuances of the planet's rotation, the seasons, the habits of the animals around them.

They noticed the obvious things: day, night, cold and heat, but they didn't notice the difference between eight o'clock's shadows and nine o'clock's. They couldn't feel the slight change in barometric pressure on the night before a storm. They didn't look for danger when birds stopped singing.

Abby had been no different. Like everyone else, she'd gone into panic mode whenever she misplaced her cell phone. She'd relied on the weather app to tell her things she could have learned by walking out the front door. Her phone was one of the hardest things for her to leave behind, but she was glad she had. She'd discovered this ability to read the environment her second day in the anchorhold, and it had grown since.

She braced herself for the reaction of the person coming down the path. She could tell by the heavy tread it was a man. Her natural inclination was to warn him, but she squelched it. What was done was done. The girl was dead, and revealing herself wouldn't change anything. No one knew Abby was tucked away behind the wall of swallows' nests. No one but her father. She might give this poor man a heart attack if she called through the squint. Finding a body was bad enough, no sense making it worse.

The man came into her line of vision at the same time the dead girl came into his. He was a garden volunteer. She'd seen him several times over the past four weeks. He looked to be in his thirties, blond hair pulled into a lazy bun at the back of his head, beard and mustache. His name was Steven. She'd heard other volunteers and employees interact with him and was sorry he was the one to find the girl. Abby liked his kind way and his humor. She was sure the girl's agonized expression would stay with him for the rest of his life. It wasn't an image easily forgotten.

Abby smelled the tang of fertilizer from the bag he carried, heard his sharp intake of breath, saw his face grow almost as pale as the body's. He set the bag down and took a tentative step toward the corpse. "Are you... are you okay?"

Of course, he got no answer. She didn't think he really expected to. The higher the sun rose in the sky, the more dead the girl looked.

"Hey. Do you need help?" He moved closer and stood for several moments with one hand on his head, the other on his hip. He pivoted and looked up the path the way he'd come as if expecting help to manifest. He turned to the body again and squatted on his haunches. He put a finger on its shoulder and gave it a gentle nudge.

It rocked stiffly and thudded back in place. Rigor must have started. He leaped away and rubbed his hand on his jeans. He pulled a cell phone from his pocket and began punching numbers as he ran up the concrete path and out of sight.

When the shadow of the Great Stone Church ruins had shifted fifteen degrees—about a half hour later—Abby's quiet world was invaded. A battalion of uniformed and plainclothes officials arrived on the scene. Four police officers, a Mission security guard, two paramedics,

Grant Hawthorne—the Mission Director—and a female detective, all hovered around the perimeter of the crime scene tape they'd just installed. Abby pressed herself against the wall of her cell, restricting the view from her squint. She could see the detective, a petite, athletic looking black woman, who stood only yards away, but not much more.

"Detective Sylla, what do we know about this?" Grant moved into view. The half of his face Abby could see looked distraught.

"Not much. The crime scene techs are on their way." Her voice was clipped. Her accent British.

"Who is she?" Grant asked the question at the front of Abby's mind. She felt a connection to the girl. She was, after all, the last person to talk to her. Or try to talk to her. She wanted to know her name.

"That we don't know. She doesn't have any I.D. on her. Unless somebody claims her. . ."

"How did she die?"

"There's no sign of violence." Sylla shrugged. "We'll have to wait on the ME for the cause."

"Could it have been suicide?"

"She was alive when she got here," Sylla said. "You can see that by the disturbance in the dirt." She gestured toward the body. "But I don't think she climbed that wall herself. Not in that condition."

"So, what are you saying? You think it was murder? I thought you said there weren't any signs of violence." Grant's voice shook.

"She could have been starved, or poisoned, or just ill and left to die. We won't know until after the autopsy."

"Why would someone leave her here? At the Mission?"

"I could ask you the same question. She look familiar? Volunteer? Relative of an employee?"

"No. I've never seen her before."

Neither said anything for several minutes. Abby dropped to the floor, her back against the wall. Was it murder if the girl was alive when she was left on the grass?

"The mayor is concerned—" he said.

Detective Sylla interrupted, "You can tell the mayor, it's a crime to dump a body on public property whether you murder it first or not."

"I understand that, but there is a distinction."

"The ME is here." Sylla's words were abrupt, as if she didn't agree. The determined crunch of her footsteps moved away from Abby's window.

Sylla was right. This was a crime, officially and certainly, but Abby sympathized with the Director. There was a distinction between murder and other crimes. Just like some sins were venial and some were mortal. If this was murder, Abby would have to reveal herself, tell the police what she saw and heard. If it wasn't... Well, if it wasn't, she would have to weigh the cost.

It had taken her over a year and all her savings to put this plan into action. She'd begun formulating it when she read Mike Yankoski's book, *Under the Overpass*. Mike had left his middle-class existence for five long months to live with the homeless, without resources, wandering from city to city, sleeping on the streets. Then he wrote about it. The story moved Abby in a way few others had, and it provided the missing piece of her puzzle—how to approach the book she wanted to write.

Two years ago, she'd read an article in the paper about the archaeological excavation of a medieval anchorhold in England. She hadn't known such a thing existed. She was fascinated. What kind of person would consign themselves to a small cell for the remainder of their lives?

As she researched the men and women who became anchorites, her fascination turned to admiration. To walk away from the lure of society, to cease playing the game, that took strength of character. Did she have that strength?

Abby knew she couldn't give up the entirety of her life, but could she do it for a time? A significant amount of time? Not a day or a week, but for forty days—the period of Lent? The challenge grew in her like the challenge of running a marathon grows in some people. She wanted to try. She wanted to hide in the midst of people. She wanted to observe life and resist the temptation to be a part of it.

It was a wild idea, but it appealed to her. Ever since she graduated from the local junior college with an AA in English, she'd been seeking a career path. She'd always dreamed of becoming an author but had no idea what to write about. Until she'd discovered anchorites, then it had taken her another year to figure out how to approach the project.

If she exposed herself now, not only would her race be over before she reached the finish line, but she'd have a lot of explaining to do. The world would find out about her anchorhold one day, but she'd hoped it would be as part of a marketing plan for her new book. She planned to pay the Mission Foundation to forgive her trespass by donating a percentage of her royalties—an indulgence.

If she came out of hiding now, with no literary agent, no publisher, she would be dismissed as an eccentric. A crazy woman. The Mission would probably press charges. Her father would lose his career.

It had been quiet outside for too long. Curiosity brought Abby to her feet. She sidled over to her window and peered out. Two men talked with Detective Sylla. They stood too far away for Abby to hear their conversation. When the huddle broke up, one of the men began unpacking a black bag. The other snapped shots of the area with a long-lensed camera.

Sylla walked toward the squint where Grant still stood. Abby retreated into a dark corner. They couldn't see her. Abby and her father had tested the window several times in all different kinds of light. As long as there was no candle lit, no one could see in, but having people so close to her hiding place made her nervous, nonetheless.

"Three to four hours," Sylla said.

"I can open after that?" Grant sounded relieved.

"Yes."

"Can I count on your discretion with the press? This month is the Swallows Fiesta. It's the height of tourist season."

"I avoid the press whenever I can."

"Good. I'll call the mayor."

"Give him my best." Sylla's voice carried a tinge of sarcasm.

Abby sat on her bedroll since she'd destroyed the chair. She'd take this time to pray through her devotions. She wasn't devout. Not like her father. But she tried to keep the Ancrene Rule, the book of laws and prayers that guided the anchorites of the Middle Ages. She wanted to make this experience as real as possible. The prayers laid out in the book took close to four hours. It had taken her a week of practice just to stay awake for the process. Now she found it soothing. Like meditation.

She would add prayers for the passage of the girl's soul to her list.

She felt a responsibility, since she'd been the only one in attendance at her death. She'd also pray for wisdom about her current predicament. Should she, or shouldn't she, break her own vows, come out of her cell and tell the police what she knew? She hoped the answer would be made clear. She closed her eyes and began.

$$3.1.4$$

THE MID-MARCH DAYS WERE LENGTHENING. Her father wouldn't come until after dark, and impatience drove Abby to pacing. She hadn't learned anything else. The ME and paramedics zipped the girl into a body bag, placed her on a gurney, and rolled her away. The crime scene techs had been the last to go. They completed their investigation, packed up the tools of their trade, gathered their evidence bags, removed the tape, and the Mission filled with blissfully ignorant tourists.

Abby guessed the girl's death hadn't been violent, as Sylla had said, or the Sheriff's department wouldn't have released the scene. But she was no closer to knowing what had caused her death, or who she'd been. She'd have to wait until her father arrived with food and water. He'd have news. But the waiting was driving her to distraction.

Paul Travers, Abby's father, managed the Mission's gift shop. Employees would be informed about the event, if for no other reason than to brief them on how to talk to tourists. But he had an added reason to find out everything he could since the body was left right outside Abby's hiding place. He must be worried about her. He and Grant Hawthorne were friends. She had no doubt her father would know everything Grant did by the end of the day.

The end of the day. That was forever from now by her reckoning.

The hardest part of this entire experiment had been the waiting. She'd never realized before what a hard taskmaster time was. Outside, distractions were everywhere. Her cell phone alone had made hours fly by like seconds. But inside time crept inch by slow moving inch across her cell in bands of light. She'd been in her anchorhold less than a month and was counting not just the days, but the hours and the minutes until her release.

How had the anchorites of the Middle Ages managed to live a lifetime like this? The anchorhold was their home as long as they were alive and often their grave when they died. The saving grace, she supposed, was they had social interaction. Unlike hermits, or those who entered monasteries, the anchorite did live in the center of town. Their holds were built onto cathedral walls. The public streamed by their windows, and often stopped for prayer, wisdom, or to buy small handcrafts the anchoress made. Abby didn't have that luxury.

She'd chosen the Mission for her anchorhold, because it was the closest thing to a cathedral in Southern California. It was busy during the days, not with parishioners but with tourists. Still, it allowed her to watch. To observe humanity. This was an important task for the anchorite, and one Abby could do. But when the tourists left, time slowed and grew fuzzy around the edges.

She shared the far wall of her cell with the Old Stone Church. It had collapsed in 1812, taking forty souls with it. The ghosts said to inhabit the ruins never appeared to her, but she often thought she heard their whispering voices and saw flickers of otherworldly candles.

Night in the anchorhold had taken some getting used to. It was filled with unease and mystery. Vibrations of an invisible world hummed in the stones around her. Time seemed a thing without borders or meaning.

Darkness finally began its descent, and the last of the visitors faded into the dusk. A security guard thudded past in his heavy boots. He was making his final circuit before locking up. Once while she'd been secluded here, she'd heard him roust a homeless man out of the bushes. He'd checked the perimeter of the Mission grounds at the same time every evening since, walking past her small cell oblivious to her presence.

Soon the birds began their bedtime songs. The chirp of crickets filled the spaces between the noises of the cars passing on El Camino Real. The scent of night blooming angel's trumpet flowers, and the sour smell of her camp toilet permeated the air. Her father was late. As if responding to the thought, her stomach rumbled. It was used to being fed at eight o'clock. Based on the sharpness of her hunger pangs, it was past that now.

About a half hour later, Abby heard the soft tread of tennis shoes on the gravel path outside. She ran to the squint. Her father looked toward the window and nodded. He couldn't see her but knew she'd be there.

She tripped across her enclosure to the loose stone and slid it from its place in the wall. She didn't dare leave it open during the day for fear someone would notice, but at night it was a blessed relief. Fresh, clean air streamed through the opening.

"You must be starved. Sorry I'm late. I was at a committee meeting for the Swallows Day Parade. It ran over," her father said.

The aromas of rosemary and beef gravy made the rumbles begin again. A covered bowl appeared on the floor in front of her, followed by a plastic bag she knew would contain silverware, napkins, and a metal bottle filled with iced tea or juice.

She pulled the food into her lap and breathed a prayer of thanks. She loved her father's beef stew.

"Want to hand me the camp toilet? I'll dump it while you eat." Her father took it to the public restroom at the end of the path each night and cleaned it for her. It had taken her several days to get over the embarrassment, but it was part of the humbling process.

An anchoress must learn to receive the ministrations of others with gratitude. According to the Ancrene Rule, her role was to devote herself to intercession and holiness, not to worldly tasks. Of course, she believed her father would be blessed for helping her. That was the only thing that assuaged her guilt about asking for this sacrifice from him. She slid the toilet out.

When he returned, she asked him about the girl between bites of food.

He sighed. "It's tragic."

"Yes, but who was she? How did she die?"

"Nobody knows who she was. She died of some kind of illness."

"Not murder?"

"They don't think so, but they can't be sure until after the autopsy. But murder or not, the girl had been horribly neglected."

An image of skinny arms jutting from a threadbare shirt came into her mind. "She was thin."

"She'd been starved, at least that's what the medical examiner said."

"I thought maybe it was cancer."

"They don't think it was cancer. She might have been anorexic, but the state of the clothing makes it more likely she'd been living in poverty." He paused. "Or captivity. But, as I said, they don't know the cause of death yet."

"And they have no idea where she came from?"

"No. Nobody's reported anyone of her description missing."

"She couldn't have been in the States long. She didn't speak English." The memory of the night before hovered close, threatening to overwhelm Abby again. She shut her heart against it, dug a piece of crusty bread out of the bag and began mopping up gravy with it.

"What?"

"I tried to talk to her—"

"You talked to her?" He sounded shocked.

"Yes." Abby almost choked on the word. It sounded terrible. It sounded like she hadn't cared, hadn't been frantic to help.

"She was alive? Talking?" His voice was louder this time.

"I tried to get out, to get to her." Guilt and grief engulfed Abby. She set the bowl and bread on the floor; appetite gone.

"You saw the people who left her here." It was a statement, not a question.

"Yes." Her voice dropped to something just above a whisper.

"How many?"

"Two. I didn't see them clearly. It was dark. They were in the shadows."

"You have to come out. You have to tell the police."

"But if it wasn't murder—"

"It doesn't matter. These men might have been able to save her if they'd taken her to a hospital instead of throwing her over a wall. That's

got to be manslaughter, or criminal neglect. I know it's some crime."
Her father was angry. She heard the growl in his voice she'd heard so
many times through her bedroom wall before her mother died.

He was right, of course, but Abby was torn. She'd invested so much,
given up so much, to be where she was. And, she only had two more
weeks. The end was in sight. Part of the premise of her book was that
the forty-day period was a sacred time, a time of renewal. If she didn't
complete it, the entire experiment would be a loss.

Then what would she have? All her savings had gone into building
the anchorhold, and she wouldn't be able to return to it if she left. Her
father had agreed to help her once. She didn't want to ask him to do it
again.

She had her job at St. Barnabas but had put any thought of career
growth on hold until her dream of becoming an author either came to
pass or died. She'd put Carlos on hold. She'd put everything on hold.
The idea of abandoning the book now was more than she could bear.

Not to mention, if she did reveal to the police where she was when
she saw the men... She groaned audibly. She had no other choice, but she
dreaded it. It would reinforce what people already thought, that there
was a crazy gene in the Travers family.

Her father's voice broke into her thoughts. "What if I went to the
police?"

"What good would that do? You didn't see the men," she said.

"What if I said I did? You could tell me everything you saw. I could
say I left work late—"

"You didn't, though. Tallulah always locks up. She probably saw you
leave."

"Then I forgot something and went back for it." Her father paused.
"I forgot my phone." He gained confidence as he spoke. "On my way
home, I saw two men near the east wall of the Mission on El Camino
Real. I didn't think anything about it at the time, but when I heard
about the girl, I realized it might be connected."

"Dad." Her voice sounded weary. "You've supported me through
this whole thing, but it's over. It's gone far enough." She paused. "Did
you bring the crowbar?"

He had supported her. He'd even presented the proposal to Grant

Hawthorne as if it had been his idea and took on the task of building the hold. Prior to her father's improvements, there had only been a flimsy false wall supported by scaffolding to house the swallows' nests. He'd made a beautiful structure that was both more stable and that blended with the Old Stone Church ruins.

Abby's grandfather had been in construction, and her father had worked for the family business when he was young. He had experience in stone masonry and bricklaying and offered to build the structure at no expense to the Mission. Miraculously, both the Diocese and the foundation agreed. Even the city released permits for the project, which Abby had interpreted as signs from the Divine.

She hadn't wanted to test God any further, however. She didn't believe anyone would agree to her plan to move into the hold for six weeks. She'd entered in secrecy, which suited her just fine. "Do your good deeds in secret, and God will reward you openly." That's what the Bible said. However, prayers and miracles notwithstanding, she couldn't have done any of this without her father.

"But don't you see, it's perfect. The police will get the information they need. You can finish what you've started. And I have a rational reason to have been here late at night."

"It's my civic and moral duty to report this." Abby said the words with as much conviction as she could muster.

"You could be prosecuted if you come forward."

"For vagrancy. That's a fine, nothing more."

"You didn't call out to the police when they were here. Isn't that aiding and abetting, or something illegal? Not to mention, I could lose my job for aiding and abetting you."

It was her turn to be quiet. He was right. He could lose his job, and going to the police now would mean public humiliation even if she wasn't in legal trouble. Their family had experienced enough of that. "Well..."

"I'm going to do this. For both of us," he said. "Tell me what you saw."

Abby exhaled and began.

3.1.5

THE NEXT MORNING feathers of sunlight slanted through Abby's squint and brushed against her closed eyelids teasing them open. The first week she'd been in the anchorhold, she'd slept hard, and a lot. Maybe it was inactivity, maybe the desire to plant her itchy fingers on a keyboard again, but she'd only slept five or six hours a night since.

She stretched, pulled her knees to her chest and rocked into a sitting position. Coffee. She missed coffee. She reached for the thermos of water her father had left for her the night before and took a sip. It was lukewarm and tasted stale. She almost spit it out but resisted. It was all she had until after dark.

She dropped her chin to her chest and rolled her head, first right and then left. Sleeping on the ground had made her painfully aware of joints she'd hitherto taken for granted. Her back especially, injured in a ski accident years earlier, ached for the first hour of the day.

Footsteps and voices floated through her window into the anchorhold. It had to be garden volunteers. They were the only ones who came to the Mission this early in the morning.

She stretched, then stood and took the two steps to her window. Steven, the man who'd found the girl's body, and a woman stood at the flower bed across from the restroom. The woman was petite, forty-ish and Asian. Abby could hear the rise and fall of voices, but not the words. Based on the gestures, Steven was explaining the morning chores.

She'd gotten very good at lip reading and body language in the past three weeks. Abby tested this new talent regularly. She'd watch people as they came up the path from the Old Stone Church exhibit, watch their expressions, their gestures, opened her heart to theirs. It was easier to intuit when emotion was high. However, she'd know what they were talking about more often than not, even when the conversation was casual.

She didn't understand why she was able to do this, but she had a theory. Truth became obvious when one had no opinion or agenda. As an observer, her heart was a blank page for others to write on. Of course, it could also be that when one sense is limited, others grow stronger. The deaf are better at reading body language than most. The blind are more sensitive to the shades of meaning behind people's words. Abby's growing talent was people-watching.

Steven and the Asian woman walked around the corner and out of her field of vision. Abby turned her back to the window, took a hairbrush from the backpack that contained her clothing and toiletries and began to brush the night tangles from her hair. It was Thursday.

On Thursday nights, her father brought the prior week's laundry to her, washed and folded, and she gave him her soiled things. On Thursday mornings, she poured water into the large plastic bowl she used as a sink, washed and put on her last fresh outfit.

She took her time, enjoying the feel of cool water on her skin and the smell of clean clothes. The floor of her anchorhold was packed dirt. She was always dusty except for a brief period after bathing. She knew by evening she'd feel grit on her scalp and under her fingernails again. She slipped on a flannel shirt and fastened the first button.

"Abby." A hushed voice shot past her.

"Dad?" She held her shirt together and moved to the squint. "What's wrong?" When she entered the anchorhold, they'd decided her father would only come to her after dark and after the Mission closed. It was dangerously close to opening time.

"I went to the police this morning."

"What did they say? Did they believe your story?"

"They had no reason to doubt it."

"Good. So, everything is good."

"No, everything isn't good. They want me to sit with a sketch artist and try to come up with a picture of the man I saw on Tuesday night. Thank God, the artist wasn't available today. But I'm supposed to meet with her in a couple of days. You have to come out tonight. Talk to her." Abby didn't say anything. Her thoughts were spinning.

"If I come out now, what am I going to tell them? I didn't come forward when I should have, and you lied to the police?"

A look of startled dismay crossed his face. "Damn it." Abby flinched. Her father rarely cursed since her mother had died.

"This is why I said—"

"I know," he barked.

"Lies breed more—"

"I know, but what's done is done. Let's think about the next step."

"The next step should be honesty."

"How is honesty going to help that poor girl? She's dead. Making a public spectacle of ourselves isn't going to bring her back." He paced in front of her window.

He was right. In Abby's experience, public spectacles didn't just blow over. They took years of effort to overcome.

"Those men can't be allowed to go free," she said.

"I agree, but you didn't see them clearly. You said the younger one had high cheekbones. He looked a little exotic. His hair was dark. That was it, and you didn't see the older one's face at all."

"They say you always see more than you think you did. Sketch artists know how to ask questions, how to pull things out of your subconscious."

"What if there's nothing in your subconscious? You said you saw his cheeks and eyes. No nose. No mouth. You can't give them what you don't have, Abby."

"Well, what are you supposed to do then? They're going to ask you things you never—" She clamped her mouth shut.

Abby had seen movement behind her father. Steven and the woman walked toward them, eyes fixed on him. She didn't know how long they'd been there, on the path. Long enough to see him having a heated conversation with a wall based on their faces.

Her father must have heard their footsteps. He glanced around. "Steven. Good morning." He stepped away from the squint and onto the path.

"Hey, Paul." Steven's eyes were wide and questioning.

"I thought I'd found a quiet place to practice my address to the Swallows Day committee. I'm a little nervous about it. Politics, you know."

For someone who hated lying, her father did it smoothly. Steven's face relaxed. "This is Mimi Jackson. Mimi, this is Paul Travers. He runs the gift shop."

"I know who Mimi is, although we've not officially met." He shook her hand. "You're my new neighbor. I've been meaning to come by with cookies or a plant."

"I thought you looked familiar," Mimi said. "Please, stop by. You don't need to bring a thing. I'd love to pick your brains about the history of my new house. I understand it's a bit nefarious."

Abby sat up straighter. Mimi must have purchased Sage's house. Her father hadn't told her it sold. It had been abandoned months ago when Sage left town. Actually, rumor had it she'd left the country— gone to live with relatives in Mexico. Abby couldn't blame her after everything that had happened.

"It's not a happy history," Paul said.

That was an understatement.

The three stood in awkward silence for a long moment. "Well, we were just heading out," Steven said.

"I'll walk you as far as the gift shop," Paul said.

"I don't know what your talk is about, but you certainly sounded persuasive," Mimi said as the three walked out of sight.

Abby collapsed on her bedroll. How had this spun so far out of control? The last thing she wanted to do was cause problems for her father. He'd had enough of them in his life. He was a strong man, but Scottie's accident and her mother's descent into madness had almost killed him at the time. It had taken years for him to heal. Those old memories were revived by the same events that had driven Sage from her home. Abby didn't have to run, the way Sage had, but she'd felt the need to take some kind of action.

Her solution was the anchorhold. She would bury those painful days in its walls. She would rewrite, if not their past, their future. Her book would launch a new chapter for both her and her father. Now she wondered if that was still possible.

3.1.6

BY AFTERNOON the temperature had risen. March's usual pleasant seventy degrees had spiked to eighty. Abby's nose began to itch. The dry Santa Ana winds must be on their way.

She was restless, more restless than usual. Another sign the winds were coming. She circled the small enclosure like a tiger in a zoo.

A laugh rang through the air, loud in the aridity. She knew the laugh. It was Tallulah's.

She ran to the squint and peered through the bars, seeking the woman belonging to the voice. A moment later she appeared, coming from the direction of the Serra Chapel.

Abby was never certain what Tallulah's job title was. She assisted her father in the gift shop, ran interference for Grant Hawthorne, and flitted from department to department like a hummingbird seeking sustenance. Abby loved Tallulah, and she loved Tallulah's fashion sense. Every outfit was entertainment, and Lord knows, she needed a distraction.

Abby smiled as she watched the woman who'd been more of a mother to her than her own had come into view. Her dark skin glowed in the warm afternoon sun. Her tall, elegant frame was swathed in black and white stripes today—more Parisian than zebra. She walked side by side with another woman, almost as tall, but not dressed with half the panache.

The second woman was white, but her cheekbones and eyes gave her an ethnic appearance. Short, dark hair curled around a delicate face. Her smile was wide.

"Bridezilla?" Tallulah asked.

"No, Momzilla." The ethnic-looking woman said in an alto voice. "She's planning the wedding. The daughter roped me into doing the decorating, so I'd be the one banging heads with her mother. I don't do events often. Now I remember why."

"My mother planned my wedding. I wore white, carried star lilies, and the guests ate chicken whether they wanted it or not." Tallulah punctuated each item with her finger. "It never occurred to me to argue."

"I'm from New England. In my family you married the way your mother, grandmother, and great grandmother married before you. If you were lucky, you got a new dress and didn't have to wear one of theirs, but there were no guarantees."

Tallulah's musical laugh rang out again. "I take it this wedding is a bit more complicated."

"Let's say, I've got a new respect for tradition. The mother-of-the-bride has changed her mind about everything from the flowers to the color of the table linens at least five times. I told her yesterday she's running out of time. The wedding is in three months. She's got to make some hard decisions."

Abby pressed herself against the wall as the women passed her hold leaving behind a whiff of spice and lavender. "Makes me thankful I only have a son. His future wife's mother can do all the heavy lifting," Tallulah said.

"I have both, but I hope and pray my daughter and I will behave ourselves when the momentous occasion arrives."

"You tell that Momzilla she'd better not be wishy-washy about the venue, Rosie. We've got people waiting in line for that June date."

Rosie paused by a star jasmine and fingered a blossom. "I can imagine. It's beautiful here. The flowers are spectacular."

"A lot of it is maintained by our gardening volunteers."

"One of my clients just joined the team. If I could squeeze the time out of my schedule, I'd do it with her."

"Who's your client?"

"Her name is Mimi. You know the house at the end of Los Rios? The one that's been vacant for the past couple of months?"

Abby was startled. Rosie was talking about Sage's old house. Strange, the new owner had been on the path just this morning.

Tallulah's eyes widened. "The one where…"

"Yeah." Rosie nodded. "That one."

"That place sold?" Tallulah put a hand on her heart. "It has some bad juju."

Rosie shrugged. "The Jacksons didn't ask a lot of questions. They were happy to get it. Homes like that don't exist in Orange County anymore. Not this close to the beach."

"I wouldn't live there."

"The yard needs some help. It's gotten overgrown since the woman who owned it moved. I've recommended Carlos Rojo for the job."

Abby peered at Rosie through her squint. She'd heard Carlos talk about an interior designer who threw business his way on occasion. Rosie must be that designer.

"Carlos is wonderful. He's my gardener." Tallulah's tone lifted, and Abby smiled.

"You work for Paul Travers, correct?" Rosie asked in an abrupt change of subject.

"Yes. You know him?"

"I've met him, and I've heard Carlos talk about him. And his daughter Abby, of course."

"Paul loves that boy," Tallulah said. "In fact, he would be the happiest man on earth if those two would tie the knot."

Tallulah loved Carlos. Abby's father loved Carlos. Everybody, it seemed, loved Carlos. Abby's brow furrowed. She was pretty sure she loved him too, but it was complicated.

The two women made a right and disappeared from view, their voices trailing off. Abby threw herself on her foam mattress. Like the bride Rosie was working for, Abby had dreamed of a June wedding at the Mission when she was a little girl. Now. . . Now she didn't know.

She wondered if marriage and children were a wise decision for her. Emotional stability didn't run in her family. Her mother had walked steadily into insanity after Scottie was killed. Her father had been hospitalized due to a breakdown after her mother died.

When Carlos asked her to marry him, she panicked. She knew he wanted children—lots of them. As much as she loved the idea, she wasn't sure she was the right one to bear them. If there was such a thing as a "crazy" gene, she didn't want to inflict it on the next generation. She'd asked him for time, and she'd had it. A month had passed, but she wasn't any closer to an answer.

She hadn't told him where she'd be thinking things over, about her decision to cloister herself at the mission for Lent. She'd known he wouldn't like it and had avoided the topic while she was getting the anchorhold ready. Procrastination set in. No time ever seemed like the right time. She'd planned to tell him the day before Lent started, but they got into that stupid argument.

She couldn't talk to him about the book. Every time the subject was raised, his jaw clenched and that little muscle in front of his ear twitched. He hated it. He thought she was obsessed with anchorites.

Oh, he didn't use the word "obsessed." He wouldn't. He knew Abby associated that word with her mother's behavior. But it's what he thought. Abby rolled onto her side and squeezed her eyes shut. How could they ever marry if he had no respect for her life's work?

Her life's work. Is that what this was? Or was it just a vain attempt to hide from her past? Or worse, to avoid making decisions about her future? The past stretched out behind her, the future in front, and she was paralyzed between them. She didn't know how to interpret the messages of her family history. She was uncertain about what was to come.

She'd removed herself from society, to gain insight into her life. But had she? She felt just as unsure today as she had on the first day of Lent. She hoped the last two weeks would give her clarity, but instead doubt had crept in. Did solitude hold the answers after all?

At this moment, she longed for a conversation with Tallulah. Wanted a heart to heart over a cup of spiced tea. Wanted to ask her opinion about anchorites, and June weddings, and Carlos, and police investigations.

Entering the anchorhold had seemed like such a good idea at the time, brilliant even, but the girl had changed everything. For the past two days, whenever Abby closed her eyes, she saw that dead face and the shining, black ponytail spreading out behind it.

MOLLY: Before we end the episode, I have two emails to read from the woman we are calling The Wife. The first is a record of what happened the day before the girl was dropped outside Abby's squint. The second continues her story the next day.

the wife

REGARDING OUR PHONE CONVERSATION, I agree. Having a written record of these events is important. I want someone to know my side of the story. I'm afraid it's going to get ugly.

On the night my life began to slide into hell, I sat on the couch in my living room savoring my last ten minutes of peace. My husband would be home soon, and that meant dinner, dishes, and all the usual evening chores.

When I heard the front door open, I slipped the magazine I'd been reading under the couch cushion. My husband doesn't approve of *O*, or Oprah. Women who never marry or, worse yet, create empires are dangerous aberrations as far as he's concerned. I find Oprah fascinating, but I kept those thoughts to myself. It was better to keep the peace.

"Where are you? I have a surprise for you." He sounded cheerful.

I hurried to the front hall, and almost collided with him. Behind him, hiding in his shadow, stood a bedraggled wraith of a girl. He pushed her forward. "This is Hannah. Seb brought her all the way from Egypt just for you."

The girl was emaciated and unnaturally pale. Her eyes were sunken. Her clothes were little more than rags, and she carried a backpack that looked like it should have been thrown away a decade ago. "I don't understand," I said, but I was afraid I did.

"Hannah will help you with the house, so you can focus more on work, the kids, committees. . ." He waved away the details of my life like he would a gnat.

I didn't know what to say. He was so proud of his gift, and I had complained that the house was a lot of work. Of course, I'd expected him to hire weekly cleaners--not bring me a live-in maid. When we decided the yard was too much, we'd hired Rojo Landscaping. We hadn't moved a laborer into the garage.

"She's happy to be here, aren't you Hannah?" my husband said.

The girl's face was filled with confusion. She looked on the verge of tears.

"Her parents need help to raise her younger siblings, and Hannah is a good girl. She knows it's a privilege to work to support her family."

She was so small, and although she had none of the baby fat of American teens, I didn't think she could be more than fifteen. "She looks so young. I don't like taking her away from her family." I immediately regretted my words.

"You don't like my gift?" His lips turned down like a spoiled child's.

"No, no, of course I do." I was quick to mollify him. Hurt feelings had a way of spinning into annoying temper tantrums that could last for weeks. "But is it legal?" I had to know.

"Legal? Would I do anything illegal? I can't believe you'd ask such a question." His eyes flashed.

I cleared my throat. "She has a green card then?"

"Of course. She has a passport, and a visa, and all those kinds of papers. Seb's nephew works at the American Embassy in Cairo. Seb owed me a favor, so he had his nephew pull a few strings."

This did not set my mind at ease. I'd only met Seb Skandalis on two occasions. My first impressions weren't positive. He reminded me of a weasel, small and nervous with eyes that never rested. Even his name, Seb, made me think of a sebaceous cyst—a slow growing abnormality according to Webster's. I didn't trust him, but what could I do now? The girl was here, and looked as if she didn't lie down soon, she'd fall down. I would have to come up with a permanent solution later.

"Where will she sleep?" I said the words without thinking.

A storm cloud crossed my husband's face. "Can't you handle anything? I made the arrangements, paid the money—no small fee—and picked her up from Seb. I assumed you could take care of the domestic details." He sniffed. "You don't seem very grateful. Maybe I should send her back."

Yes, please. I wished he would, but I didn't want to push him into a full-blown pout. Instead, I hurried to his side and kissed him. "I am grateful. It will be wonderful to have help." I'd learned to manage his moods the first year of our marriage, a little affection, a stroke or two of the ego, and he purred like a kitten.

"You were the one who said the house was too much to handle on your own."

"I know. You are so thoughtful." I patted the sullen lines of his cheek.

"I was only thinking of you."

"Of course, you were. I'll take her to the garage and make a bed in the laundry room." We didn't have an extra bedroom—besides I didn't want her in the house when we were sleeping. The previous home-owners had put a lock on the laundry room door for some unknown reason, maybe they stored valuables there when they went out of town. Tonight, I was glad. I would feel better knowing she was secure.

"I knew you would think of something." He brightened. "I'll get my own drink while you take care of Hannah."

Magnanimous of him, I thought, but said, "Come," to the girl. She followed me out to the garage. I opened a cupboard along the back wall and took two sleeping bags from a shelf. "Have you eaten?" I asked. She didn't answer.

I placed the sleeping bags one on top of the other on the floor of the laundry room. "I'll find a pillow for you, but for now you can use your backpack." She swayed on her feet, so tired or ill she could barely stand. I reached for the pack. She clung to it but only for a moment. When she released it, I placed it on the sleeping bags and gestured to the pallet. "Lie down. I'll bring you some dinner in a bit." I closed the door behind me when I left. The click of the lock was reassuring.

It was quite a while before I was able to follow through on my promise to bring her dinner. My husband was buoyant now that his gift was received with what he considered to be the correct spirit. We sat for dinner in the dining room. It was just the two of us that night. I would have preferred to eat in front of the television, but he wanted to talk.

"It was last week; remember the night you were so upset because the vacuum was sitting in the front hall when I got home?"

I nodded, although I hadn't been upset. He was the one who'd been upset, but it wasn't worth arguing about.

"The next day I told Seb, I said, 'Seb, my poor wife is working herself to the bone with this big house. What is the good of all the money I'm making if I can't take care of my wife?' Do you know what Seb said?"

Was this a rhetorical question? But he looked so expectant I said, "No. What?"

"He said, 'I have the solution to all your problems.' Then he told me about Hannah. Her parents are dirt poor. You can see by how skinny she is they haven't been able to feed their children adequately. Seb assured me we'd be doing both Hannah and her family a great service by bringing her to America." He bragged about the cleverness of his acquisition the way some women brag about their shopping conquests.

"What did Seb charge you for that?" I kept my voice light.

He dropped his gaze to his plate and stabbed at a piece of meat. "There were fees, the airfare, the cost of the visa and the passport. I was happy to cover them."

"How did she get her paperwork so quickly?"

"I told you," He said between bites, a shadow of his former pout around his eyes. "Seb's nephew works at the American Embassy in Egypt. Those guys can get anything done."

I didn't believe that. More likely the passport was a forgery and the visa nonexistent.

"Anyway, now all I have to pay is two hundred dollars a month into an account. Seb will send that home to her family, minus a small cut for handling everything for us. Even considering the initial investment, it will save us in the long run. Those cleaning services are very expensive, besides Hannah will live here. She'll be on call twenty-four hours a day, seven days a week. And she can do more than clean. Seb tells me she's a very good cook." He rocked his chair onto two legs and beamed an expansive smile in my direction.

I stood and carried the dinner dishes into the kitchen. I couldn't bear to listen anymore. But he followed me. "She's seventeen. That's young, I know, and she doesn't speak a word of English." That explained why she didn't answer any of my questions. "We'll have to teach her and take care of her until she's at least eighteen. But I should make back my investment by then."

He frowned as he did the numbers in his head. "Well, maybe she'll live with us until she's in her twenties." He brightened at the thought. "But we can cross that street when we need to."

I love my husband, but sometimes he is as naive as a child, certainly more naive than mine. He believed what he wanted to believe. Women don't have that luxury. Society holds our feet to the fire, requires more, and gives less. In my experience, a suspicious nature isn't always a bad thing.

Two Days Ago

My nose wrinkled as I entered the garage the next morning. Hannah didn't smell good. First order of the day would be a shower, and then I'd show her how to use the washer and dryer. She could start with her own clothes. I opened the laundry room door, and the stench slapped me in the face. Under the sour odor of unwashed body was something else— something worse.

She lay curled in a fetal position, the top of her head poking out above the sleeping bag. "Hannah." The child didn't move, didn't open her eyes. "Hannah." I used the same firm voice I use to wake my children for school when they oversleep, but still no response. "Hannah." I pulled back the sleeping bag and shook her by the shoulder this time.

The girl groaned and rolled toward me. I caught my breath. She looked more ill than she had the night before, if that were possible. Her eyes were black holes. Her face flushed. Beads of sweat stood out on her forehead. I touched her skin with the back of my hand the way I did with the children when they complained. She was burning up.

I pulled my cell phone from my pocket and called my husband. He answered on the third ring. "Did Seb tell you what to do if she gets sick?" I said.

"She's not sick. She's just tired and malnourished."

"She has a high fever."

"So, give her a couple of Tylenol."

"She needs to go to the doctor."

There was a long silence on the other end of the line, then he said, "I don't think that's a good idea."

"Why?" But I knew the answer.

"Seb didn't give me her papers. He said he'd have them for me at the end of the month. She misplaced them after she landed. His nephew is sending copies, but they'll take a few weeks."

It was my turn to remain quiet. "What have you gotten us into?" I finally said.

"Hold on, now." I could hear the trumped-up indignation in his tone. He was as nervous as I was. "Hannah spent one night at Seb's house. He doesn't have a wife. It's a bachelor pad, messy, you know? He thinks her papers may have gotten thrown out with the junk mail or something."

"Sure." I couldn't keep the sarcasm from my voice. I didn't know what Seb was up to, but I knew it wasn't good.

"I'll talk to him as soon as we hang up, okay? I'll find out what we should do. I don't think the hospitals can turn her away even if she doesn't have papers."

"And how do we explain who she is, and why she's with us?"

Another long pause. "I'll return her. Make Seb give me my money back. She's not well. She's defective."

"She's not a toaster!" It burst from me. Hannah moaned and rolled onto her side. "She's a human being. You don't buy them, sell them, or return them when you're through with them."

"I didn't mean it like that. I only meant Seb is the one who brought her here, she's his responsibility."

"But he brought her for you, because you asked him to."

I heard my husband inhale. "Yes, and no."

"What do you mean, yes and no?"

"It's not the first time Seb has done this."

"He's a slaver, a trafficker, that's what you're saying?"

"No. No. Nothing like that. People talk to his nephew, because of his position at the Embassy. They want to come to America. They're poor. They need help. His nephew tells him about these people, and Seb makes arrangements for them. It's very altruistic. A win-win. Good for everyone."

Everyone but the girls. He knew the truth as well as I did, but he wouldn't admit it. "Well, he must take her back. We don't need a refund. If we get it, we get it. If not, it's a good lesson for us. I don't want to be involved in this kind of thing."

"I'll call him." My husband sounded contrite. I hoped I'd convinced him to let go of the money. The child needed help, and we weren't in a position to help her. I had to believe Seb would do it, even if only for monetary reasons. Once she was healthy again, he could sell her to someone else.

I heard the chime of the doorbell and closed my eyes. Who could it be? I left the girl, carefully closing the door behind me. I was fairly sure she was too sick to follow me, but one couldn't be too careful.

Before I reached the hallway, I heard the front door open. I stopped. Maybe my son could handle this on his own, but no. A moment later, I heard his voice.

"Mom."

"Yes." I bustled toward him as if I was just now coming from the garage.

"Someone at the door for you." He headed up the stairs without a backwards glance.

It was Carlos, our gardener. His broad, handsome face broke into a wide grin, and he held out a hand. I looked at it for a long moment. What if the girl was contagious? I hadn't had a moment to wash my hands. I clenched and unclenched my fingers, thinking. Then, I grabbed his hand and shook.

"I'm sure it's an oversight," he said, "but I stopped by to let you know your payment is overdue." He handed me an envelope.

I took it. "I'll give it to my husband."

"I was hoping to collect."

I didn't have time for this. "My husband has the checkbook. I'll make sure he gets this." I waved the bill and returned his smile. "But how are you? How is business?" I did my best to make small talk, to act like nothing was wrong.

We chatted for several painful minutes before I was able to shut the door firmly in his face. I backed up to it and dropped my head to my chest. Why had my husband spent money on a sick child, but hadn't paid the gardener? What was happening in this house?

I hurried to the kitchen to make the girl a cup of broth. My hands shook as I put the cup into the microwave. When I returned to her with the soup, two Tylenol, and a glass of water, she was so weak, I had to lift her head and bring the water to her lips. She gagged on the pills, but finally got them down. I wondered if she'd ever taken a pill before, if she'd ever had any medical help in her short life. She only managed a few spoons full of the broth before falling onto the sleeping bag, exhausted.

As I pulled the top bag over her, I saw a glint of metal in her hand. I reached for it, thinking she might stab herself with whatever it was while she slept. When she felt my tug, she gripped the object so tightly her fingertips turned white.

"It's okay. I won't take it," I said, but her grip didn't loosen. It wasn't until later in the day when I went in to check on her that I saw what the object was. Her hand had fallen open while she slept and revealed a Coptic cross.

My husband came home from work early. The jovial attitude of the night before gone. Before I could ask what had happened, he held up a hand and said, "I talked to Seb. After dark, I'll take her to him."

"He'll get her medical help?" I said.

My husband nodded. "He has a doctor who works with him on these things."

"Then he'll keep her? You made sure he knows we don't want her back."

"I told him." My husband walked into the living room, his steps heavy, his shoulders slumped. He collapsed on the couch.

"She's worse," I said. "I've been giving her Tylenol every four hours, but it doesn't seem to be doing much. She can only take small sips of water and broth. She's been asleep most of the day."

"Get me a lemonade, would you? I'm so thirsty."

As I poured the liquid into a glass, I remember my handshake with Carlos and had a terrible thought. When I returned to the living room, I pressed a hand to my husband's forehead. "Could she be contagious? Do you feel ill?"

He took my hand and pressed it to his lips. "I'm fine." He didn't look fine, but I suspected it was more a matter of his heart than his health. "I'll take her in a couple of hours. Let me rest."

"What about dinner?"

"I'm not hungry."

My husband is always hungry. The only time his appetite wanes is when he's stressed and upset. He was probably both, and that was good. Maybe next time he'll talk to me instead of making such a big decision alone.

He had to carry the girl to the car that night. She was too weak to stand. I didn't like it, but our son had to help him. My husband said he couldn't manage alone, not with his back.

As soon as they drove away, I went into the garage. I scooped up the sleeping bags and took them directly to the outside trash cans. When I returned, I saw her backpack in the corner of the shed. I lifted it by one dirty strap. It seemed heartless to throw it away. It was all she had.

I opened a cupboard and tucked it behind a bag of clothes I'd meant to take to Goodwill. Maybe I could return it to her somehow. I closed the cupboard, walked into the house, into the downstairs bathroom, and washed my hands for a long, long time.

MOLLY: A little reminiscent of Lady McBeth, or Herod, right? You can't wash that kind of guilt off your hands.

Speaking of guilt, what are your thoughts on Abby's decisions? I don't mean locking herself in the anchorhold. That's not something most of us can relate to, I get that. However, she could have yelled out to Steven, the garden volunteer, when he found the body. She also could have announced her presence to the detective when she arrived.

Instead, she let her father go to the police. Granted, he wanted to go, and she did try to talk him out of it, but . . .

I don't know. She could've put her foot down. Insisted on coming out. There were financial considerations. She'd invested all her savings in the building of the anchorhold. There were also social ramifications. If people heard what she'd done, it could revive the rumors about her mother and her family. And, finally, there was the worry that her father would lose his position at the mission. He shouldn't have been helping her camp out on the grounds. Do those things outweigh her obligation to report what she saw to the police?

What do you all think? As in previous seasons, I'd love to hear your thoughts on the question of the week. I'll drop the link to the Facebook Group in the show notes. Let's chat there.

(cue music)

VO: If you enjoyed this episode, please leave us a five-star review on your favorite podcast service—it really helps. *Murders Under the Sun* is edited by Jim Wilbourne, theme music is by Eclectic Blends, and I'm your host, Molly Shure.

part three

MURDERS UNDER THE SUN
  SEASON THREE; EPISODE TWO

MOLLY: Welcome back to *Murders Under the Sun*. This is Molly Shure, your host.

Before we get into this episode, I just want to mention what went on in the Facebook group this week. Feelings about Abby's decision to remain silent ran high. It was pretty divided. Some thought she did the right thing. Some thought she should've come forward. But you were all really adamant about your position.

I love how invested you are. It's going to be a great season, because all I can say is, just wait. It gets worse. Abby's mistakes start piling up quickly. Spoiler alert: Things get real personal for her in this episode.

Speaking of personal, I received another listener email regarding the disappearance of my college roommate, Melissa Shilling. For those who are tuning in for the first time this season, I told listeners in season one how I got involved with crime reporting.

In the 2005 - 2006 school year, my roommate went out to party one night and never returned. I spent several long months grieving and doing my very unprofessional best investigating. I never turned anything up, and neither did the police. Mel is still a missing person.

Since I mentioned this, I've received several messages regarding other students who disappeared from CSU Fullerton that year. I've continually encouraged listeners to send this information to the police. I'm not an investigator. I'm a journalist.

However, you're wearing me down. Listen to the latest email I received on the topic.

Dear Molly,

I'm writing to tell you about my son, Raphael Jimenez. My son Raphael also disappeared from CSU-Fullerton in 2006 just like your friend Melissa.

The police think it was drugs or a girl or he stole something and ran away. I know this isn't true. My son was a good student. He knew how hard I worked to pay his tuition. He would never do those things.

Raphael was getting a degree in Cinema and Television. He loved his classes. When he got his AA, he was going to transfer to a U.C. to become a filmmaker. He wanted to make Hollywood movies like Mr. Stephen Spielberg.

I have attached a picture of my son. I pray for him every day. Please, find out where he is.

Sincerely,
Camilla Jimenez

Here's my response:

Dear Ms. Jimenez,

My heart breaks for you. Your son Raphael sounds like a wonderful person.

However, I'm not sure what I can do about this. As I've said to other family members of missing students, I encourage you to take your concerns to the authorities.

Having said that, I don't want to get your hopes up—my resources are limited—but I will ask a few questions of those who've contacted me and see if I can find any common links. My guess is that these are random cases. CSU-Fullerton had and has a huge student body, but I'll let you know if I find anything significant.

    Best wishes,
    Molly Shure

There you have it. I will look into this to the best of my ability. Now let's get back into Abby's story.

3.2.2

MALAISE CHASED Abby around the anchorhold like a starving cat. Hot Santa Ana winds were blowing outside. Inside, her cell was stifling. She'd stripped down to a pair of shorts and a tank top and pulled her hair on top of her head in a messy ponytail. She was still miserable.

She held her face as close to the squint as she dared. The winds made her sneeze, but she had to have air, or she'd scream. The tourists were out in full force. It was only a week until the Swallows Day Parade, and the birds were having their annual fifteen minutes of fame. This morning alone three young boys, two teenage girls, and one adult male left the path and walked right up to the exhibit wall. They were so close she could hear them breathe.

She couldn't see them, but she knew they were checking the man-made nests to see if any swallows had moved in. None had. There were very few swallows at the Mission these days thanks to all the development in the area. Those that had returned had built their own nests rather than use the artificial ones. Luckily for her, the foundation hadn't given up hope in the project.

She ducked as a man with a Canon around his neck snapped a picture of her enclosure. He couldn't see her from that distance, but she didn't know how cameras worked. Maybe it picked up things the human eye couldn't. She didn't want a shadowy image of her face plas-

tered all over the internet, "New photograph proves San Juan Capistrano Mission is haunted." That's all she needed.

Abby stepped away from the window and paced across her cell four
times, but the exercise made her break out in a sweat. She took up her
perch at the window again and waited for a breeze. This was the hardest
day she'd experienced yet. It wasn't just the scorching wind, or the dirt
itching her scalp and crunching between her teeth, or that her head felt
stuffed with puffy balls of pollen. It was that she didn't like herself very
much today, and there was no escaping herself.

She shouldn't have allowed her father to talk her into staying silent.
She should have made her presence known to the police. Instead, she
put him in the compromising position of having to lie to them. Actually, she should have called out to Steven, the garden volunteer, as soon
as he found the girl. She could have made up a story about how she'd
gotten trapped in the hold by accident. Asked him to get her father. But
she didn't.

She didn't.

That should be engraved on her tombstone—a perfect and succinct
description of her life. The number of things she'd left undone was staggering. She should have let Carlos know where she was going. She
didn't. She should have said yes, or even no, to his proposal. She didn't.
Were marriage and children going to fall into the category of things she
didn't do but would regret later?

She should have gone away to college, escaped the small-town labels
attached to her family name. But she didn't. She'd stayed and hoped
somehow her mother's legacy would disappear from the communal
memory. It didn't.

Her greatest sin of omission, however, the sin that had knocked over
the first domino, the one that brought the whole line tumbling down,
was ever present in her mind. She'd thought, hoped, and prayed that she
could shed the guilt by devoting herself to this time of renewal. But so
far it hadn't worked.

When Abby was small, she'd been gregarious and competed with
her big brother for attention as most kids did. But all that changed when
he died. She'd gradually become more and more inward. At seven years
of age, she decided invisibility was something to strive for.

The idea came to her on a Sunday after Mass. She and her father and mother went for ice cream. The day stood out in her mind because they hadn't gone for ice cream for a full year. Not since Scottie died. They stepped out of church into the bright sunshine, her dad looked at the sky and in a quiet voice said, "I feel like a cone."

Abby came to attention. That was what he always used to say on warm Sundays after Mass. Scottie would answer, "Vanilla, or chocolate?"

Dad would say, "Pistachio."

Scottie would say, "Booger ice cream," and Abby would say, "Gross."

They had the same conversation a hundred times. She'd almost forgotten about it. But when Dad said, "I feel like a cone," it came back like the words of a song you used to know but hadn't sung in a long time.

She'd stopped walking and looked at her parents. She wanted to see if they were really going, or if Dad was just remembering. Her mom and dad did a lot of that these days. But Dad turned right on Camino Capistrano instead of left, and she knew it was real.

She took Dad's hand and skipped next to him. Not a big, full, leaping skip, more like a walk with a hop in it. She figured ice cream meant she was allowed to act a little bit happy.

Her mother sat in the same booth they used to sit in, and Abby and her father went up to the counter. "What do you want, sweetheart?" he said.

She used to get vanilla with sprinkles, but she didn't want to upset her mother. A vanilla cone with sprinkles might remind her of Scottie. She considered the choice as carefully as if she was holding one of the delicate figurines from her grandmother's mantle. "Vanilla," she finally said.

"Sprinkles?" he asked.

"No." Plain was her compromise.

They carried the ice cream to the table, Dad's pistachio cone, Mom's bowl of chocolate and Abby's vanilla cone.

"So, what's coming up this week?" Her father asked them both when they were settled. Lots of people ask how your day was, or what you did last week, but Dad always asked about the future. She liked that.

Abby stole a glance at her mother. She was staring at her bowl of ice cream, not eating. She didn't look angry or upset. She didn't look *anything*. Abby swung her legs to get some of her nerves out, and said, "I have to make a diorama."

"Of what?" Dad said.

"A tide pool. Our class went to the Marine Museum last week."

"Great. That's great." Dad sounded more cheerful than he had in a long time.

"Yeah, it was fun."

He smiled. It seemed like talking about the Marine Museum put him in a good mood, so Abby kept going. "They have this octopus in a big glass aquarium, and the lady there told us how it kept escaping. They'd come in the morning and find it on the floor. Once they found it on a bookshelf. They had to put a big rock on the top of the aquarium to keep the lid on."

"I've heard octopi are pretty smart," Dad said.

"Octopuses," Abby corrected him. "They are."

"What else did you see?"

Abby's cone started to drip on her hand because she was talking so much. She licked the drips before she went on. "They have scallops too. When something bothers them, they clack through the water like this." She opened and closed her free hand like an angry scallop.

"Wouldn't want to get snapped by one of those." Her father made a face like he was scared, but she knew he wasn't. Happiness warmed her from her toes up. She'd forgotten how good it felt.

Then Dad laughed. It wasn't a big laugh, but it was the first one she'd heard from him for as long as she could remember. Abby felt a grin spread across her face. She swung her legs harder and laughed too.

Whack.

Her mother slammed her spoon onto the table. Dad's mouth snapped shut like one of those scallops. Abby's laugh choked in her throat.

Her mother glared at both of them. "Stop." The word was quiet, but it rang with rage.

"Honey," Abby's dad said, and put a hand on her mother's.

Her mom yanked hers away. "It's not right."

"Scottie wouldn't want this." Dad's voice was soft.

"Scottie will never eat ice cream, or crabs, or go on field trips again. How can you...?" She didn't finish her sentence. How could he *what*? Eat ice cream? Or laugh? Or be happy?

"No, he won't. But we have another child, and she will." Her father's voice quivered with emotion.

Abby wrapped the rest of her ice cream cone in a napkin and set it on the table. She didn't want it anymore.

"Well, I can't go on. Not as long as the person responsible walks around as free as you like."

Dad winced as though Mom had stabbed him. "We have a life to live, Mary. We have each other. We have a daughter to love. It's time to move on. To let go."

That's what Father O'Brien had said in church that morning. Abby didn't usually listen to the sermons, but when Father O'Brien said God had forgiven us, so we had to forgive others, Dad had reached across her and taken Mom's hand.

"I will not rest until the world knows the truth." Mom stood and picked up her ice cream. She marched toward the street, stopping only to dump the still full bowl into the trash on her way out the door. Everyone in the shop was staring at them.

Abby's throat ached from holding back the sobs that were trying to get out. If she cried right then, she'd draw even more attention to their family. She wanted to disappear. Desperately. She wanted to pull an invisibility cloak around her shoulders and poof! Be gone. Because Abby knew she was, at least in part, responsible for Scottie's death.

She'd only been five, and he'd sworn her to secrecy. But if she'd have tattled, told her mother about the bike jump at the railroad tracks, Scottie would be alive today. If Scottie were alive, the ripple effects of that accident would never have occurred.

That day at the ice cream shop was the first time Abby had longed for invisibility, but it was far from the last. The further her mother burrowed into her pain and rage, the more erratic she became. The last two years of her life, she walked the streets of San Juan Capistrano talking to Scottie—who really was invisible.

In the beginning Abby's father had tried institutionalizing her. They'd keep her for a month and send her home with a bottle of pills she'd immediately stop taking. Back in she went. Then out again—a revolving door of anxiety and shame—until her father gave up the fight. After that Mad Mary became a town institution. Kids taunted her. Women shook their heads. Men averted their eyes.

When Abby was ten, her mother died of cancer. Abby hardly grieved. Not because she hadn't loved her, but because she'd been losing her by inches for so long there wasn't much left to grieve.

And now, Abby had disappointed the man who'd become everything to her—her father. She'd talked him into helping her with this project at the risk of losing his job and reputation. She'd allowed him to lie to the police for her.

She'd make it up to him, she promised herself. When her book was published, their family name would be associated with something good. Something noble. Something honorable. If she'd been discovered in the anchorhold before her manuscript was ready, everyone would assume she'd gone crazy, like her mom. Sometimes she felt as if the town watched her, waiting for it to happen.

The clack of shoes on cement broke into Abby's thoughts. A dark-haired, dark-eyed woman rounded the path near the restrooms. Her steps were short and rapid. Her gait purposeful, unlike the usual rambling of visitors to the Mission. She stopped before the swallow exhibit, but only gave the nests a casual glance. She turned in a slow circle, as if searching for something.

After making a three-hundred and sixty-degree turn, her gaze locked onto Abby's squint. She stepped forward. Abby stepped back. The woman looked in both directions, then walked off the path and headed straight for the window.

Abby slid into the darkest corner of her cell and cursed her lack of clothing. Her arms and legs, pale from not having seen the sun in weeks, seemed to glow in the dim light. Her gaze fell on the navy-blue blanket on her bedroll—a camouflage.

She reached out a hand, but before she could grab it, she heard scratching and inhaled a whisper of unfamiliar perfume. Abby turned. The woman's face was pressed against the bars of the squint. Pulse racing, Abby scrutinized the anchorhold. What did the woman see?

Abby kept her possessions stowed against the walls where daylight wouldn't touch them. A precaution. But she'd grown sloppy. The strap of her dark green backpack lay coiled in the light like a heat-seeking snake. One scuffed white sneaker sat exposed in the center of the space. She squeezed her eyes shut like a child playing peek-a-boo. If she couldn't see them, maybe no one else could either.

"Excuse me, ma'am." It was a man's voice.

Abby's eyes popped open in time to see the woman's face disappear from the window.

"You're not allowed to touch the exhibits, ma'am." It must be a docent, or a security guard.

"I was just curious," the woman said.

"I understand, but you need to stay on the path."

"I didn't know." Her voice was haughty, unused to censure.

Short, rapid footsteps receded into the distance, followed by the clump of a heavier tread. Abby snatched up her shoe, dragged her backpack into the shadows, and huddled into her corner again. She didn't move until the sunlight narrowed into the thin sliver that meant it was noon.

3.2.3

"ABBY." A whispered voice nudged her awake. Had it been part of a dream? She stared at the ceiling waiting for it to come again. It did. "Abby."

"Carlos?" She scrambled to the squint. A waning crescent moon hung low on the horizon. The little light it gave glinted off his black hair. A mix of joy and consternation filled her when she saw him. "What are you doing here? Where's Dad?"

"I have bad news."

The joy fled. "About Dad?"

Carlos nodded.

"What's happened?"

"He's been in an accident. He's at Mission Hospital."

Abby's throat seized up, but she managed to choke out a question. "How bad?"

"I don't know, but he managed to call, to tell me where you were. You have to come."

"Did you bring a crowbar?" Carlos's eyes narrowed in question. "I can't get out unless you pry one of the stones loose."

"You've been trapped in there all this time?" Disbelief rang in his tone. "What if there'd been a fire? An earthquake?"

"There wasn't." Abby's words were terse. "You need a crowbar if I'm going to get out of here."

He snorted like an impatient racehorse. "I'll be back."

Abby watched Carlos recede through the shrubs. He disappeared the same way the men who'd dropped the girl's body did three nights ago. Was it only three nights? It felt like a lifetime.

Anxiety crept over her. She hadn't asked anything about the accident. Where it had happened. How it had happened. The questions would have to wait until she was on her way to her father.

She looked around the anchorhold as if seeing it for the first time. She should pack. She shouldn't leave things here for people to find. She wouldn't be returning, and it no longer mattered. Only her father mattered.

She dropped to her knees and began gathering up the few things she'd brought with her. She shoved the candle, matches, and her books into the backpack with her clean clothes. There were only two protein bars left in the box her father had brought her. She threw them into the backpack too. Food would attract rodents and rodents would attract mission staff members.

She folded her blankets and put them in the bag of dirty laundry. She rolled up the foam mattress but couldn't squeeze it into the bag. She stood and surveyed the space. She'd have to leave the toilet, broken chair, and mattress. Get them after dark tomorrow. Or on the next night. She didn't like leaving the toilet. Didn't want the smell to attract attention. She had just replaced the disinfectant tablet, but there was an odor.

Abby pondered that for a long moment, then pulled a spoon from her backpack. She moved to the corner where the dirt was loose and began digging. She managed to scratch out a cup or two of soil, just enough to bury the waste inside. When she was done, she closed the lid and rubbed her hands on her jeans.

She reached for the laundry bag, pulled out a flannel shirt, and wiped down the exterior surfaces of the camp toilet. She picked up the broken chair and swiped at the metal supports. She did the same with the bars of her squint and the rough stone walls.

It was unlikely anyone would find this space, but if they did, and if the police heard about it, they might wonder if the person in this room had anything to do with the dead girl. Abby worked in a school. Her prints were on file in some database somewhere. Wiping everything clean was probably an unnecessary precaution, but it set her mind at ease. A little bit, anyway.

By the time Carlos returned, Abby had done everything she could to erase her presence. "I got it." His voice was hushed.

"Go to your left. Over by the Great Church wall. I'll slide out the bottom stone," she said.

A moment later, Abby heard the crack of grout as Carlos pried at the wall. A second stone fell, and the opening widened. She slid the backpack and the laundry bag through, then dropped to her belly and crawled out.

Carlos grabbed her with rough hands and helped her to her feet. A chill of night air embraced her. The world felt huge, a place without borders or fences. Opposing emotions tore through her. She wanted to return through the hole in the wall to the protection of the shell she'd left behind. She wanted to run into open spaces, giddy and drunk with freedom.

She turned toward Carlos to hug him. They hadn't seen each other in a month, and she wanted the comfort of his strong arms. But he stepped back, avoiding her embrace. "We should hurry," he said.

A stab of rejection hit her but worry for her father followed quickly and dampened all other emotions. She shouldn't think about their relationship, not while her father was in the hospital. "We have to put the stones back," she said.

"Your dad will be out of surgery soon."

"I know, but someone might notice."

Carlos squatted by the wall. He pulled one stone into place and balanced the second on top. "I can come back some night soon and grout them, but this should be okay for now."

Abby followed him through the shrubs. He knelt at the foot of the wall separating the mission from the world outside. She stepped onto his knee and hoisted herself to its top. Before dropping to the other side, she caught a glimpse of the squint. Its bars were dark slashes against the gray inside.

3.2.4

ABBY AND CARLOS stood without speaking all the way up the elevator. The doors slid open, and the overhead lights of the hallway made her eyes ache. She turned right, then left, then right again following the arrows on the wall like a tourist in a foreign land.

"Excuse me." Abby's voice sounded unnaturally quiet in the busy hive of scrubs and electronic beeps. She was unused to talking. The only conversations she'd had for the past three and a half weeks had been with her father, and most of those were held in hushed tones. She cleared her throat. "I'm here to see Paul Travers. Is he out of surgery yet?"

A thin faced woman typed on a keyboard. "Not yet. Third door on your left is a waiting room. I'll make sure the doctor knows you're there."

"How much longer?"

The nurse glanced up from her computer, sympathy in her eyes. "I can't say." She continued her typing. That was no answer at all. Abby opened her mouth to say: Could you find out? But Carlos took her arm and steered her away.

After guiding her onto an orange and green couch next to a coffee table littered with magazines, he said, "Can I get you something?

Coffee?" She shook her head. Her stomach was a mess. Putting anything into that swirling sea of acid seemed a recipe for disaster.

Her eyes wandered to the television mounted on the wall. It was tuned to a telenovela. She didn't understand the language, but it was easy to imagine the plot. Two melodramatic actors spat Spanish invectives at one another, slapped each other's faces, then fell into a passionate embrace. It could have been *Days of our Lives*, or *As the World Turns*, the soaps her grandmother used to watch.

The round wall clock had only moved seven minutes since she'd sat. Time was doing that thing again. That thing it had done in the anchorhold, staggering forward one slow second at a time, like an arthritic old man. She closed her eyes and tried to pray.

An eternity later, she felt Carlos's hand on her shoulder. A woman only a few years older than Abby came into the room. She was in full battle gear: pale green scrubs, cap, booties, face mask dangling around her neck. "Abby Travers?"

"Yes."

"I'm Dr. Trudeau. I'm your father's doctor." She didn't hold out a hand. "We can talk in here." She gestured to a room leading off the waiting room.

Abby dragged herself from the couch. Her limbs felt weighted and stiff. With Carlos following, she walked ten feet into the other room and reseated herself, this time in a hard chair pulled up to a laminate-topped table. It seemed a waste of energy. Why couldn't the doctor have spoken to her in the waiting room?

It wasn't good news. That's all Abby could think. Not good news. If the doctor had good news she'd have told her straight out. Dr. Trudeau didn't want Abby to make a scene in public. The telenovela stars were paid to make scenes, but Abby had to be shuffled here into this little room with the closed door.

"The injuries from the accident weren't as extensive as we'd feared—three broken ribs, some lacerations, no internal bleeding. Your father should recover from them just fine."

Relief washed over Carlos's face. It was such a guileless, little boy look it almost broke her heart. Abby knew the bad news was coming. If this were all the doctor had to say she wouldn't have brought them into this private room. She would look happier.

"However." She paused. Abby tightened, prepared. "There was some head trauma."

Abby didn't respond.

"There's only minor swelling, but we won't know the extent of the damage until he's awake. He did regain consciousness briefly before the surgery, which is a good sign."

"When will he wake up?" Abby said.

"When he's ready." Dr. Trudeau gave her a guarded smile.

Abby and Carlos followed the doctor's directions to Paul's room. It was as dim and quiet as a cathedral. The soft inhale and exhale of a compression device and the occasional blip from an array of monitors were the only sounds. At the center of it all, buried in a tangle of wires and tubes, was a figure swathed in pale blue and white.

Abby stepped closer. All she could see of her father, his face and the arms that rested on top of the blanket, were a mass of purple bruises. Her legs felt weak. "Dad." She whispered the word.

Carlos moved behind her, a solid, reassuring presence. She wanted to lean on him, feel his arms around her, but she stayed still. "He's going to be okay, Abby. The doctor said it wasn't as bad as they thought."

"But he looks. . . He doesn't look like himself."

"He's been in an accident. He just got out of surgery. Give him time."

Abby covered her face with her hands and gave herself over to the emotion she'd been holding in since she'd first heard about the accident. Had he been so distraught over the events of the past three days, so distracted by having to lie to the police, it had made him careless? Could this have been avoided if she'd left the anchorhold? Guilt, grief, and loss washed over her in waves.

She felt a tentative hand on her back, then an arm moved around her shoulders. She turned and pressed her face into Carlos's chest. She cried for what felt like a long time, but it didn't bring relief.

When she was done, she pulled away and wiped her eyes on the sleeve of her flannel shirt. "I don't know what to do," she said.

"There's nothing you can do. Go home. Get some sleep. Take a shower."

"What if he wakes up?"

"There's a staff of nurses and doctors who'll take care of him."

"He'll wonder where I am."

"You'll be spending plenty of time here, and you're going to have to make lots of decisions. You're not in any condition to do that right now."

Abby gazed down at the length of herself. She hadn't realized until that moment how ragged she was. Her jeans, her shirt, her hands were all brown with dirt. She could imagine what her face looked like after her crying jag. Her hair hadn't been washed with shampoo in almost a month, and neither sun nor makeup had touched her skin in the same amount of time.

The weariness that often comes after strong emotion enveloped her. Carlos was right. She had to rest, had to get cleaned up. She'd come back in the morning.

"I'll take you home," he said.

She placed a hand on her father's leg. "I'll see you later, Daddy." There was no response, not a flicker of an eyelid. Not a twitch of a finger. "I'll be back." Her voice caught. She stood for another moment, composed herself, and then turned. "Okay."

3.2.5

CLEAN, but only somewhat more rested, Abby made her way through Mission Hospital's maze of hallways to the ICU. She prepared herself as she walked. She already knew her father's condition was precarious, no surprise there. She would control her emotions, make cool, clear-headed decisions. She'd be there for him the way he'd always been there for her. She took a deep breath, stepped through the doorway into his room, and stopped short.

The lights, bright today, beamed onto a bare mattress. The bank of computer monitors no longer blinked and beeped but stood quiet and dead. Where was he? Surely, someone would have called her if he'd taken a turn for the worse—if he'd. . . She shoved that thought away.

She spun and walked with rapid steps through the corridor to the medical station. Her phone. She'd been so exhausted the night before; she hadn't bothered going to her father's house in San Juan Capistrano to get it. Her purse with her car keys and wallet were at her apartment, so she went there. She'd crept in so she wouldn't wake her roommate, collapsed on her own bed, and fallen into a dead sleep. But she didn't have her phone. What if they'd tried to call her? She broke into a run.

She turned a sharp corner and collided with a cart loaded with breakfast trays. Mumbling an apology to the orderly pushing it, she jogged the final distance to the desk. "Paul Travers." The words came in panted breaths.

"What room is he in?" said the almost pretty woman seated behind the counter.

"That's what I want to know," Abby said.

The nurse stared at the ceiling for a moment, trying to curb her annoyance, Abby thought. "Is he in the ICU?" she said through pinched lips.

"He was in room 302."

The woman took an immense amount of time plugging information into her computer. Abby resisted the urge to scream. A phone at the woman's elbow trilled. She answered it with a crisp, "ICU," listened for a moment, and relaxed into her chair as if settling in for a nice long chat. "Again?" she said in mock reprimand.

Abby stared at her.

"Don't worry. Your secret is safe with me." A ripple of laughter erupted from her no longer pinched lips.

Abby said, "Paul Travers?"

The woman raised a silencing hand and frowned. "Yes, *Doctor*." She emphasized the word "doctor" and glared. Apparently, Abby, who had no initials after her name, should understand her status. "I'll hold you to that." The smile returned as the nurse turned her attention back to her phone conversation. "I most certainly will. Yes. See you tomorrow then. Okay. Okay. Goodbye."

The grin slipped from her face as the receiver dropped onto the cradle. "Paul Travers was moved into the general population. He's on the second floor. Room 212." Abby darted toward the elevators without a thank you.

She found her father in the first bed of a double room. He was still ashen beneath the bruises, but his open eyes looked alert. Relief almost buckled her knees. He reached a hand toward her. She took it and sank onto the edge of his bed. "How did you get out?" His voice was a rasp of sandpaper.

"Carlos."

"Good. I thought I called him, but it's a bit of a blur."

Abby squeezed his hand. "How did this happen?" She was afraid to ask, afraid he would say that the accident was his fault caused by his distraught state of mind. But she had to know.

"I was crossing El Camino Real to get a cup of coffee at that shop near the mission. A car—" His words were interrupted by a coughing jag. He wrapped an arm around his ribs and yelped with pain.

Abby reached across him for the plastic cup of water on his bedside table. She helped him fit the straw between his dry lips. "You were walking?" She asked when he pushed the glass away.

"Yes. Car came out of nowhere."

Her father had become a man of extreme caution after Scottie's death, and he'd drilled that caution into her. Abby never rode bicycles, was afraid of heights, was a nervous driver, and wouldn't even consider hopping on the back of a motorcycle. She only swam in pools or on beaches attended by lifeguards, and never on red flag days. She carried a canister of pepper spray in her purse, although she'd never taken it out because she never went anywhere alone at night.

Needless to say, she always waited for the light, crossed at crosswalks, and looked both ways before stepping off the curb. And her father did the same. The accident couldn't have been his fault. "Was the driver drunk? On drugs?" she asked.

"I don't know." His eyes closed.

She felt a stab of guilt. "Of course you don't, and you don't need to bother about that now. Get some rest."

His head tipped, and then nodded. His breathing became steady and deep in moments. Abby slipped her hand from his when his fingers relaxed their hold. She needed to speak to his doctor or nurse. To someone who might know the answers to her growing list of questions.

She blinked in the bright light of the hallway and wondered where the nurse's station was on this floor. She turned right, back the way she'd come. But before she reached the end of the corridor, she heard a familiar voice coming from a patient's room. Dr. Trudeau stood in a doorway, one hand on the jamb, poised to leave. "I'll be back tomorrow," she promised someone Abby couldn't see. "Ms. Travers." The doctor smiled when she caught sight of Abby.

"My father's awake. He's lucid," Abby said.

"I know. I heard. I was just headed that way."

Abby fell in alongside the doctor. "He said he was hit by a car while he was walking. I didn't know that. I'd assumed it was a collision."

"I was told the same thing. An investigator visited last night. She wanted to speak to your father, but he wasn't awake. I talked to her briefly, confirmed the injuries were consistent with the eyewitness accounts."

"An investigator?"

"Her name was Sylla, I believe. She's with the Orange County Sheriff's Department."

Sylla? Abby stopped in her tracks. Sylla investigated homicides. She'd come the morning they'd discovered the girl at the Mission. Did she investigate other kinds of crime as well? Dr. Trudeau disappeared into her father's room. Abby hurried to catch up. Either way, it was the police's business to find the idiot who hit her father. Her job was to take care of him.

3.2.6

ABBY NOSED her car up the gravel drive in back of her father's house. Dr. Trudeau had said if her father continued to progress at the rate he'd been progressing, Abby would be able to bring him home in a day or two, but he'd need care. She still had two and half weeks before she had to return to work, so she could stay with him.

Her plan today was to take stock of the food situation and make a list of things she needed to get from the store. She'd also do a bit of cleaning. Her father was tidy, but he'd never be confused with Mr. Clean.

She entered through the back door and headed straight to the kitchen. The musty smell of day-old garbage and dirty dishes greeted her. As she dropped her purse onto the table, she saw her phone. She'd left it in the desk on the far kitchen wall and wondered why her father had moved it. Was he checking her messages? She must have a lot of them. She'd told her employer and most of her friends she was going to a remote cabin in the mountains to work on her book. That cell reception was sketchy there. But she hadn't told everybody.

She pressed the power button, but nothing happened. She took it to the desk, found her charger in the drawer where the phone should have been and plugged it in. She hadn't told Carlos. She'd been hurt and angry, which wasn't much of an excuse. Truth is, she would have felt guilty lying to him. They were too close for lies. But she hadn't been up to facing his disapproval either, so she hadn't said anything about where she was going.

Abby threw open the dishwasher with more force than she needed to and began loading the dishes from the sink into it. In their early days together, it seemed as if she could do no wrong. He'd thought everything about her was wonderful. He'd listened to her author dreams and her musings about books she might write with rapt attention. They never disagreed about anything more serious than which restaurant had the best tacos.

Sometime toward the end of their first year together, things began to change. He listened less, switched topics more, and they'd started bickering now and then. She guessed it was to be expected. Something that happened to most couples once the honeymoon phase was over.

In some ways it showed their relationship had become deeper. The more serious things were, the greater the stakes, and the more important it was to know where the other stood.

But recently, his opinions about what she should and shouldn't do had become too strong. They felt less like love and more like disrespect. She flipped the dishwasher on, took the trash bin from under the sink and dragged it over to the fridge.

As she discarded leftovers and wilted vegetables, the words she'd used the night they'd fought ran through her head. "I'm not wearing a ring," she'd said. "I need time," she'd said. If he'd accepted that, maybe things wouldn't be so awkward between them now. But he hadn't, and he'd said some things she was having a hard time forgetting.

Abby lifted the garbage bag from the can and walked to the back door. She rounded the corner of the house, heading for the outside trash cans, and was startled by a car in the driveway of the house next door.

She hadn't known it had sold until her father had introduced himself to the Asian woman at the mission. She was glad it had. The house had terrible secrets. But she'd never held it against the place. Like her, it seemed an innocent victim of its terrible past.

She hoped it would have a new life now, one filled with happiness. And, on a more practical note, it was good that her father wouldn't be here at the end of the long drive all by himself. A neighbor who could look in on him from time to time would ease Abby's mind.

She dumped the trash in the can and replaced the lid. Maybe she should go over and introduce herself? They might wonder who she was. Later. She'd do it later, after she had a chance to finish cleaning up and run to the store. She'd buy them a houseplant or something. It would give her an excuse to stop by.

Her phone had half-power by the time she entered the kitchen. Enough to check her messages. She had eight. Five were from Carlos. They covered a wide range of emotions: from casually apologetic, to irritated, to angry, to worried, to bereft. She chewed her bottom lip as she listened. Maybe she'd been too hard on him.

There was one message from the principal's office at St. Barnabas, the school where she worked. The head librarian had come down with the flu, and the secretary was wondering when Abby would return. The last two messages were from Detective Sylla, both requesting Abby contact her as soon as possible.

She made herself a pot of coffee. She'd slept hard the night before, but she hadn't slept long. She didn't think she could face the police without caffeine. She doctored a cup with a dollop of half and half and sat at the table.

What would she say if Sylla wanted to know where she'd been? She could give her the same story she'd told everyone else about the Big Bear cabin. But what if she wanted to know who owned the place? Wanted the address? It didn't seem like a good idea to lie to the police.

She could be vague. Why would it matter to Sylla where she'd been? As far as the detective knew, it wasn't relevant. She'd say she was away. She didn't need to say anymore.

Abby picked up her phone with more confidence, but her finger hovered over the "call back" message. She was approaching this call all wrong. She was on the defensive, focused on hiding information. She set the phone down.

Weren't investigators trained to pick those kinds of things up? She'd watched enough episodes of *Criminal Minds* to know they all studied psychology. She had to get her head on straight before she called. She blew on her coffee and sipped.

What if she *had* been away at a cabin in the woods working on her book? What if she'd come down the hill to find her father in the hospital and two messages from the police on her phone? She narrowed her eyes. She'd be frantic. She'd rush to call them, full of worry and questions. She would think of them as allies.

Detective Sylla was an ally. She had to remember that. Sylla wanted to find the person who'd hurt Abby's father. She wanted to find the men who'd left that poor girl to die. She wasn't after Abby. Abby picked up the phone and dialed.

After speaking with two different people at the Sheriff's department, she found out Sylla wasn't in but was supposed to return shortly. Abby told the man on the phone she'd come by. She had to go out to run errands anyway. She hung up, made a grocery list, grabbed her car keys, and left the house. She'd go to the police station first, then to the market.

WHEN SHE RETURNED to her father's house two hours later, Abby could see the Rojo Landscaping truck before she turned in the driveway. Carlos had come to see her. He must be ready to apologize, to reconcile. Relief washed over her, but it was short-lived. When she got to the top of the hill, she saw he wasn't parked in her father's driveway. He was parked at the house next door.

Her gaze strayed to the neighbor's as she unloaded groceries. She listened for his voice as she traveled back and forth from the car to her father's house. She wouldn't go over. She'd wait for him to come to her. He was the one who'd created the rift between them. Yes, she'd run, and she hadn't told him about the anchorhold. How could she after the things he'd said? But she missed him, missed being able to talk things out with him. Especially now.

When Abby had arrived at the police station, Detective Sylla had seemed concerned, compassionate even. The longer she was there, however, the more pointed the investigator's questions became.

She began by inquiring about Abby's father's health, his disposition, moved to questions about his normal routine and relationships, and finally, asked whether he had any enemies. A disgruntled employee maybe? When Abby asked why she wanted to know, she was evasive.

The conversation had left her feeling uneasy. There wasn't anything specific she could put her finger on, but a sense of disquiet came over her while she was at the station. It followed her out the door when she left and clung to her like a bad odor while she ran errands.

Abby finished putting the groceries away and locked the house. Next on the agenda was a trip to her apartment to pack the things she'd need while she was at her father's house. Sharona, her roommate, would be delighted she was moving out again. She hadn't been exactly over-joyed to see Abby when she stumbled out of her bedroom that morning.

As she walked to the car, Abby saw Carlos standing under the shade of the big oaks. Their gazes locked, but it was Mimi Jackson who called out to her. "You must be Abby." She strode out of the shelter of the trees with her hand extended. "I'm Mimi Jackson, your father's new neighbor."

A momentary confusion passed through Abby's mind. Why was she introducing herself? Abby already knew who she was. She gave her head a quick shake. She'd seen Mimi from her anchorhold. *Get it together, Abby*. The woman had been completely unaware of her presence.

Abby took her hand. "Nice to meet you."

"I heard about your father's accident. I'm so sorry. Is there anything I can do?" Mimi said.

"No. He's still in the hospital. Thanks, though."

"How's he doing?"

"Surprisingly well. The doctor said I can bring him home in a day or two."

"That's such good news," Mimi flashed her a broad smile. "I'll bring something over when he's released."

"You should take her up on that." Carlos moved into their circle. "She's the descendant of a Chinese herbalist."

"Don't worry." Mimi held up a hand. "I'm descended from one, but I'm not one. I plan to bring chicken soup."

"Chicken soup would be great," Abby said.

"Where are you headed?" Carlos said, a coolness in his tone she was unaccustomed to.

"To my place. I have to get some clothes and things."

"Are you moving in?" Mimi said.

Abby nodded. "Just for a few weeks. Until Dad is up and around and can take care of himself." She turned her gaze on Carlos. "I just spoke to the police."

"Did they tell you anything else about the accident? About the driver?" he asked.

"No." Abby widened her eyes, hoping Carlos would understand this wasn't something she could talk about. The police had asked her to keep it quiet until they learned more.

Mimi looked shocked. "Was it a hit and run?" Abby didn't answer, and Mimi launched into a story about a distant cousin on her husband's side whose son was the victim of a hit and run. Part way through the list of surgeries the poor kid had to endure, Abby's mind flitted away.

She wanted to talk to Carlos, by himself, but she couldn't figure out how without seeming rude. Carlos solved the problem for her.

"What time will you be back?" he asked Abby when Mimi finished her story.

"I'll be in and out all day. But I'm sure I'll be ready for a break around 5:00," Abby said.

"I should be done here by then. Is it okay if I come by?"

"I'll make a pot of coffee."

"Do you have anything stronger?" He smiled for the first time since he'd gotten her out of the anchorhold. He had a great smile.

"Wine." Abby's father had a cupboard he kept stocked.

"That'll work," Carlos said.

Abby said goodbye to Mimi and drove away with a lighter heart than she'd had for days. Carlos wanted to talk.

3.2.8

ABBY SAW Carlos coming up the path and opened the door before he knocked. He smelled wonderful like grass and herbs and dirt. He looked even better. She was glad her own hair was clean and combed.

She thought about kissing him, but she didn't. Instead, she made room for him to walk past her into the house. "I opened a red blend. It's not one of Dad's usual wines, so I hope you like it." She sounded nervous and cleared her throat.

They hadn't talked about the fight yet. Hadn't used the word, "us". Her father's accident had pushed everything else to the side, but he was out of danger now. Maybe they could focus on other things.

Carlos followed her into the kitchen. There was a small lamp lit on the counter, and the last rays of the sun slanted through the window. It looked cozy. Nice. She put a wine glass into his hand, and he sat at the table.

"Want cheese and crackers?" She couldn't help noticing the way the lighting made his bronze skin glow.

"No."

She dropped into the chair across from him. "I'm glad you're here."

He didn't respond, just sipped his wine. Then, his eyes grew wide. "Wow. This is good."

"It is." Abby gave a low laugh. "I'm afraid I must have opened something Dad was saving for a special occasion. This isn't his usual ten dollar a bottle stuff. It's called Red Ravish." She rolled her r's when she said the name.

"It is a special occasion." Carlos said with a brief smile.

Abby raised her eyebrows. Was he referring to the end of her anchorhold experiment?

"Your dad is going to be all right," he added quickly.

"Yeah," Abby agreed. "But I wish we were sharing this wine with him."

"He's on too many pain meds. I'll buy him another bottle when he's better." Carlos rested his elbows on the table and leaned forward. "Tell me what happened at the police station."

So, they weren't going to talk about their relationship. The topic was still on hold. She pushed aside her disappointment and began to recount her visit with Sylla. As she spoke, Carlos's frown deepened.

When she finally paused for breath, he said, "It sounds like the police don't believe it was an accident."

Abby gave him a sharp look. "What do you mean?"

"It sounds like they think someone ran him over on purpose."

"The detective didn't say that."

"But she asked about enemies, unhappy employees."

"Yeah, but—"

"Did the witnesses say how the accident happened? Did it seem like your dad was targeted? Or was the car driving erratically before it hit him?"

"I didn't ask." Abby's voice grew quiet.

"Maybe you should."

"But Dad doesn't have any enemies. Everybody loves him." As soon as she said the words, she realized how silly they sounded.

Carlos shook his head. "Paul is a good guy, but he isn't Mother Teresa."

"Okay, well not everybody, but certainly nobody dislikes him enough to kill him."

He twirled the stem of his wine glass and stared at its contents. "Maybe it has something to do with the girl."

Abby stood, walked to the wine bottle on the counter, and brought it to the table. Their glasses weren't empty, but she needed to move. "How could it?"

"Your father was the one who said he'd seen two men near the mission wall the night the girl was left there. Maybe those men are afraid he'll I.D. them."

"But nobody knows that. Sylla said the police kept his identity quiet."

"Maybe your father said something to someone. News travels fast around this town."

Abby gulped the last of her wine, then set the glass down hard. "I'm going back to the station."

Carlos leaned back in his chair abruptly. "Why?"

"Because I'm going to tell them the truth. I'm going to tell them it was me, not my father, who saw the men." She stood, pushing away her chair. "Then we can make that public. I can't allow him to be in danger."

"Is it better you're in danger?"

"He lied to the police for me." Abby took her purse from the counter and moved toward the door.

Carlos rubbed his forehead with one hand. "Hold up a minute. Sylla won't even be there at this time of night. We have time to think this through."

Abby paused, hand on the door, impatience coursing through her. She couldn't sit still and wait for another attack on her father.

"If those men staged the accident, and we don't know that's true, what's to stop them from coming after you?"

"That's not the point." She heard the irritation in her own voice.

"It is the point." Carlos shot her an exasperated look. "Your father would no more agree to exposing you to killers than I would. He loves you. You're his kid."

"I love him."

"I know you do, and he needs you now, here, to help him when he comes home from the hospital. Not only that, but we don't know what will happen if the police find out you guys were lying to them. What if you or your dad end up in jail, or named in a lawsuit? He could lose his job."

Abby's resolve wavered, but the fear for her father's safety stayed strong. She returned to the table and dropped onto the edge of her chair. "So, what do I do to protect him?"

"What do we do, you mean?"

"I can't let you get involved with this. It's bad enough my father is in the hospital because of my poor decisions."

"Shut up." Her face snapped toward his. Carlos softened his voice. "I mean it. Shut up and listen. I don't know what's going on between you and me. We'll have to figure that out when all this is over. But you and your dad are family. This is what family does."

Tears sprang into Abby's eyes. She wiped them with the back of a hand. "Thanks."

"Your father is safe while he's in the hospital. I'm pretty sure it's only in the movies that hit men dress up like doctors, sneak in, and kill patients. And these men are no pros."

"How do you know that?"

"If they were, he'd be dead, and the girl would be at the bottom of the Pacific."

She nodded, thoughtfully. He had a point. "Okay, but what about when he comes home?"

"We keep a close eye on him. Keep the doors locked. We stay alert and aware."

"I have to go back to work in two weeks."

"Hopefully he'll be back to work then, too."

Fear injected a jolt of adrenaline into her bloodstream. "Will he be safe at work? That's where the accident happened."

"I don't know." Carlos reached for her hand. "But I have to believe this will blow over. Either the guys will get caught, or they'll decide your father isn't going to nail them and just go away."

What if it didn't blow over? "I don't know."

"I don't know either, but what else can we do?"

Abby closed her eyes for a minute. She needed time to think. Disconnected thoughts bounced around in her head. Nothing made sense. When she opened her eyes, she said, "I'm going to get some dinner and go check on Dad. Are you hungry?"

Carlos pushed away from the table. "I promised Mama I'd be home for dinner." Abby walked him to the front door. He paused before stepping into the night. "Maybe you should stay at your apartment tonight."

"Why?"

"It might be safer."

"I'll be fine. Nobody's after me."

He looked as if he was about to argue but clamped his jaw shut. She was glad. They'd argued too much lately.

"Goodnight." She raised herself up on tiptoes and kissed his cheek.

He gave her a weak smile. "Goodnight." He walked through the dark front yard to his truck and drove away.

3.2.9

WEARINESS SETTLED on Abby's shoulders. She pushed open the front door, then kicked it closed behind her with one foot. After a visit to the hospital, she dropped by her apartment to pick up some clothes. She was finally in for the night.

The house was dark, but Abby's arms were too full to manage the light switches. She'd gotten used to living without electricity though and made her way by the streetlights coming through the windows without a problem.

She entered her old bedroom, dumped the load she was carrying onto the bed, and then felt up and down the bedside table lamp, fingers seeking its stem. She found it, turned it on, and a soft glow lit the room.

Her father hadn't changed a thing since she'd moved out two years ago. Botticelli's *Birth of Venus* and Monet's *Water Lillies* still hung in cheap frames on the walls. A bookshelf filled with epic fantasy novels and medieval European and early church history books sat near a window.

The room smelled unused and musty. She walked to the window and lifted the sash. Cool night air washed her face, and she marveled at the luxury. The anchorhold had been so small and had no cross ventilation if the stone near the floor was shut up. It had often been stifling.

Abby looked across the expanse of brittle grass outside her window to the neighboring house. Lights were on, and she could see Mimi move through the living room and disappear into what she knew was the hallway. A moment later a man followed her. The man was dark haired and dark skinned. She couldn't tell his ethnicity from a distance, but he definitely wasn't Chinese like his wife.

She moved away from the window and began to unpack the bag of clothes she'd brought from her apartment. The gentle croak of frogs and chirruping of crickets kept her company. When she was done, she slipped her empty suitcase onto the closet shelf and slid the door shut.

A thump sounded from somewhere in the house. Abby froze. Had it been the closet? A trick of sound? She listened for a long moment, but everything was quiet.

The conversation with Carlos had left her feeling jumpy—the idea that her father's accident hadn't actually been an accident. But he was in the hospital, and no one was after her, she reminded herself.

She turned to the bed to finish putting away her things, and she heard it again. A soft thump, and then the creak of a floorboard. Someone was in the house.

Abby reached for the lamp and switched it off, heart beating like a scared bird's. What should she do? She glanced at the open window. Climb out? Run to the neighbors for help?

Another creak, and a footstep. Whoever was there was coming down the hall. She wouldn't make it out the window before they got to her room if that's where they were headed.

Hide.

She ran to the corner behind the door and held her breath.

"Who's there?" A hushed voice broke through the pulse pounding in her ears.

"Tallulah?" Abby said.

A small shriek, then, "Abby?" Abby came out from behind the door and switched on the bedroom lamp. "Good Lord child, what are you doing? I saw your car, but the house was dark. I thought you must be out with Carlos. You scared the life out of me."

"I was unpacking. I heard someone in the house."

"So, you hid?"

Abby ignored her question. "What are you doing here?"

"I came over to drop off cookies. They wouldn't let me leave them at the hospital. But I didn't see any lights. I didn't know you were here."

"How did you get in?"

"The door was open. I was going to use the hide-a-key, but I didn't need it." That's right. Abby's hands had been full, and she hadn't bothered to lock the door behind her. She wouldn't do that again. "I thought maybe Paul forgot to lock up, so I was going to do it for him but then I heard a noise back here." Tallulah put a hand over her heart. "Can I have a cup of tea? You gave me quite a scare, girl."

Abby laughed. "I think I need something stronger."

They walked to the kitchen turning on lights as they went and were soon seated at the table with steaming mugs of tea, a bottle of whiskey, and Tallulah's plate of molasses cookies.

"I don't know what on earth is going on around here these days. First, that poor child is left at the Mission to die, then your daddy gets mowed down." Tallulah bit into a cookie.

Abby nodded. She didn't know what to say. Sylla told her the police hadn't disclosed who had tipped them off about the two men. If her father's accident was connected, he must have said something to someone. Could it have been Tallulah? She was a wonderful woman, but she had loose lips. She was everybody's best friend. "It is strange. Makes you wonder." Abby was fishing. She wanted to know how far news about her father's trip to the sheriff's station had spread.

"It does, doesn't it?" Tallulah said.

That was no answer. Abby tried again. "You don't think the two things are related, do you?"

Tallulah shook her head and stared into her mug like she was trying to read the tea leaves. "I don't know."

"I mean, how could they be?"

"These things usually are."

Abby sat up straighter. "What do you mean?"

"They come in threes," Tallulah said in a soft voice. "When those pearly gates open for one soul, they don't shut right away. Others get invited in." Her eyes met Abby's. "But your daddy, he decided not to go."

A shiver ran up Abby's spine. Would others go? She exhaled and dragged herself back to the task at hand—discovering what Tallulah knew. "So, you don't actually know anything that might link my father's accident with the girl?"

Tallulah's eyebrows raised. "No. Why would I?"

Abby stood and took her cup to the sink. She didn't want to face Tallulah when she lied. The woman read her, read most people, like a text message. "No reason. It was just what you said, you know, about the strange things happening lately."

Tallulah pushed her chair away from the table and stood. "I don't *know* anything, honey, but I *feel* lots of things. I'm unsettled in my spirit. That's all I'm saying."

Abby walked her to the door. "I was just going to make a late dinner. You sure you can't stay?"

"No, I promised Jordan I'd be home by nine, and it's past that already. We're going to watch a movie. I've got to spend as much time with that boy as I can when he's home."

Jordan, Tallulah's son, was in his first year at Berkley. Abby knew she missed him. They kissed each other's cheeks, and Abby watched her walk toward her car. Before she reached it, she turned. "You lock up now. You hear me?"

"I will," Abby said, and did as soon as Tallulah's taillights disappeared. She hadn't needed the encouragement. Tallulah's words about the pearly gates and souls departing in threes didn't sound like an old wives' tale tonight. They spooked her.

She stared at the locked door until the emptiness behind her crept forward. It slid up her back and tickled the hairs of her neck. She spun to face the vacant house. Memories flitted from room to room.

Scottie's sneakered feet slapped down the darkened hall to his old bedroom. Five-year-old Abby with cotton candy hair, wearing Scottie's too big hand-me-down jeans trailed after. Her mother's voice floated from the kitchen, "Pick up your things, Scott Raymond Travers." The anchorhold had taught her to hear ghosts, and she wasn't sure that was a good thing.

MOLLY: Poor Paul. I think this falls into the "No good deed goes unpunished" category. He's trying to help his daughter and ends up getting mowed down in the street. Of course, we don't know if the accident was connected to the girl who died at the mission or not. Tallulah's words were pretty ominous, however.

But before I ask your opinion, let's hear from The Wife. She may give us more food for thought.

the wife

THREE DAYS LATER, I decided to make a special dinner. I was so relieved the girl was gone for good I felt like celebrating. It didn't appear she'd be coming back.

I remember dicing an onion with my favorite knife. The one my husband had given me for Christmas two years ago. It was so sharp I'd almost sliced my finger off before I'd learned to use it correctly. But I had learned, and now I loved it.

We hadn't heard anything for days. I did feel a pinch of guilt, but I don't know what more I could have done. I'd spent an entire day nursing her. I would've taken her to the doctor if I could have, but she had no papers.

Seb had connections. That's what my husband said. He knew a doctor who wouldn't ask any questions. I was so tired of hearing about Seb and doubted half of what I'd heard. I'd just read an article in the news about refugee camps in Greece and traffickers who made a living from them. Wasn't Skandalis a Greek name? I was beginning to believe it more likely Seb's nephew was in Greece forging papers than working in the American Embassy in Egypt.

I did hope the part about the doctor was true, however. I wanted to imagine Hannah in a clean bed with antibiotics coursing through her system, on the road to recovery. It assuaged my guilt.

What if Seb wanted us to take her back when she was well? My hand shook, and my cup clattered to the counter. That couldn't happen. I wouldn't let it happen. The burden of her presence far outweighed the burden of caring for the house. The past two days had been a reprieve, so calm after that storm. I wouldn't allow the peace of my home to be disrupted again.

The radio was on, dialed to a local news station. My husband liked to listen while he had breakfast in the mornings. I walked across the kitchen to turn it off but stopped with my hand on the dial.

A newscaster's voice said, "A witness has come forward who claims to have seen two men on El Camino Real the night before the body of an unknown woman was discovered at the San Juan Capistrano Mission. They are not suspects, but the police would like to talk to them. If anyone has any information in this unusual case, please contact the Orange County Sheriff's Department."

Cold crept up my arms. A premonition, an inner voice, her ghost maybe, something told me the mysterious girl was Hannah. It couldn't be. I tried to push the thought from my mind, argue myself out of believing it, but the feeling was as insistent and insidious as a plague.

I turned off the radio, ran to the living room, grabbed the remote from the coffee table and aimed it at the television. After flipping through several stations, I found one that covered local news.

Perched on the edge of an easy chair, I listened to a story about gang violence in Santa Ana, a commercial for dish soap, and then a feature about the increase in Orange County's homeless population. The third story covered what I'd tuned in to hear.

A well-groomed man in his forties stood at the mission gates. "The mystery at the San Juan Capistrano Mission deepens," he said. "Yesterday a young girl, who appears to be of Arab descent, was found dead inside these walls by a volunteer. At this time authorities believe she died of natural causes, but they would like to know who she is, who left her there and why.

"This morning, we learned that an unnamed mission employee reported seeing two men, possibly a father and son, on El Camino Real near the mission wall late Tuesday night. If anyone has any information regarding these men, they're asked to contact the Orange County Sheriff's Department. It's a slim lead, but it's all they've got at this point. Back to you, Becky."

I clicked off the TV and stared at the blank screen. Tuesday night. Two men. Father and son. How could he have done such a thing?

I walked to the kitchen in a fog, forgetting why I'd entered. I turned to leave and remembered. My phone. I had to call my husband, had to hear it from his own lips. I found it on the counter and began to dial the numbers with trembling fingers. The sound of the front door opening made me pause. I waited. A moment later, he entered the kitchen.

His face was as white as death. He opened his arms to me, but I didn't go to him. Instead, I sank into a chair, my legs about to give way. "I thought you were taking her to Seb."

"I did. He wouldn't take her."

"So, you decided to heave her over the wall at the mission and let her die, alone and afraid." The words came out in a monotone, a simple statement of the facts. My emotions were tied up tight in a corner of my heart. I couldn't afford the luxury of giving them free rein.

"No. It wasn't like that."

"What was it like?"

My husband sat in the chair opposite me. "Is there any coffee made?" I jerked my head toward the pot on the counter. He could get his own. But he didn't. He put his elbows on the table and dropped his head into his hands. "I brought her to his house, like I told you I was going to do. But he told me to go away. He said she was my problem, not his. I would have left her anyway, but he had a gun."

"A gun?" I stifled a laugh. This was a television crime drama, not our life.

"Yes, a gun." His voice rose. He stood, opened a cupboard, slammed a mug onto the counter with such force I was surprised it didn't break and filled it.

He took a large gulp, then turned to face me. "He said if I took her to a doctor, I would be arrested. He said if I told the authorities where I got the girl, he and I would both go to jail. But before the police took him, he'd kill you and the children. I didn't know what to do."

"So you took her to the *mission*?" That decision made no sense to me.

"Not at first. I drove to the emergency room. I thought I could leave her there, maybe in the parking lot. But there were too many people, too much light. There was no way. Then I remembered you said you found a cross on her." His eyebrows raised as if I should understand why this was relevant.

"Yes?"

"Those are her people. The Catholics. I figured someone would find her and take care of her."

"It's a museum, not a hospital." I closed my eyes, but the scene continued to play in my mind. My husband and my son taking that poor girl and leaving her out in the cold night air to die. It was murder. A murder of neglect. And he'd made my son a party to it. "You did a terrible thing."

"Maybe it was a mercy. She was half-starved. Sick. Her family didn't want her. We didn't want her. Nobody wanted her."

"She wasn't a dog to put out of her misery. You had no right."

"What else could I have done? You tell me? You said, 'Get rid of the girl.' But you didn't say how. You didn't offer to help."

My emotions came unleashed, and I stood. "I didn't bring her here in the first place. I don't understand how you could have thought for one minute that buying a girl was a good idea. It's not only illegal, it's immoral." He didn't say anything, just stared at the floor. He knew I was right. "And you were seen."

"What?" His head snapped up.

"You were seen. I heard it on the news right before you walked in."

"Who? When?"

"A mission employee. The person said they saw two men near the wall on El Camino Real late Tuesday night."

"I don't see how that could be. There was no one there on the street. We looked."

"You've been missing the obvious lately."

"There was no one there, I'm telling you."

I didn't argue with him. There was someone there, and that someone saw him and my son. I hoped and prayed for my child's sake, the police would have no way of discovering the truth.

MOLLY: Okay, can we all agree the husband isn't the brightest bulb on the tree? Seriously, people, leaving the girl at the mission because she was a Catholic, that's… Well, it defies reason. I'm truly at a loss for words.

About the only thing I can say for The Wife is she's not as big a boob as her hubby. Something she said raised a flag for me. It was the sentence: "A premonition, an inner voice, her ghost maybe, something told me the mysterious girl was Hannah."

In the intro to the podcast every season I say that I want to understand the connection between these crimes. Since I don't see a logical one—at least, not yet—I'm willing to entertain any possibility.

So, cast your minds back to Season One and even earlier. Think about the story *The Dark Room* that was written about a crime that occurred before the events of *The Cliff House*. In both, the people involved felt there might be a supernatural influence.

The Dark Room mystery absolutely screamed supernatural. The drawings on the walls depicted scenes from hell. You don't get much more supernatural than that. *The Cliff House* was less so, but still Gwen Bishop felt something in that basement.

If you haven't read *The Dark Room*, there will be a link for a free digital copy in the show notes in the last episode of this season of the podcast. I don't want to give away the end, but it was postulated that a force from another realm was set free to roam south Orange County. An evil force. I know this is a crazy theory, but give me a better one. It almost seems that a wave was set into motion, a pebble thrown into a dark pond. It's as if each person touched by one ripple is soon surrounded by the next—an ever growing circle.

But enough pontificating. Let's talk about the question of the week. Do you think Paul Travers' accident was an accident? Or do you think hubby had something to do with it? He seems pretty oblivious, but maybe he's smarter than we're giving him credit for. He might be a good actor. Or possibly, the mysterious Seb Skandalis plowed Paul down. Let's talk about it on Facebook.

Join me next time for more *Murders Under the Sun.*

(cue music)

VO: This episode is brought to you by The Fishbowl, your place for Pilates in the OC. *Murders Under the Sun* is edited by Jim Wilbourne, theme music is by Eclectic Blends, and I'm your host, Molly Shure.

part four

MURDERS UNDER THE SUN
SEASON THREE; EPISODE THREE

MOLLY: Welcome back to *Murders Under the Sun*. I'm Molly Shure, your host. Danger is mounting for Abby and her father today. Some of her less than brilliant decisions are beginning to bear fruit. Her story is a cautionary tale if there ever was one. Turns out, not doing the right thing can be just as detrimental as doing the wrong thing.

Before we get into all that, however, I wanted to mention that I loved hearing your thoughts on my supernatural musings at the end of the last episode. I can see most of you aren't convinced. I'm not sure I'm convinced either. It's definitely a crazy explanation, but as I said, "Give me a better one." None of you could, and it did raise an interesting debate.

More interesting than the comments raised by the question of the week. Everyone was in agreement on that. None of you thought Paul Travers' accident was an accident. You all thought it was related to the death of the girl at the mission. As one very astute listener pointed out, why would I spend so much time on it if the two weren't connected? Two points for that.

Last, but not least, I want to thank you for your votes of confidence regarding my ability to find out something about the missing CSU-Fullerton students that the police haven't. As I said to Ms. Jimenez, don't get your hopes up. I'll do some asking around and if I learn anything I'll report back.

Now, let's get back to the topic of our podcast. Here's Abby.

3.3.2

SIGNING her father out of the hospital the next day had been a four-hour affair. Abby had arrived at 11:00 that morning. She'd known she had to wait for the doctor to arrive to release him, which happened about 12:30. Then prescriptions needed to be written, care procedures reviewed, tubes detached, clothes donned, the last hospital lunch eaten, and finally reams of paperwork done.

"Sight for sore eyes," her father said as soon as the house came into view.

"Wait until you get inside. I spent the weekend cleaning and cooking."

"It needed it?" His eyes squeezed into tiny smile-shaped arcs. He knew very well it had. He reached over the center console of the car and patted her thigh. "You're a good kid."

"Are you hungry?" Abby turned off the engine.

"Nope. I already ate lunch, remember? But I could do with a cup of coffee."

"Can you have coffee with those meds you're on?"

"They didn't say I couldn't."

Abby helped her dad, who was still walking stiffly, to the front door. "Smells good in here," he said as soon as he entered.

"It's amazing what happens when you take out the trash."

"I take out the trash, but it never makes the house smell like cookies. Chocolate chip?"

Abby agreed—she had made several batches on Sunday. "And Tallulah dropped off molasses. I'll give you some of both with your coffee. Let's get you settled in bed first."

"I'm not getting in bed in the middle of the day." His voice took on a stubborn edge.

"But the doctor said—"

"I don't care what the doctor said. I don't see what difference it makes if I'm in bed, or I'm in my recliner."

"Maybe she wants you to lie flat. Your ribs and all."

"I wasn't flat in the hospital bed."

Abby couldn't argue with that. He'd been pretty handy with the buttons that controlled the bed angles. "How about the couch?" she said, aiming for a compromise.

"No, ma'am. I've been dreaming about my chair since Saturday." He collapsed into it with a groan and a sigh. "Now stop fussing over me, and hand me the TV remote."

Abby smiled despite her worry for him. Her father was on his second recliner, but this spot, in front and just to the right of the TV and to the left of the big picture window, had been his for as long as she could remember.

After delivering the coffee and cookies, she went out to the car to retrieve his bag. Two figures were walking up the long gravel drive. One was taller than the other, but both displayed the slenderness and loose stride of youth. They must be Mimi's sons. She'd mentioned she had children.

Abby waited by the car, deciding to introduce herself. She wasn't gregarious. What she wanted to do was ignore them. Based on what she knew about high school students from working at a school, that would be their preference too. But she'd decided to make friends with the neighbors for her father's sake. The more people keeping an eye on him, aware of his presence in the house, the better.

As the boys drew closer, a pebble of anxiety plunked into her chest. Not because of her general anti-social nature, but because there was something familiar about the oldest. Something she couldn't put her finger on. Something that brought with it the miasma of a memory. A bad one.

A jolt of recognition snapped up her spine. Could he be? No, she dismissed the idea. But the eyes. The cheekbones. "Hello," she said when they were only a few yards away. "You must be Mimi's boys." She wanted to hear his voice.

The oldest looked at her with suspicion, but the younger smiled brightly. "I'm Evan," he said and held out a hand.

"Abby. I'm Mr. Travers's daughter. I'm going to be staying with him for a while." After shaking Evan's hand, she turned to his brother and examined him. The night had been so dark, and the boy had been in the shadows, but the eyes were the same—dark and exotic.

"Chad," he mumbled and shook her outstretched hand.

"Just getting home from school?" Abby addressed the question to him, but Evan answered.

"Yup. We go to Capo Valley. I'm a freshman, but Chad is a senior."

"Good for you. Do you like it there?"

"It's great. Much better than our old school. Or, at least, better than my old school. Chad liked his okay."

Evan obviously handled communication for the both of them, but she wanted to get Chad talking. "So, you're graduating this year? Do you have college plans?"

Chad stared at his shoes. Evan said, "Chad's good at math. He's probably going to go to UC Irvine next year."

"Really? UCI is a great school for the sciences."

The scratch of a screen door interrupted the conversation. Mimi called to them from her front porch. "You boys bothering Ms. Travers?"

"She said we could call her Abby," Evan said.

"Absolutely," Abby said.

Chad was already halfway across the yard when his mother said, "Well, come on in and let her get back to whatever she was doing. Evan will talk your ear off." Evan gave Abby a lopsided grin and loped off after his brother.

"How's your father doing, Abby?" Mimi said after the boys disappeared through the door she held open.

"He's being very stubborn."

"That's usually a good sign."

They said their goodbyes and Mimi promised to stop by with chicken soup soon. Frustration followed Abby inside the house. She'd wanted to hear Chad speak. *This is stupid.* That's all she'd heard the boy at the Mission say, but it was something. If the eyes and the voice matched. . .

So, what if they did? It didn't mean anything. There were probably dozens of dark-haired young men with exotic-shaped eyes and sullen voices. Didn't most high school males have sullen voices?

She couldn't go to the police based on a vague resemblance, with eyes, cheekbones, and a sullen voice. Carlos was right, it was better for her to stay with her father, take care of him, protect him, than get both of them in trouble. If she had something definitive, something that cast real suspicion on someone, it would be worth it. And solid information would most likely soften the investigator's attitude toward them.

But this wasn't definitive. She was being yanked around by her expectations, seeing what she wanted to see. What was the likelihood that the first boy the right age, with the right coloring she bumped into was the one she'd seen at the Mission? The truth was she wanted so badly to find the men who'd abandoned that girl, who may have tried to kill her father, she was superimposing her desire on the circumstances.

Worse still, she was falling victim to The Other-Race Effect. Most people had a hard time distinguishing the subtle differences in appearance between people of other ethnicities. They all look alike, right? It sounded so racist, but like it or not, and she didn't like it, it was true. Abby was Dutch and British. She was fair and had light brown hair and eyes. Mimi's son was Chinese and whatever ethnicity her husband was, but he wasn't her culprit. Abby put that notion out of her head as the back door slapped shut behind her.

"Abby." Her father's voice rang out. She locked the door before running to the living room. She'd check the windows as soon as she had a minute. They'd never been vigilant about buttoning up the house. They'd never had to. That was about to change.

Her father's face had taken on a gray tinge since she'd left him. "Maybe I was overly optimistic."

"What's wrong?"

"I'm not feeling too good. Can you help me get into bed? I need to rest."

She walked him to his bed, put his pajamas out, and closed the door. The afternoon and evening were spent running back and forth between his room and the kitchen. Caring for her father drove all other thoughts from her mind.

3.3.3

AFTER HIS DINNER, her father finally fell into a fitful sleep. Abby turned off his bedside table lamp, walked straight into the kitchen and poured herself the last glass of Red Ravish. She took it out to the small porch that faced the Jacksons' house and collapsed into the old rocker.

The Jackson house. She didn't know if she'd ever get used to calling it that. Her whole life it had been "Sage's place" or the "Hartman house". The home had been in Sage's family for several generations and was famous in these parts for its garden. The cloying scent of angel's trumpet blew across the yellowed grass and wrapped around her head now.

Sage's grandmother had been San Juan Capistrano's medicine woman and had made herbal remedies for everything from the common cold to postpartum depression. In her day, many people believed she was a witch. Today, some thought she haunted the garden and the house. Abby had never seen her. She believed the house was haunted, but not by a ghost. By memories. The past shrouded the place like a thick fog.

The year after Scottie died, Sage's husband, Doug, died. Abby's family had nothing to do with the man after he tried to poison their dog, Pepe, but it wasn't until the day of his funeral that Abby learned her mother blamed him for Scottie's death as well. It was terrible. And the first time she saw the bitterness that ended up consuming her mother like rust corroding a tin roof.

Abby's mother had worn her favorite yellow dress that day. Usually, she saved it for parties and special occasions. The first thing Dad said when she came out of the bedroom in it was, "Mary, don't you think that's disrespectful?"

Abby didn't know why wearing the yellow dress was disrespectful, or why her father was so upset. She loved the dress. The yellow was such a happy color.

"What?" Mom opened her brown eyes wide.

"His family is grieving."

Mom shrugged and waltzed into the kitchen swinging the skirt around her legs. A little bit later she called them in for breakfast. She'd made pancakes and bacon and gave Dad orange juice with bubbly wine in it. It was like Christmas morning, except Dad didn't look very merry. His mouth was tight and pinched.

Mom hummed as she set the plates of food on the table. She was happier than Abby had seen her since Scottie's death. Abby poured extra syrup on her food and watched from the corner of her eye to see if her hand was going to get slapped, but her mother didn't seem to notice. Dad was busy pushing his food around with a fork.

Mom's cheerful mood didn't last long.

That afternoon, Abby sat in the sun on the back porch and watched cars park all along one side of their long driveway and down on the road. People, in groups of twos and threes, women in black dresses, men in black suits, trooped up to Sage's house carrying platters of food. The ladies wobbled on the gravel in their high heels. The men's shoes crunched loudly.

Her mother came outside, threw herself into the rocker and began to rock, hard and fast. Abby didn't turn around, but she could feel the change in temperature like when a storm cloud covers the sun.

"Emma," Mom called out to one of the women walking up the drive. Emma Williams gave Mom a quick glance from under the brim of her hat.

"Mary," she said so softly Abby almost missed the word.

After Emma Williams came the Carrillos, husband, wife, and two teenage daughters. Mom called out to them too, but not in the friendly, easy way she usually did. The Carrillos nodded, looked at their feet and walked faster. After the Carrillos came Mr. and Mrs. Dempsey, then the Fields family. Mom said hello to all of them in the disappointed voice she used when Dad came home late and smelled like beer, or when Abby got an "Unsatisfactory" on her report card.

She didn't understand why her mother was mad at them. Those people were their friends. They saw them in church. They saw them at school events. But she didn't ask. She didn't want to hear what her mother would say. Somewhere in her seven-year-old mind she understood the answer would change everything.

The screen door slapped open. Dad walked out. "That's enough, Mary."

"I'm just greeting our friends, Paul. It's the neighborly thing to do."

"I said, that's enough." Dad's voice was so cold it could freeze water. Abby had never heard him talk like that to Mom before.

"Get in the house," he said to Abby, his tone softer. She knew better than to argue. She darted inside, but stayed close to the door so she could hear the rest of their conversation.

"You're making a spectacle of yourself," her father said.

"If by spectacle you mean I'm setting an example for these hypocrites, then I agree."

"I haven't said much, because I know what you believe, and I didn't want to upset you. But this has to stop now. The police said it was an accident. The medical examiner said it was an accident. There's no proof Doug had anything to do with it."

Mom's voice raised. "Hey there, Scarlet. Hey, Greg. If you're bringing that pasta salad you brought over when my boy died, Sage is going to be real pleased. Wonderful salad. I love those artichoke hearts you put in it."

"You're shaming our family." Dad's words came out in a hiss.

"They're the ones who should feel ashamed, Paul. Paying respects to a man who doesn't deserve any."

"Let it go, Mary." Dad's voice was pleading now. "Think of Sage and the kids. They haven't done anything wrong, and it's them you're punishing. Doug is gone. He's in God's hands now. If he's guilty, he'll pay. Sins that aren't punished in this world are punished in the next."

"Then I guess I'm going to have to go to hell, so I can watch." And in many ways, Mary Travers had done just that.

The porch door across the grass opened, and a woman stepped out interrupting Abby's trip to the past. Abby couldn't see the woman's face, but she saw Mimi leaning from the doorway. "I'll see you later in the week, then?"

"Absolutely. I'll bring the tile samples as soon as I get them. What day is good for you?" The woman's alto voice rang a familiar chord.

"Thursday?"

"Okay. I'll call."

"Goodnight, Rosie." Mimi disappeared into her home, and Rosie walked along the path to the driveway. When she reached her vehicle, Abby recognized her. She was the interior designer who'd walked by her squint with Tallulah. The interior designer who'd recommended Carlos to Mimi. She watched from the shadows as Rosie got into her car and drove away.

Abby drained the last of her wine and looked at the empty glass. She should get herself something to eat. Put something inane on the television. Rid her mind of morose memories.

The only thing she could do to right the wrongs of the past was to get back to work on her book. Tomorrow, hopefully, her father would be more comfortable, and she'd be able to write. She'd written a lot in her journal while she was in the anchorhold. She wanted to get those notes onto the computer and fleshed out while the experience was still fresh in her mind.

It was already fading. Why was it so hard to forget the things you wanted to forget, while good memories evanesced? Perhaps if she went to the mission next week and sat on the bench between the restrooms and her cell, remembrances of her days there would revive the way older, darker times had revived sitting on this porch.

She stood and stretched. Imagining that small bit of world visible from her squint comforted her. She walked into the kitchen and began reheating spaghetti left over from her father's dinner. Now that she was clean, had slept in a soft bed for a couple of nights, and eaten some hot meals, she missed her hidden life. She'd had nobody to please, no decisions to make, no knotty relationships to untangle. Things were so much less complicated in the anchorhold.

3.3.4

THE NEXT MORNING, Abby sat at the kitchen table, laptop in front of her, journal at her right hand. She'd been at it for nearly two hours, and she'd only transcribed three or four pages so far. Her father was feeling better today. Consequently, he'd wanted coffee, breakfast, help dressing, and assistance to his chair. He was there now, remote in hand, watching an old Turner Classic movie. She hoped, with a guilty twinge, it would keep him busy for a while. She sipped a fresh cup of coffee, and dove in.

> Often the decision to become an anchorite had traumatic roots. Julian of Norwich, 1342 - 1416, survived an attack of the plague, while her entire family died. At thirty, Julian got very sick. She was near death. When the priest came to administer last rites, she had a vision. As the priest raised the crucifix, she saw the figure of Jesus. He was bleeding. This event was followed by sixteen separate visions of Jesus. They are recorded—

A knock at the door interrupted her. Really? Was she ever going to get anything done? If it wasn't her father, it was the phone, or someone selling solar panels. "Abby," her father called from the living room. "Door."

"Got it," she said on her way past the living room. She swung the door open and the we're-not-interested expression she'd donned slid from her face. It was Detective Sylla. "Oh."

"Sorry for the surprise visit," Sylla said and flashed a set of very white teeth. Clearly, she wasn't.

"Can I help you?" Abby said.

"Can I come in?"

"Oh," Abby said again, suddenly aware of her rudeness. "Of course." She stepped aside and the investigator entered.

"How's your father doing?"

"Much better, thank you."

"Who is it?" her father yelled, as if on cue.

"The police. Detective Sylla." Abby led the woman into the living room. "She wants to know how you're doing."

He flipped off the TV, disguising his disappointment with a smile. "A bit sore and slow moving, but I'm not at death's door. Nice of you to check on me, Detective."

"Glad to hear it." She walked to a chair opposite Abby's dad's, but didn't sit. "I was hoping you could answer a few more questions for me, now that you're on the mend."

"I'm afraid I told you everything I remember about the accident while I was in the hospital."

"Do you mind if we run over it one more time?"

He sighed and nodded.

"Can I get you a cup of coffee?" Abby asked. She ought to be polite.

"That would be lovely," Sylla said.

"Refill, Dad?" He handed her his mug.

"Going back to the day of the accident. You headed to your favorite coffee shop at about three."

"It's not my favorite, but it's the closest to work."

"Right, well. You're walking across El Camino Real . . . "

The conversation became a muffle of voices as Abby entered the kitchen. The coffee pot was all but empty. She dumped the remainder, rinsed the carafe, and set up a fresh pot. She thought about returning to the living room, but decided to wait until the coffee was brewed. She'd heard the story of the accident more times than she could count.

Instead, she sat at her laptop and typed another paragraph from her journal into her manuscript, editing as she did.

When the pot sputtered out its final drops, she stood, poured two cups, put them on a tray, added a container of half and half and a sugar bowl. Not very fancy, but her father had given all her mother's china to a thrift store. Besides, it wasn't a social visit.

"I have all the receipts." She could hear her father's indignant words from the hall. Receipts for what? Abby couldn't imagine what receipts had to do with the accident.

"I'd like to see them, if possible." Sylla's body language belied her pleasant tone of voice. She stood where she'd been when Abby left the room but had assumed the position of a soldier at ease—feet wide, hands clasped behind her back.

"Why on earth would you need them? Everybody knows I was the one who modified the exhibit."

Abby's hand shook as she set the tray on the coffee table upending the container of half and half. She righted it before any spilled.

"I'm simply surprised you paid for all the supplies. Wondering why you didn't request the Diocese or the foundation to contribute."

"I tithe to the church. I decided to take my tithe money for the year and apply it to a worthy project. Upkeep on a historic site, like the mission, isn't cheap. I felt I was doing my part. I don't see what this has to do with anything."

Abby heard the defensiveness in her father's tone. If she could hear it, it screamed to a trained law enforcement officer. She tried to catch his eye, to warn him, but he avoided her gaze. How had the conversation taken this strange turn?

"Noble of you." Sylla's voice was deadpan. "Would you mind if I collect those receipts? Then, I can let you get back to your movie."

"I have to find them, make copies for my tax records. And as you can see, I'm not exactly up to—"

"I could come back tomorrow." She paused, then added, "With a warrant."

"Your coffee," Abby broke in before her father could say anything else. She held out a mug to Sylla. She didn't take it, didn't even look at it.

She'd locked eyes with Abby's father. Tension ran between them like taut rubber bands.

"I'll bring them down to the station this afternoon," Abby said.

Sylla didn't speak for several long moments, as if she was waiting for Abby's father to protest. He didn't, thank God. "Fine," she said, breaking the silence. "You'll come round by three."

It was more of a command than a request, but Abby said, "Three is fine." The investigator showed herself out. Abby lowered herself onto the couch before her legs gave way.

3.3.5

HER FATHER'S discomfort intensified after lunch. Abby helped him to bed, gave him a painkiller and wrested the whereabouts of the receipts from him before he nodded off.

She called Carlos several times, as she dug the receipts out of a file box in the closet and got ready to go. He didn't pick up. Equipment on job sites was so noisy he often couldn't hear his phone. She hated to leave her father home alone, but didn't see that she had a choice. This was an emergency.

She locked the door behind her just in time to see Mimi pull up their shared driveway. Should she ask Mimi to keep an eye on the house, check in on her father? Did they know each other well enough? She chewed on her lower lip and made a decision. Abby couldn't live here forever. She should forge a relationship with the neighbor for her dad's sake. She approached Mimi's car.

"Abby, hi," Mimi said, as she exited.

"I have a big favor to ask. I'm on my way out. I have to run some errands."

"Do you need me to check on your father while you're gone?"

Abby was relieved she didn't have to ask. "That would be great. He's asleep now, but if he wakes and I'm not there. . ."

Mimi raised the rear door of her vehicle and reached in to retrieve a shopping bag. "I'll put this stuff away, and pop over."

"I locked the front door, but there's a hide-a-key under the third brick on the right." Abby pointed to the brick-lined walkway.

"Perfect," Mimi said.

"I'll hurry."

"You don't need to. I'm in for the day."

Abby thanked her and left. She would hurry despite Mimi's reassurances. Mimi wasn't aware of the potential danger, and Abby couldn't tell her.

She made it to the office supply store in record time, copied the receipts and headed to the station. She left the envelope at the front desk with instructions to deliver it to Detective Sylla and ran out the door. She had no interest in seeing the woman.

Her phone jingled as she crossed the parking lot. It was Carlos. "What's up?"

"Sylla came by. I wanted to tell you about it. I'm just leaving the station now."

"Your dad is home alone?"

"Mimi is keeping an eye on him."

"What happened?" His voice was tense.

"Where are you?"

"The office. Why?"

"I'll come by now. I don't think I want to talk about this on the phone."

"But your dad—"

"I won't stay long." Eleven minutes later, Abby pulled up to Rojo Landscaping. It was in a long, narrow stretch of parking lot between an auto-mechanic's shop and a tire shop. She hadn't been there in months, but nothing had changed.

She opened the glass door and was met with a blast of cool air. A young girl sat at a desk only feet from the entrance. She looked at Abby through unfriendly, Kohl-lined eyes and popped her gum. "Can I help you?" Her voice was familiar. Her face was familiar too, but Abby couldn't place her.

"I'm here to see Carlos," Abby said.

"I'll see if he's available." She reached for the phone with a hand adorned with nails the most terrible color pink Abby had ever seen.

"It's okay, Gab." Carlos appeared in the doorway of his small office. "This is Abby."

The girl's hard expression transformed into a broad grin. "Your girlfriend?"

"Yeah." An uncomfortable expression crossed his face.

"Wow. So good to meet you." The girl stood and pumped Abby's hand. "Tia Connie is always talking about you. How pretty you are. How smart you are. How Carlos should—"

"This is Gab," Carlos interrupted her. "My cousin."

Abby smiled. Cousin. That explained it. She had the Rojo look under all that makeup. Her jaw was almost as square and stubborn as Carlos's, and her eyes were every bit as wide and beautiful. She must have seen Gab at a family function. When the entire Rojo clan gathered, Abby generally hid in the kitchen with Connie. The crowd was daunting.

"Come on back." Carlos extended his arm toward the room behind him. Gab looked disappointed. He shut the door, took his phone from his pocket and typed something into it. A second later, country music blared from a speaker on a bookshelf. "She's got big ears." He nodded his head in Gab's direction.

Abby moved close to him and spoke sotto voce. "That detective came to the house today. She said she wanted to ask Dad about the day of the accident. I left them alone together, just long enough to make a pot of coffee. When I came back, she was grilling him about the Swallows Nest exhibit at the mission."

Carlos's chin jerked to his chest. "What did she want to know?"

"She wanted to see all the receipts from the supplies it took to build it. She seemed to think it was strange he paid for the whole thing, didn't ask the Diocese or the foundation to chip in."

"Do you think she saw the anchorhold? Looked inside?"

"I don't know. But even if she did, why would she care?"

"She might think it has something to do with the girl they found."

"What, like the men were seen from the anchorhold, not from the street? How would she get that idea?"

"I don't know, but it makes me nervous."

A muscle in Carlos's cheek contracted. He was as worried about her father as she was. His protectiveness was endearing when it was directed at someone else. Abby wanted to stroke his face, to calm him, but she didn't.

"We have to get the rest of your stuff out of there," he said.

"That's what I was thinking. If the police found the toilet and the mattress, they'd know someone was living there."

"I'd guess it was a homeless person if I was that detective. But homeless or not, he or she might have been there the night the girl showed up. I'd want to find the person. Talk to them."

Abby hugged herself and groaned.

He put a hand on her arm. "I can't go tonight. There's a family thing at my aunt's house. I have to take my mother. But I'll go tomorrow night."

"I'll go with you."

"No. You stay with your dad."

"But I don't want you—"

"I can handle it."

Abby's eyes shifted away from his. She hated this. She had no idea when she moved into the cell at the mission it would end up putting everyone she cared about at risk. She'd had good intentions, but what was that expression? Something about them paving the road to hell.

Carlos put a hand on hers and took a pen from her. She hadn't even realized she'd taken it from his desk and been flicking it up and down. "I was going to go back and grout in the loose stones anyway. Might as well clean out your stuff while I'm there." He held her hand a moment longer than necessary.

"Okay. But I don't like it," she said.

He looked into her eyes. "I know." There was nothing romantic about his words, but an ember of hope flickered to life inside her. He hadn't mentioned marriage since their argument. She didn't know whether to be upset or relieved about that, but she did know she missed what they'd had. Maybe they could go back to the way things were. She'd been comfortable then, before he'd pressed her to make decisions.

3.3.6

BY TEN THE NEXT DAY, the sun had burned off the morning gloom. Abby lifted the newspaper from the edge of the driveway and breathed in damp earth, manure from the petting zoo on nearby Los Rios Street, and sage—the scents of her childhood. Her father was doing better today. He was up, dressed, in his chair, and calling for the paper. He wanted to peruse it with his coffee.

Abby told herself she would write today. But more and more, it seemed like she was working on a travel guide to a country she'd never visited. Avoiding this disconnect was the reason she'd entered the anchorhold. If she could spend some time at the mission, maybe her enthusiasm would return. But how was she going to do that? She couldn't leave her father alone. The mission, although only minutes from the house, might as well be in a foreign land.

"Here's your paper, Dad." She placed it on the end table next to his chair with his reading glasses.

He put a hand on hers and squeezed it. "Thanks, honey."

"Are you good?"

"I'm good. You go write."

Abby plastered a smile on her face, nodded and went to the kitchen. Her laptop was already on and opened on the table. She'd booted it up while she was fixing her father's breakfast, so she'd have no excuses.

She sank into a chair, placed her hands on the keyboard like a pianist readying herself to begin a recital, and stared at the blank screen.

An anchoress, although solitary, did rely...

Abby paused for a moment, then deleted the words. She typed, *The anchoress would have been lost without aid from—* She hit the backspace key, stared at the screen for another long minute, then leaped from her chair.

It was hopeless. She didn't care who the anchoress relied on, and in fact was beginning to think those women would have been a lot better off if they'd handled their own affairs instead of burdening everyone else.

She strode through the house to check on her father, who was reading his paper placidly. He glanced up and sent her a questioning smile. "Just making sure you don't need anything," she said.

"No. I'm good. Don't bother with me. You have things to do."

"Right." Abby pivoted and returned to the kitchen. Her laptop grinned at her from the table like a mocking sprite. She breathed deeply and moved toward her chair. But before she sat, the doorbell rang. She almost ran to the front hall.

"Abby, someone's here," her father called.

She knew that. You could hear the bell from every room in the small house, but she answered with the words he expected to hear. "I've got it."

Tallulah stood on the stoop, a covered baking dish in her hands. Today she was wearing a kimono-inspired dress—a fitted red silk print with a Mandarin collar and a pair of black ballet slippers. Must be what all well-dressed people wore to deliver meals. "Is he up?" she said.

"Yes. He's doing great today. Come on in." She was so thankful for the interruption; she kissed Tallulah's cheek and gave her an extra hard squeeze.

"I've brought you my famous fava bean casserole." Tallulah thrust the dish at Abby.

"Yum. Dad will be so excited." Her father hated fava beans, but Tallulah had no idea. He always made a fuss over the dish, so she kept making it. And Abby kept throwing it out. "He's in the living room."

Abby walked past her laptop on the way to the refrigerator but didn't look at it. After putting the beans away, she hurried to the living room.

"Everyone wants to know when you're coming back to work," Tallulah said.

"I have a doctor's appointment next week. I'm hoping she'll spring me," her father said.

"I doubt it," Abby said. "You need to rest, get those ribs healed up."

He shook his head. "I'm doing better every day. I'll go crazy if I have to stay on house arrest much longer."

Tallulah settled on the couch and crossed one long, black-stockinged leg over another. "Why don't you go run errands or something, Abby? You've been trapped in this house as much as he has."

Freedom. It sounded wonderful. "Are you sure?"

"I wouldn't say so if I wasn't." She jogged her leg up and down. "I have the day off, and I don't have to be anywhere until four."

Abby had wanted to go to the mission, had wanted to sit on the bench near the anchorhold in the sunshine. She was sure her muse would return if she could relive some of those days she spent in her cell, soak up the atmosphere. "If you're—"

Tallulah held up a hand to interrupt her. "How can I fill your daddy in on all the gossip from work while you're standing there? Go on. Get out of here."

"Thanks." Abby rushed to her bedroom to grab a sweater, and then to the kitchen to pack her laptop into a tote bag. She stopped by the living room to kiss her father on top of his bald head, waggled her fingers at Tallulah and headed to the front hall.

"Don't let that door hit you on the way out." Tallulah's laugh was cut short by the closing of said door.

3.3.7

THE BENCH WAS PARTIALLY SHADED by a bougainvillea. Abby sat on the sunny end, closed her eyes, and immersed herself in sensory luxury. The scents of roses and lavender replaced the manure and sage of her father's front yard. She smiled at the familiar trills and chirps of the birds that had been her roommates for a month. A breeze cooled her warm skin.

For a moment, she was inside her anchorhold in the days before the girl. A ghost of the restless excitement that had been her constant companion then, hovered on the edges of her mind. She willed it to come close, to sit by her on the bench, to revive her desire to write.

The distressed caw of a crow caused her to open her eyes. She watched the large black bird dodge as a mockingbird swooped and dove around it. A squirrel scurried onto the grass in front of her, stopped short and eyed her. "No peanuts, friend," she said. The squirrel flipped around and disappeared into the foliage.

"Who are you talking to?" A voice behind her made her jump. She twisted in her seat, and saw Steven, the garden volunteer.

"A squirrel. He was begging."

"They're bold. We tell the tourists not to feed them, but they do it anyway." Steven made his way around the bench to stand in front of her. "Steven Homestead. I'm a garden volunteer."

Abby suppressed a smile. She'd seen Steven three to five days a week for the entire time she was in the hold. It was a strange feeling, knowing people who didn't know you at all. It was kind of like meeting your favorite soap opera star. "Abby Travers," she said.

"You're Paul's daughter?"

She nodded.

"How's he doing? We all heard about the accident." Steven's handsome face crinkled into concerned lines.

"Better. He's still moving slow but we've cut back on the pain pills. He's only taking them at night now."

"Wow. Crazy, right? So weird it happened right after that girl died here."

"Yeah. Crazy." Abby scooted closer to the edge of the bench and Steven sat next to her.

"Do you think the accident had anything to do with it? With the girl?"

Abby tensed. "What do you mean? Why would it?"

He shrugged. "Paul was the one who reported seeing the guys who did it. Maybe they found out."

"What makes you think my father saw anything?" She sounded sharp and angry.

Steven glanced at her, surprised. "I saw him at the police station." He paused. Abby waited for him to continue. "I was the one who found the girl, you know." He sounded almost proud. "So, I was in and out of there for a couple of days. They kept asking me the same questions, and I kept giving them the same answers."

He paused again, longer this time, like he'd forgotten the original question. "My dad?" Abby prompted him.

"Right. The morning after we found the body, the police asked me to come in to answer a couple more questions. I saw your dad leaving the station. The next day the media said a mission employee had come forward as a witness. I figured it was Paul."

Anxiety knotted Abby's stomach. "I hope you didn't say anything to anyone. The police were keeping his identity a secret."

He rubbed dirt off a fingernail. "No. I mean, I don't think so." He studied his other nail beds. "I might have mentioned it to one or two of the other volunteers, but they wouldn't . . ."

"Someone did." Abby's face shot toward his, her peace shattered. "Who did you talk to?"

"I don't know. Everyone was talking about your father's accident at the St. Joseph's Day meeting. I might have said something."

"Think. Who was there?"

He stared at his shoes. "A lot of people. Tallulah. She's the—"

Abby's heart fell. "I know Tallulah." And she loved her, but Tallulah was the biggest gossip at the Mission.

"And a bunch of volunteers. I didn't know everybody's names." He looked her in the eye. "I'm serious, I don't remember. I'm not even sure I said anything. I know I thought it."

Abby tried to keep the irritation from her voice. "If you hear anybody talking about it, put out the fire. Okay? Tell them it's just a rumor."

"I'm really sorry." He looked it. "I'd feel awful if I had anything to do with your dad's accident."

"Just don't say anything to anyone else," Abby said and hurried to the exit. Suddenly it didn't seem safe to leave her father with anyone, not even Tallulah.

By the time Abby got home, her father was hungry. She hugged Tallulah goodbye, went directly to the kitchen, and threw together a tuna sandwich for him. Then she did the breakfast and snack dishes, cleaned the counters and stove top, and swept the floor. By the time she'd done all that it was 4:30. Since she hadn't gotten anything done at the mission, she decided to work until it was time to start dinner.

She turned on her computer and opened her journal. Forty-five minutes and only two pages later, there was a knock at the kitchen door. Abby closed her eyes. Her project seemed doomed. Even when she had time to spend on it, she couldn't get anything accomplished.

Mimi and her husband stood at the door, pot in hand. "I brought the chicken soup."

"You're so sweet." Abby ushered them in. "Let me take that."

"This is my husband, Bradley."

Abby set the pot on the stove, turned, and shook his hand. He wasn't a tall man, dark-haired, olive-skinned and older than Mimi by some years. Their boys had inherited Mimi's eyes but had their father's deeper skin tone. "Nice to meet you," Abby said.

"How's your father?" Mimi asked.

"Come and see." Abby led them into the living room. "Dad, the neighbors are here."

She left them together and went to look for a bottle of wine. She'd heard her father's version of the accident too many times. In the kitchen, she rifled through his cupboard looking for a nice red. There wasn't anything as fancy as the bottle she and Carlos had drunk, but she found a decent mid-priced Cabernet. She uncorked it, took three glasses from the cupboard and carried everything to the living room.

"I have better wine than that. There's one called Ravishing Red, or Red Ravish—some crazy name—in the cupboard." Her father turned to Mimi. "Your real estate agent gave it to me."

"Who, Gwen Bishop?" she asked.

"Yeah. I kept an eye on things for her while the place was on the market. Called her when the fliers ran low. Let her know when people came by. She brought me that bottle of wine when the house sold. Nice lady. She said the wine was one of her favorites. I was saving it for a special occasion."

"Ah," Abby said. All three sets of eyes turned to her. "Carlos and I drank it. Sorry, Dad. I didn't know. We'll get you another bottle."

He waved away the suggestion. "Doesn't matter, as long as somebody enjoyed it."

Bradley gestured to the bottle Abby carried. "We drink this at home. Love it." He had a subtle accent, but Abby couldn't place it.

Bradley and Mimi settled on the couch. Abby took the chair across from her father's. His bruises were livid in the maroon glow of evening light coming through the big picture window. The Jacksons must have noticed this as well, and the conversation flagged. She sipped her wine, using the moment to think of something to say.

But her father spoke first. "So, what do you do, Bradley?" The classic male ice-breaker.

"I work for Boeing. I'm in customer relations," Bradley said in his cultured tone.

"Interesting work?" her father asked.

"Most of the time. I'm getting a little tired of all the traveling. When I was younger, I thought it was exciting. Now . . ."

"Most of his clients are in the Middle East," Mimi said. "Makes for very long flights."

"And a lot of TSA hoopla," her husband added.

"He misses out on so much with the boys."

"Only been to one of Chad's basketball games this year." Bradley shook his head.

"I met your boys the other day," Abby said.

"Let me guess," Bradley said. "Evan talked your ear off, and you couldn't get a word out of Chad."

"They were both very polite, but, yes, Evan did do most of the talking."

They chit-chatted about their busy schedules and how everyone was adjusting to life in San Juan Capistrano as the elongated rectangles of sun painted across the carpet dimmed from red to gray. It was past six. Abby was content to sit in the dying light. She'd given up the battle with time in the anchorhold and embraced the changes the hours brought, but she stood and turned on lamps for the others.

Worry nibbled on the edges of her mind. Carlos was going to the mission that night. For her. What if the police were keeping an eye on things there? What if the night security guard had become more vigilant since the girl had been found? What if he was caught?

"Abby." She jumped. Her father's expression was quizzical.

"Sorry. Thinking." He must have said her name more than once.

"Our guests are leaving. Can you see them out?" He looked at his lap as if to explain why he didn't go himself.

"No need," Mimi said.

"Let's not be so formal," Bradley said. "We're neighbors."

In the doorway, Abby thanked them again for the soup and promised to bring the pot back soon. Mimi said not to hurry and took off across the yard. Bradley followed close behind, his solid silhouette so much stockier than her petite form.

Solid.

Stocky.

A memory of the night the girl was left outside her window paraded through her mind. *Two men, builds so similar she guessed they were father and son—the heavier man a preview of what the younger would become in time.*

The vision had a soundtrack. Mimi's voice: "Most of his clients are in the Middle East. Makes for very long flights." The police had said the girl appeared to be of Middle Eastern descent.

Chad had exotic eyes and high cheekbones.

Circumstantial. There were probably dozens of families in San Juan Capistrano who had exotic looking sons with stocky fathers and some connection to the Middle East. But she wasn't going to ask Mimi to sit with her father anymore.

MOLLY: Poor Abby. Seems like she's getting paranoid. Doesn't know who to trust anymore. Every family she comes in contact with that has a connection to the mission and a teenage son with high cheekbones is suspect.

Abby's life is spinning out of control. Not only is she plagued by doubts about everyone around her, but Detective Sylla is asking questions about the construction of the anchorhold. What's that about? Maybe that should be the question of the week.

But before I sign off, I have a couple of emails from The Wife to read to you. They are chilling.

the wife

I **WAS SO UPSET,** I raced through a yellow light just as it turned red. I'd just heard a terrible rumor and needed to get home and talk to my husband, find out what he knew. Fear surged through me in waves. He'd kept so much from me over the past week, I didn't trust him anymore. Did he know about the accident?

The girl's death was terrible, an act of criminal neglect. But this, if it had been successful, would have been first-degree murder. A fuse of anger sparked within me on the short drive. By the time I walked into the house my panic was gone, replaced by a quiet rage.

My husband sat in the living room, a basketball game blaring on the television. "I need to speak to you," I said.

He grunted a response, but didn't take his eyes off the screen.

"Now."

"Shoot the ball," he yelled at the TV.

"I need to speak to you." I raised my voice.

"Aw!" He slapped his leg in disgust.

"It's important."

"Honey, this is. . . Move, move, move."

I picked up the remote and turned the TV off.

"Hey." A dark look marred his features. "Can't it wait ten—"

"Paul Travers, a mission employee, was hit by a car. There are rumors that he was the one who saw two men the night Hannah died. That the accident wasn't an accident."

The look of shock on his face appeared genuine. "They can't think it has anything to do with her."

"It's quite a coincidence," I said, repeating the words I'd heard.

"That's what it must be." His voice wasn't as confident as his words.

"You didn't have anything to do—"

His head snapped around. "Good lord no. What do you think of me? You've been married to me all these years and don't know me better than that?"

"I didn't think you were the kind of man who would purchase a child to do my housework. I didn't think you'd leave that same girl out in the cold to die alone. Honestly, I don't know who you are anymore."

His face hardened, and he opened his mouth as if to defend himself but closed it without speaking. What could he say?

I sat on the couch and trained my gaze on him. For once, I didn't care about his ego, his mood, his sensibilities. I wanted the truth. A long minute passed before he spoke. "It's possible Seb had something to do with it."

I watched him squirm as he chose his next words. "He called me yesterday."

"What did he say?" My voice held a hard edge I'd never heard before.

"He wanted to know what I knew. If I saw anyone at the mission that night. If anyone could have been close enough to get a good look at us. He'd heard a witness had gone to the police." He turned up his palms. "I would have sworn in a court of law no one was on the street when we climbed over the wall."

I waited.

"After he yelled at me, Seb said not to worry. He'd take care of it."

"He'd take care of it?" I said.

"I... I didn't think about what that meant. I was just relieved. You know?" He turned toward me, a plea for understanding in his eyes.

"How would he know who the witness was? The news didn't name him."

My husband shrugged. "I told you; he has connections."

I stood, too full of adrenaline to sit any longer. "What kind of man have you gotten us involved with?"

"He's a financial planner." My husband's words ended in a sob.

I paced across the living room, thoughts churning through my mind. What did this accident mean to my family? How would these new developments impact us? "Well, he didn't take care of it," I finally said. "The man who saw you, who saw our son—" My husband groaned. "Saw our son," I repeated. "That man is still alive. Seb Skandalis is not only ruthless, he's inept."

My husband buried his face in his hands. "I'm sorry. So sorry."

"Sorry does nothing." I continued my pacing. "You need to call Seb."

He raised damp eyes. "I can't."

I stopped moving and returned his gaze. "Why not?"

"It's safer if we have no more contact with him. That's what he said. We don't want the police to make any connection between us. It's for our own protection."

My laugh was bitter. "He's protecting himself, not us. He wasn't spotted at the mission that night. You were. He would sacrifice you to save his own skin in a heartbeat. You'll call him."

"I can't. He was very adamant on that point," my husband said.

"I don't care what he's adamant about. We need information if we're going to protect ourselves."

"I don't think he knows any more than we do." My husband's mouth formed a thin, stubborn line.

"He knew who the witness was."

"We don't know that for sure. Maybe the accident was a coincidence," he said with no conviction in his voice.

"But he has connections. At least, that's what I've been told over and over. You've assured me, he can find out anything."

"What do you want me to say?"

"I want you to ask him if he was the one who tried, and failed, to kill Paul Travers. If so, I want to know why he did it. I want you to ask him if he knows, exactly what, if anything, Paul saw that night."

My husband looked horrified. "I can't do that."

"Why?"

"He won't like it. He's not the kind of man you want to have angry at you."

I put my hands on my hips and spoke in a firm voice. "If we went to the police now, we might have to suffer some consequences, but we could put him away for a very long time. He needs to cooperate with us."

My husband looked sick, but didn't argue.

"Call him tomorrow." I stalked from the room. I wasn't the kind of woman you wanted to have angry at you either.

Tuesday, March 20, 5:15 PM

I wore a rut in the living room carpet waiting for my husband to get home from work the next evening. He'd cut me off on the phone earlier. He'd said he had to go. Seb was on another line. I thought he'd call me as soon as they hung up, but he hadn't.

The front door opened at exactly 5:15. His step was heavy. I didn't go to him the way I usually did. He could come to me.

"What did he say?" I was afraid I already knew. My husband's face was somber.

"Can I have something to drink first?"

I stomped into the kitchen, threw a few ice cubes into a glass and filled it with iced tea. I knew he preferred his ice crushed, but I wasn't in any mood to pamper him. Cubed was quicker.

When I returned, I found him on the couch. He was a husk of the man he'd been only a week ago. His usually well-groomed hair looked greasy and needed a cut. His shirt was wrinkled and had perspiration stains in the armpits. His hand shook as he took the iced tea glass.

"Well?" I tried to keep the impatience from my voice.

"Paul Travers is home from the hospital. It seems he wasn't injured as badly as Seb had hoped."

I inhaled sharply. "He did try to kill him then."

My husband nodded. "He saw our boy."

My son. Why him? If Paul Travers had to see anyone, why couldn't it have been my husband? "What are we going to do?" I heard the panic in my voice.

"Seb wants me to finish the job."

"What?" The question exploded from me.

"What's going on?" The son we'd been discussing stood in the doorway. My heart skipped a beat. I hadn't heard him come home. I had no idea how long he'd been standing there.

"Nothing." My husband and I said the word simultaneously.

He looked at each of us for a long moment, turned and disappeared down the hallway. I'm sure he knew it wasn't nothing. He was young, but he wasn't stupid.

My husband lowered his voice to a stage whisper. "He says he can't try again. He can't take a chance. There were witnesses. They saw his car. It's gone, sent to Mexico, but if something else goes wrong the police may put two and two together."

"So he wants you to do it?"

His face transformed into a parody of the Tragedy Mask of Greek Theater. "How could I? How would I?"

My heart turned to cold stone. I felt no pity for him, only contempt. "Those are two completely different questions. One is a moral question. The other a practical one. Which do you want the answer to?"

He threw his hands up and let them drop into his lap. "I don't know."

"How could you? That one is easy. You're already a murderer."

"I'm not. I didn't . . . She was alive when I left her."

I waved a hand in the air, erasing his excuses. "And she might have been alive the next morning if you'd taken her to the hospital." His jaw tightened. "The point is, you've proved you're willing to do what you have to do to protect your reputation, your position in the community."

"I would have gone to jail."

"Maybe. Maybe not. Even if you did, it wouldn't have been a long sentence. You could have gone to the police with the whole story. Told them Seb Skandalis had tricked you into believing you were simply taking in a girl from a foreign country, offering her a job. You were told she was here legally. But you didn't."

He shrank deeper into the couch. "I don't know what to do. I don't know what to do." He repeated the phrase like a mantra, which it certainly wasn't. He looked more and more miserable with every utterance.

"You did what you thought you had to do to protect yourself."

"I don't know what to do." His keening tone grated on me.

"I understand that." I tried to soothe him, but my words sounded harsh.

"I don't know what to do."

I was done with this. "Be a man. Do what you have to do to protect your family."

His head snapped as if I'd slapped him. He turned his tear-streaked face to me. "What is that? Tell me? I don't know anymore."

I sat next to him, took his hand, and softened my voice. "You're going to do exactly as I say."

MOLLY: Is she scary, or what? I've always heard male bears can be dangerous, but never ever get between a mama bear and her cubs. And this mama bear wants Paul Travers dead. Turns out Abby was right to be paranoid. The circle is closing around them.

Which brings me to the question of the week: Why do you think Sylla wants to see the receipts for the anchorhold? Why does she care if Abby's father built the thing? What difference does it make? Pop into the Facebook group and let me know your thoughts.

Join me next time for more *Murders Under the Sun.*

(cue music)

VO: If you enjoyed this episode, please leave us a five-star review on your favorite podcast service—it really helps. *Murders Under the Sun* is edited by Jim Wilbourne, theme music is by Eclectic Blends, and I'm your host, Molly Shure.

part five

MURDERS UNDER THE SUN
SEASON THREE; EPISODE FOUR

MOLLY: Welcome to Season Three of *Murders Under the Sun*. This is Molly Shure, your host.

We are at the halfway point of our story today, which seems like a good time to do a little recap. What have we learned in the prior three episodes?

The mystery, of course, is who left that poor girl on the grounds of the San Juan Capistrano Mission to die. We know a little about them. Actually, we know more than Abby did at the time thanks to The Wife's emails.

We know a man bought a young Coptic Christian girl from Egypt to be his domestic slave. He'd have said servant, but when the person has no choice, they're a slave. We even know who he bought her from. A man called Seb Skandalis.

We also know he has a teenage son he roped into helping him get rid of the girl, and a wife who's proving herself to be pretty cold and calculating. What we don't know is who the man and his wife are.

Neither Abby nor Detective Sylla are privy to this information at this point in the narrative. They are each trying to solve the mystery without a lot to go on, and for different reasons. Sylla wants to prosecute the person who mistreated and abandoned the girl. Abby wants to protect her father.

You'll see in today's episode that even though Abby doesn't know anything about The Wife's proclamation that hubby needs to man up and get rid of Paul Travers, she becomes even more frantic to figure out who might be after him.

Is it a premonition? Or is the guilt getting to her? After all, Paul wouldn't be in the middle of this if Abby hadn't come up with her hair-brained scheme to live in an anchorhold at the mission for 40 days. Whatever the reason, her past seems to be catching up with her, and she's very emotional. Sylla, on the other hand, is as cool and controlled as Abby is a hot mess. Danger and uncertainty have that effect on people.

Which reminds me, thank you to those who sent comments and emails this week about your personal experiences. It's sad how many of us have been impacted by crime. I believe if we can find the reasons behind them, capture the perpetrators, mete out justice, it will go a long way toward healing our hearts. This is why I do what I do.

Having said all that, I did report that I would look into the missing CSU-Fullerton students, but I absolutely can't get involved in all the mysteries mentioned in the group. As absolutely devastated as I am to hear your stories, I simply can't get involved with them all. And I don't think I'd be any help to you if I did.

Now, back to the question of the week. Why did Sylla want the receipts for the anchorhold? Your answers were all over the board. Some of you thought Sylla wanted them because she didn't believe Paul Travers made the anchorhold. Some thought she suspected him of building the anchorhold to house the girl. Some just thought she was out of ideas, grasping at straws.

Well, you'll find out what she actually thought today. You'll also find out what The Wife's instructions to her husband were. As you'll hear, neither of these revelations brings comfort to Abby.

3.4.2

AFTER SETTLING her father in front of the TV with a plate of scrambled eggs and toast, Abby poured herself a cup of coffee and sat to write. She didn't want to. The project had taken on the ambiguous, unpleasant aura of a bad dream. When she thought about it, a rush of anxiety, guilt, and other negative emotions she couldn't name flooded through her. She had begun to associate the book with the dead girl, her father's accident, and Sylla's suspicions.

Writing is work. Writing doesn't have to flow. Writing has to be done. Do it.

She'd start with the story of Christina of Markyate. It had a fairy tale quality that had always captivated her. She flipped open her laptop and eased herself into the book.

About a half hour later, rapping on the front door jarred her from her work. She sat, confused for the moment it took to time travel forward from the Middle Ages. The rapping came again. Someone was impatient. She stood, the knocks like shots from a repeating rifle assaulting the door as she made her way. Cold began at her core and seeped outward to her limbs. Something was wrong.

Sylla stood on the porch, two uniformed officers behind her. Her face was calm. Expressionless, until a closed lip smile cracked the mask. "Is your father in?"

"Of course." Abby sounded defensive even though she'd done nothing wrong. She adjusted her tone. "He's in the living room. May I help you?"

"I'd like to speak to him."

"He's still recovering."

"Abby, who's there?" Her father's voice boomed.

"Sounds as if he's on the mend," Sylla said.

Did Abby hear menace in her voice? Warning bells went off in her head. She wanted to barricade the door, but she stepped back and let the officers enter.

"Detective Sylla, good to see you. Any news on the driver?" Her father was oblivious to the clamor inside Abby's brain. Why didn't he hear and feel the danger in the air?

"No news yet." Sylla angled herself between him and the TV. He reached the remote around her, switched it off, and tipped his head to one side like a dog expecting a treat. An unexpected wave of love crashed over Abby. A fierce desire to protect him came with it. But protect him from what?

The police were their allies, their defenders. Civil servants sworn to protect the innocent. And he was innocent. He saw the best in everyone whether they deserved it or not. But the way Sylla stood before him now reminded her of a mountain lion preparing to attack.

"I need you to come down to the station with me," she said.

"He can't. He's not well enough," Abby said.

"I don't know what more I can tell you." Her father's brow furrowed, as if he only now sensed the current in the room.

"It's not about the accident."

"What is it about?" he said.

But Abby knew. It was about the anchorhold. Maybe they suspected him of building it to spy on tourists like some twisted voyeur. Maybe it was because they thought he'd lied about the night the girl died, that he'd seen the men up close, from the hold.

"I'd rather talk about it at the station," Sylla said.

"We can't discuss it here?"

"No."

"He's not well enough." Abby moved into the tight space between Sylla and her father.

Sylla shifted her weight onto one hip. "I only need a statement. I'm not putting him on a chain gang."

"I'm fine." He grabbed Abby's arm and used it to heft himself from the chair. "Just let me get some shoes on."

"I'll help you." Abby shot Sylla a cold look and followed her father into the bedroom. "Listen." She lowered her voice to a whisper. "Carlos went to the mission last night to get the camp toilet and my bedroll. He was going to grout the stones in place while he was there. I don't know what happened though. I haven't spoken to him."

Her father's eyebrows raised. Abby knelt and held a shoe while he shoved his foot in. "I think this is about the anchorhold. If it is, if they know someone was living there, tell them it was me. We can't keep this going any longer. I'll talk to them. Show them my manuscript. We've got to come clean."

Pain creased his face, and he exhaled. She waited until it passed and helped him with the other shoe. "I don't want you taking the blame for anything anymore. I know we'll have to admit you lied to them, but I'll explain. I'll tell them I coerced you. You did it for me."

She felt the weight of his hand on her shoulder. "Let's not jump the gun, okay, honey? I'll go down there. I'll see what they want. And we'll figure it out from there."

"I'm going with you."

"How are we doing?" Sylla leaned into the doorway.

"I'm ready," he said.

"I'm coming." Abby rose to her feet.

"Suit yourself." The investigator shrugged.

An image of her father getting into the back of a cop car out in front of the house, where the neighbors could see, crashed into Abby's mind. "I'll drive him."

Sylla paused, shrugged, then walked out of the doorway.

"Your sweater, Dad." Abby lifted it from the back of a chair and shoved it into his hands. She followed him to the front door, sputtering a steady stream of words. She wished she could stop but worry and guilt had overflowed the banks of her heart and there was no damning them up. "Let me just get your antibiotics. You have to take another one in an hour. I'll bring a snack too. So you don't have to take them on an empty stomach."

She stood in the kitchen window watching the black and white traverse the driveway and her father head to her car. She felt numb, useless. She'd gather his things and take him to the station. It was all she could do.

3.4.3

ABBY WAS HUDDLED in a chair in a corner of the station lobby when Carlos entered. Her eyes filled with tears when she saw him. He hurried over, and she grabbed his arm. "I was going to call you earlier, but I didn't want to leave until they were done interviewing Dad."

"What's going on?"

"I don't know. They came to the house hours ago and said Dad had to come in and make a statement."

"I need to tell you something." Carlos lowered his voice. "Come outside with me."

"What if Dad needs me?"

"We'll be right there." He pointed to the parking lot. "They can see us through the window."

She hesitated for a minute but let him lead her outside. "I went to the mission last night," he said, when the door shut. "There was nothing there."

"What do you mean, nothing there?"

"The toilet, the bedroll, they were gone."

Abby hugged herself. "Are you sure? Did you go inside? Because it's hard to see the whole space from—"

"I went in."

"How could that be?"

"They must have found the room. That's gotta be why that detective was asking so many questions about the receipts for the building supplies."

Panic filled Abby's chest. "I've got to talk to them, tell them it was me in there. Tell them about the book."

"I think you do," Carlos said. "Your fingerprints have to be all over everything. Better you tell them before they figure it out for themselves."

"I wiped everything down."

He looked confused. "You cleaned up your fingerprints? Why would you do that?"

"I know, I know. It sounds paranoid." Her voice had an angry edge. "But I was afraid this would happen. The police were nosing around where the girl was found. I was worried they'd find the anchorhold. If they did, I didn't want them to know who'd been in there."

"But now you do."

"I don't want them to think it was Dad." She turned toward the station entrance.

"Abby, wait."

She couldn't wait. This had to end now. She threw open the door and marched to the front desk like a martyr headed to her execution. Carlos entered behind her, sank into a chair, and watched.

"I need to talk to Detective Sylla," Abby said to the officer on the desk.

"She's busy," he said.

"It's important. I have important information regarding the mission case."

The officer smiled. It wasn't a nice smile. Abby wanted to wipe it off his stupid face. "The mission case? Is that, like, an official case name?"

She felt her cheeks go red. "I mean about the girl who was found dead at the mission."

"Gotcha." His expression softened. "Detective Sylla will be out soon. She's talking to your father now. I'm sure she'll want to talk to you as well. Why don't you have a cup of coffee or something?"

Frustrated, Abby slumped into the chair next to Carlos. "It's better that you wait, anyway," he said.

"Why?"

"You need to cool down, think. You're too emotional right now."

Anger flared in her gut. "What's there to think about? I got my father into this; I need to get him out of it."

Carlos glanced around and lowered his voice. "You don't know what they're asking, and you don't know what he's saying. If you go in there with a story that's not the same as his, that could be bad, Abby."

His words burned, but he was right. "What do I do then?" She buried her face in her hands. "God, I don't know what to do."

"Let them ask the questions. Don't make them wonder about things they're not already wondering about."

"But they must think Dad has done something wrong, or they wouldn't have had him come down here when he's recovering from surgery."

"Maybe, but you don't know what that is. Don't give them any ammunition, Abby."

"I'm going to lose my mind if I don't do something."

"The wrong thing is worse than nothing."

"Doing nothing is what got us here. If I'd revealed myself to the police when they got there that morning, we wouldn't be sitting out here. My father wouldn't be sitting in there."

Carlos removed one of her hands from her face and squeezed it. "I get it. But there's a middle ground."

Before he could tell her what that middle ground looked like, Detective Sylla reappeared in the doorway. "Abby Travers?"

"Yes." Abby jumped out of her chair.

"Would you follow me, please?"

Carlos gripped her hand tighter before she could pull it away. "Don't tell them you were the one who saw the men." He whispered the words. She glared at him. "It could make things worse for your father." She gave him a quick nod. "Do you want me to wait?" He spoke in a louder voice.

"No. I'll talk to you later," she said, and followed the detective.

3.4.4

ABBY HURRIED after Sylla to a small interview room with hospital green walls that smelled of burned coffee and sweat. In its center was a Formica topped table surrounded by chairs, but the chairs were empty.

Anxiety fell like a rock in her stomach. "Where's my father?"

"He's in another room. He's fine. Just chatting with one of the other detectives." Sylla gestured to a chair on the far side of the table and sat across from it.

"Are you charging him with something? If you're not charging him, you need to let him go. He has to go home. He needs his antibiotics."

"All we're doing is asking questions." An unpleasant smile appeared on her face.

Abby dropped into a chair and leaned forward. The desire to tell Sylla everything, come clean, was strong. But Carlos's words rang through her mind, *Let them ask the questions. Don't get them wondering about things they're not wondering about.*

Sylla wasn't a priest. She wasn't a confessor. She was a cop trying to solve a crime. "What do you want to know?" Abby said.

"Your father built the room around the Swallows Nest exhibit, yeah?" She didn't pause for Abby to answer. "Why do you think he did that? I mean, it seems like a big expense. Why take that on?"

"He did it for me."

"For you?"

"Yes. I'm writing a book." Abby rested against her chair back, forced her shoulders to relax and began her confession. Sylla asked. She would answer. That's all she'd promised Carlos.

She told Sylla about the anchorites of the Middle Ages, and her desire to practice the reclusive life. How she believed it was the answer to many modern social pressures. It was an experiment, one she hoped would not only give her perspective for her writing but also help her find a publisher. Sylla's face remained impassive, but several times her left nostril twitched as if she smelled something bad.

When Abby finished, Sylla leaned forward on her elbows. "That's certainly an unusual story. I wonder why you didn't come forward sooner?"

Abby looked at her hands where they clutched her thighs. The nail beds were white. She released her grip. "Because I didn't want people to know. Not until I finished the book. Not until I had a publisher."

"Why is that?"

"I didn't want people to think I was crazy, why do you think?"

"It does sound a bit... Strange."

Abby's head shot up. "Exactly. It's not the kind of thing people do every day."

"I'll give you that." Sylla pushed her chair onto two legs. "Coffee?"

Abby ignored the question. "Listen, the point is, my father didn't do anything illegal. He got the Diocese's and the foundation's permission to build the structure. I'm the one who moved in."

"How'd you eat? Where'd you get water? We found a toilet. Seems like that thing would fill up pretty quickly."

Abby paused. She didn't want to tell the truth now. She didn't want to say that her father had taken care of her needs. It made him sound like an accomplice. Which, strictly speaking, he was. When she spoke again, the words came in a rush. "My dad helped me. He didn't want to. He tried to talk me out of it before I went in, but I was strong-headed, I wouldn't listen."

"Did anyone else know you were there?"

"Not until the day I left."

"Could you leave whenever you wanted?"

"What do you mean?"

"I mean, could you come and go as you pleased?"

"No. We left one stone loose so Dad could give me food and things, but the opening was too small for me."

"So, you were, essentially, a prisoner."

"No," Abby's voice rose. "My father would get me out if I asked. He wanted me to leave."

"Was he the one who got you out when you did leave?"

Where was she going with this? Abby had expected questions about the night the girl was left at the mission, but Sylla hadn't said anything about that. "No." Abby dragged out the word.

"Who then?"

"Carlos Rojo."

"The man who was sitting with you in the lobby?"

Abby nodded.

"So, let me get this straight, your father imprisoned you in this room. You couldn't get out on your own—"

"That was all part of it." Abby thought she knew where Sylla was headed now. She had to make her understand. "The anchorites couldn't leave their holds either. If I could come and go whenever I wanted, it wouldn't have the same effect. I had to know how it felt to be... To be..."

"Imprisoned?" Sylla's tone was helpful.

Abby threw her hands up in frustration. "It wasn't like that."

"What was it like?" Abby didn't answer.

"When Rojo found out where you were, he got you out that same day?"

"I only left because my father was in the hospital. I was worried about him."

"Not because he was out of the way? Not because he wasn't a threat anymore?"

What was she saying? Did Sylla believe her father was a monster who'd locked her up and kept her against her will? "No. No. My father is the most kind, supportive man in the world. I pressured *him* into building the room, cementing the stones in place, not telling anyone I was there. He didn't think it was a good idea. I talked him into it."

Sylla shrugged, a graceful gesture. "Interesting."

"I'm telling you the truth."

"Are you? Or was the cell built for someone else?"

"What do you mean? Like who?"

"The girl we found looked as if she'd been held prisoner."

"That's crazy." The words erupted from Abby. "What would stop her from calling out for help? I was free to speak. The cell is in a public place, for God's sake. People are walking by all day long."

"Have you ever heard of Stockholm Syndrome?"

Stockholm Syndrome. Could that explain the version of events Sylla believed? Abby had read about prisoners who grew dependent on or developed affection for their captors. But to stay hidden when help was so close. She didn't buy it, but Sylla did, and that's what mattered.

Abby opened her mouth to argue, but Sylla interrupted her. "We didn't find any fingerprints. Strange that someone would wipe down everything that could hold a print. It almost seems like they were trying to hide the inhabitant's identity." The investigator rose in one smooth movement.

Abby followed her to the door in a daze. "I was the one in the cell. Tomorrow, I'll bring you what I've written," she said when she found her voice. The two women stared at each other for several moments before Abby broke the silence. "Why would I make up such a crazy story? Make myself look like a lunatic?"

"To save your father."

Abby's thoughts raced as she helped her father to the car. She would fix this. It was her fault her father was under suspicion, that Sylla thought he was a maniac. Sylla would see. She'd understand when she read Abby's manuscript.

She and her father hardly exchanged a word on the drive home. He leaned his head on the neck rest and closed his eyes. He looked drained and exhausted. She'd talk to him about it tomorrow.

She parked along the side of the house so he wouldn't have to walk as far and entered through the back door. She flipped on the kitchen light. The warm glow, the smells of home, like a hug, drew her in. She offered her father a sandwich or a cup of tea, but he didn't want anything. He went straight to his room. When she checked on him a half hour later, his light was out.

She knew she should call Carlos, but her thoughts were in turmoil. The outline of her book swam through her mind, chapters jostling for prominence. Which should she focus on? What segments would help her father's case with the investigator most?

She made herself a pot of coffee, a necessary expenditure of time if she was going to stay awake and get the job done tonight. She wasn't even close to completing a first draft, but she had to pull together what she had into some coherent whole.

She labored over the keyboard until her eyes began to close of their own accord. Her chin hit her chest, and she jerked awake. The clock said 3:15. She typed two more sentences and saved the file. She'd only completed three chapters, but it would have to do. She had to sleep. Tomorrow, first thing, she'd drop the pages at the police station.

Abby stripped off her jeans, fell on the bed and into a fitful sleep. The dark shape of the Great Stone Church ruins towered over her, blotting out the moonlight. She followed the path around the corner to the swallow nest exhibit. The anchorhold of her dreams was almost as tall as the church itself. Its stones were brown with age and lichen, the bars of the squint spotted with rust.

She peered between them. A shape reclining on a pallet of straw was within, half hidden by shadows. "Dad?" The figure moaned and thrashed on the makeshift bed. "Dad?" she said again. He shifted into the beams of light. His eyes were sunken hollows, his skin so white it almost glowed. His emaciated arms jutted from tattered sleeves. He turned his face to hers and cried out in a foreign tongue. It was the same language the girl had spoken.

"I'll get you out, Dad. I've got you." She sobbed the words, but he didn't seem to hear. The next three hours, until the alarm clock went off, were spent attempting to free him from the anchorhold. But every time she pried a stone from the wall, another would grow in its place.

3.4.5

SUNLIGHT MADE her closed lids glow red. Her eyes were sheets of sandpaper. She was so sleep deprived it was hard to think, but the night's work had paid off. At least, she was fairly sure it had. Sylla had been working the early shift, so Abby was able to hand the manuscript directly to her. The skepticism on the investigator's face seemed to lift when she saw it. Optimism might even call the new expression sympathetic or understanding.

Have you ever heard of Stockholm Syndrome? A nauseous chill rolled through Abby every time she thought of the accusation. The memory had kept her writing until three. She was determined to erase that idea, wipe it away as if it had never been.

"Abby."

Her eyes sprang open. Her father leaned on the old wooden rocking chair. She hadn't heard him come out. He didn't look well. His face was pale. A thin line of sweat beaded his forehead despite the chill in the air. "How did you sleep?" she said.

"Like the dead." For a brief moment, his lips lifted in an imitation of a smile.

"You don't look well."

"Neither do you."

"I'm just tired," she said. His eyebrows raised in question. "I was up half the night, writing."

He sank into the rocker. "I'm sorry I'm so high maintenance. I'm keeping you from your work."

Consternation welled up in her. "No. It's not that at all. I pulled together the first three chapters of the book. I wanted to do more, but I kept falling asleep. I gave them to Detective Sylla this morning, so she'd understand. So, she'd believe me that the anchorhold was my idea."

"Did she?"

"I don't know. She didn't read them in front of me. She looked them over and thanked me. But I think she was softening." Abby searched for a phrase. "Open to persuasion." She lowered her voice. "What did you tell her?"

"I told her what happened. I told her I built the anchorhold at your request, but that I also believed it was good for the mission. I told her when it came down to it, I was against the scheme, and probably should have refused to help you. But daughters and fathers and little fingers and all that."

"Did you say anything about that night?" Abby wondered if Sylla had accused him of keeping the dead girl in the cell.

He shook his head. "If I tell her I lied, I'm a liar. Why put that in her mind? If she asks me, I'll tell her the truth, but she didn't ask yesterday."

"Good." Abby was relieved. She didn't want her father to know what was in the investigator's mind. It would horrify him.

"We can't tell any more lies, Abby."

Abby's throat closed. Tears sprang up behind her eyes. "I'm sorry. I'm so sorry, Dad."

"We'll get through this, honey." The half-smile returned. "I'm supposed to be the wise one, the old sage, and I went along with it. It's as much my doing as yours."

Abby swiped her eyes with the sleeve of her sweater.

"Don't cry. They don't have anything against me. Building the anchorhold wasn't illegal. I had permission. And as far as I know, bringing you food and water wasn't illegal either."

His optimism was uninformed. He didn't know what was in Sylla's mind, and Abby wasn't going to tell him. It seemed every time she recovered from one blow, another came. She'd protect him from them as long as she could.

"I have a favor to ask," he said.

"Of course. Anything."

"Saturday is the Swallows Day Parade. I have the first shift at the mission kiosk. I can't make it. I'm not in any shape—"

"Dad." Abby interrupted him. "No one is going to expect you to be there. I'll call and let them know, but I'm sure they realize you can't attend."

"You didn't let me finish. When Tallulah came by with the fava beans, I told her I'd be there. I guess I was being overly ambitious, but it's too late for her to find someone to replace me now."

Abby understood what he was asking. "So you want me to go?"

"Yes."

"Who'll take care of you?" Abby couldn't keep the note of panic from her voice.

"I'm not a child. I can stay home alone for a couple of hours."

Neither spoke for a long time. The soft creak, creak of the rocking chair on the worn wood slates and the songs of birds filled the silence. The sun climbed over the Jacksons' roof and warmed the porch.

Her father rose from the chair with a small groan.

"Dad." Abby leaped to her feet.

He waved her off. "I'm okay. Stop fretting. I need to rest for a bit." He shuffled to the door; his pain obvious.

"Dad," Abby said again.

He placed one hand on the doorframe for a moment. "I bet you another bottle of that Ravishing wine you and Carlos drank this whole thing is going to blow over." The screen door slapped shut behind him.

"I love you," Abby called after him.

"Love you too, honey."

She sat in the rocker he'd just vacated and stared at nothing. She hoped with all her heart he was right, but braced herself for the next blow anyway.

3.4.6

HER FATHER HOBBLED down the hall to his room, and Abby went to the kitchen to scrub out Mimi's soup pot. She'd dumped its contents. Steven had said garden volunteers, of which Mimi was one, were there when he might, or might not, have mentioned he'd seen Abby's father at the police station. Abby was paranoid. Officially and clinically certifiable. But she was also frantic.

At first, she'd hoped to find out who'd left the dead girl at the mission to protect her father from them. But there were other ways to do that. She could have someone she trusted with him at all times, keep pepper spray handy, buy a dog, dump out soup and fava beans that might contain poison.

But everything had changed. The stakes had been raised. She had to know who'd committed the crime to save him from suspicion, shame, and the wagging tongues that almost destroyed him years ago.

While Abby's mother was alive, her father had kept his anxiety and rage on a short leash. When she died, grief stole his ability to hold them. They escaped and tore him to shreds.

He'd had a breakdown and been hospitalized for a month, only a month. But that was long enough for the town to make up its mind. There was something wrong with the Travers family. The superstitious believed they were bad seeds. The scientific minded thought there was a genetic defect in their line. The mockers said they had a screw loose.

She wondered now why they hadn't moved. But her father had been out of work for quite a while in the years after her mother died. Abby assumed he didn't have the money to start over. And maybe he didn't want to leave the home his son had lived in.

It had taken years, but through long-suffering, kindness, goodwill, and generosity her father had changed local perception. If this scandal came to light, it would undo everything he'd worked so hard for. Abby couldn't bear that. She had to find those men she'd seen that night at the mission before the rumors began.

A wheel of possibilities revolved through her mind. Anyone who was there the day Steven let it slip was suspect. She wracked her brain to come up with the names of ethnic-looking volunteers or employees the right age to have a teenage son. There were two that she knew of-- Tallulah and Mimi. Of course, there must have been others present, people she didn't know. Anyone in the room that day could have shared what he'd said, but Abby had to start somewhere.

Between Tallulah, who she'd known her whole life, and Mimi there was no contest. She knew the Jacksons were a nice middle-class family. How they would know the girl, never mind why they would leave her to die at the mission was a complete mystery. And, most likely, she was grasping at imaginary straws.

However, every time she talked herself out of believing it could be them, her thoughts would spin again. The wheel's flapper would slow at each damning bit of evidence. *Click.* Chad's eyes. *Click.* Bradley's cultured accent. *Click.* His Middle East connection. *Click.* Mimi's volunteer position at the mission. Then Abby's mind would settle to a stop on the Jacksons again. She had to know the truth.

She could see the driveway where Mimi and Bradley's cars were parked under the outer branches of one of the huge oaks. Sunlight shone through the leaves and dappled them like an impressionistic painting. She was going to return the pot as soon as they left. As long as she was there, she'd take a look around. She didn't know what she was looking for. She hoped she'd recognize it when she saw it.

She shook water drops off her hands and retrieved a dish towel from the oven door. When she turned back to the sink, movement through the window caught her eye. Bradley strode toward the cars, briefcase in hand. He got into a white sedan and headed down the gravel drive. Abby glanced at the kitchen wall clock—8:10.

What time did Mimi take the boys to school? At Saint Barnabas, where Abby worked, student drop-offs started around 7:30, and first classes at 8:00. It seemed late, but the boys were in high school and high school schedules varied.

She dried the pot, set it on the kitchen table, and got a pen and pad of sticky notes from the desk. *Thanks for the soup! Hit the spot.* Of course, if she'd poisoned it, Mimi would know it hadn't hit the spot as soon as she read the note. Abby shook her head. Most likely she'd wasted a perfectly good batch of chicken soup. Letting her father eat it wasn't a chance she'd been willing to take, however.

The chirp of an automatic key interrupted her thoughts. She moved to the window. Evan, backpack thumping, jogged to the car. Mimi, her steps quick and short, followed closely. Chad, moving only slightly quicker than the sloth Abby had seen at the San Diego Zoo, dragged behind them. She had the feeling their gaits were examples of how they approached life. Evan charged. Mimi walked with purpose and efficiency. Chad dug in his heels.

She had no idea how long Mimi would be gone. The night she and Bradley had dropped off the soup, Mimi had mentioned she was going to the mission one morning this week to do some weeding. It would be wonderful if this was the morning. But Abby had zoned out several times during that conversation, and didn't remember when it was.

Abby itched to race over to their house, but made herself wait. What if they'd forgotten something and came back? She had to be careful. When ten minutes had finally passed, she walked outside carrying the pot.

The sun warmed her head and shoulders, but as soon as she plunged under the oaks, the morning chill enveloped her. She hurried to the house. The porch steps creaked under her feet as she climbed. At the top, she pushed open the screen door. The musty scent of vacation beach houses, hot summer days, and childhood rolled over her in a wave of nostalgia. An old ache for her brother, for lost friendships, and lost innocence made it hard to breathe for a moment.

She and Lily Hartman had been best friends once. This porch had been their schoolhouse, white-picket-fence cottage, or haunted mansion, depending on the game. But that was a long time ago.

She set the pot on a side table between two wicker chairs. Through the front door window, she saw the hall that led to the kitchen. If she wanted to find traces of the girl from the mission, or clues the Jacksons had known her, she didn't think she'd find them here. Their home was too visible. Too many people came and went. If the girl had been here, someone would have seen her.

The screen door slapped closed behind Abby. When she reached the grass, she pivoted and faced the squat old house. Where should she begin? What was she looking for? Sylla had mentioned they believed the girl had been kept against her will, not fed properly, not given medical care. That would require a prison of some kind.

The large garden shed behind the house seemed like a possibility. Abby circled the property and let herself into the backyard through a gate. A flood of memories threatened to wash away her purpose. She closed her eyes for a moment and forced her mind to the present.

She opened them again and took in the sight before her. The garden was a shabbier version of its former self, but here and there small beds had been recently turned, planted, and labeled in Carlos's neat hand. Pride warmed her. If anyone could bring this yard to life again, he would.

She walked the serpentine paths through the various herb and flower beds to the back fence. The shed was smaller than she remembered. Probably because she'd been smaller herself the last time she'd seen it. Its redwood walls had darkened to a deep gray long ago. Dirt coated its square-paned windows. Cobwebs hung from the roof.

Abby sidled up to the window with the least spider webs and rubbed the glass with the sleeve of her shirt and peered inside. The visibility was about the same as that at the bottom of a pond when the silt had been stirred. When her eyes adjusted to the murk, she made out the outline of a bench against one wall. Beneath it were pots in various shapes and sizes, stacked one inside the other. Shelves holding bags and bottles of what must have been fertilizers and bug killers lined another wall.

There was barely enough room for one person to stand and work inside. Certainly, no room for someone to lie down. Abby backed up and looked at the door jamb. The layer of dirt coating it didn't appear to have been touched in months. The girl couldn't have been kept here.

Abby wiped her hands on her back pockets and stepped away from the shed. She turned and looked at the house again. There wasn't a basement, only a crawl space. She knew that, because Scottie and Tomas, Lily's brother, had tried to get her to wiggle into it to retrieve a ball once. She was the smallest, and the only one who'd fit. She'd poked her head under, but that was as far as she'd gotten.

Tight spaces never bothered her. It wasn't that. It was the army of spiders hidden in the dark recesses she didn't like. A city of webs swung from the underside of the house.

A breeze blew up, and the sun hid behind a cloud. Abby shivered. She'd better hurry. Mimi could return any minute.

Abby went around the far side of the house where the bedrooms were located. As she walked past them, she glanced through the windows. Although she didn't think the girl could have been kept in the house, there might be some clue as to whether the family knew her or not.

The first room was decorated in a sports motif, bed thrown together, a gym bag tossed in a corner. The next had to be Chad's. Posters of bands hung on the walls. A black quilt spilled from an unmade bed. Dirty clothes hid most of the area rug. There was nothing unusual in either room, at least nothing she could see from the window.

The third bedroom, Abby knew, was the master. But the shade was down, obstructing her view. Frustrated, she turned from the house and looked over the rest of the property.

To the right of the house was an old, detached garage. She crossed the pebbled distance and peered into a dingy window. A wall of boxes met her gaze. That explained why the Jacksons didn't park inside. They must still be unpacking.

She moved around the back of the garage, headed for its far side. If she remembered correctly, there was another window there. As she rounded the corner, she heard the crunch of tires on gravel. Mimi. Abby's heart thudded in her chest.

How was she going to explain her presence? She could say when she'd put the soup pot on the porch, she'd seen. . . An interesting bird? A raccoon? A coyote? She'd gone to investigate.

But why make up stories? It would be better to hunker down, out of sight, and wait until she heard Mimi go inside. She slid to a crouch and leaned against the garage wall.

A moment later, footsteps clacked on the porch stairs and the screen door screeched on its hinges. She waited two more minutes, then crept to the front of the garage. Should she make a run for their shared drive? It was the longer route, but otherwise she'd have to cross in front of the Jackson's house to get home.

Before she could make up her mind a silver import pulled up next to Mimi's car. Abby ducked out of sight. A car door slammed.

"Good timing. I just got home," Mimi said.

"You said 8:30, so here I am." A contralto voice answered her. Rosie, her interior designer.

"There are two possibilities in the last sample group you brought. I can't decide which I like best. You're going to have to help me."

"I'm glad it's only two." The woman laughed.

"Coffee?"

Before the contralto could say yes or no, Abby's phone sang out the guitar riff that meant Carlos was calling. It vibrated deep in her pocket. Why hadn't she put it on silent? Why had she brought it at all? Her fingers fumbled with the buttons. The riff stopped mid-note, but the damage had been done. A moment later Mimi and Rosie appeared at the edge of the garage with curious expressions on their faces.

"Abby. What are you doing?" Mimi said.

"A coyote." She stammered out the word.

"You saw a coyote? In broad daylight?" Rosie's eyebrows lifted.

"Why on earth would you follow it?" Mimi said. "I've lost so many cats to them; I've given up on pets."

The other woman nodded. "I have a shepherd mix, but I've heard packs sometimes even attack big dogs."

"I read an article about a man . . ."

Abby stopped listening. Her cheeks were hot. Could she sneak away while the two shared coyote stories? But they stood directly in her path.

What felt like an eternity later, Mimi seemed to remember she was there. "Oh, sorry. Abby this is Rosie, my decorator. Wait, you guys call yourselves interior designers these days, don't you?"

"I answer to either," Rosie smiled.

"Abby is staying with her father on the other side." Mimi waved a hand toward Abby's house.

"You're Paul's daughter?"

Abby nodded. She hadn't found her voice yet.

"He's a nice man." Rosie smiled; the suspicion she'd been wearing on her face disappeared. "I met him when Gwen Bishop had this place listed."

"You know the Bishops?" Abby said, hoping to shift the conversation off her and coyotes.

"Yes. I've done some home staging for Gwen. When this place was on the market," she tipped her head in the direction of Mimi's house, "she asked for my advice. Your dad came over to see what we were up to."

"Whatever you did worked," Mimi said.

"I'd better get going," Abby moved toward the two women. "I put your pot on the porch. The soup was great. Thanks again."

"Glad you enjoyed it. How's your father doing? I was planning to stop by today."

Abby paused. "The ribs are healing, but I'm a little concerned about the head trauma."

"Head trauma?" Mimi said.

"Yes." Abby's thoughts raced. "He's sleeping a lot." Which was true. "But he also has some memory loss. The week leading up to the accident is foggy." Which was a complete lie.

"Do the doctors think his memory will return?" Rosie said.

"They don't know. Unlikely though. Transient amnesia isn't uncommon after this kind of thing." Abby hoped neither woman would research what she'd just said. She was shooting from the hip, hoping to start a rumor that would work for her father instead of against him.

"You can't be too careful with head injuries," Rosie said. "A little boy from St. Barnabas was in an accident, hit and run, maybe a year and a half ago now. It took him a long time to recover from the brain damage."

"Are you talking about Brian McKibben?" Abby asked. He was one of her favorite students. The whole school had been pulling for him when he'd been in the ICU.

"I don't remember the name." Rosie looked apologetic. "My husband is more involved in the school than I am these days. Once my son graduated, I lost touch. Eric is still on the board. He's a financial planner, and they like to run money decisions by him."

Abby stared at Rosie. She had a son. She was kind of exotic looking. Possibly her husband and son were as well. She had a connection to the mission. Maybe her family left the girl there to die.

She almost laughed out loud. The ridiculousness of her thoughts hit her with such force, she felt hysteria bubbling under the surface. There were untold numbers of people who could have committed the crimes. This was futile. She needed to get away before she made an even bigger fool of herself. After an awkward silence, she said, "I'd better be going. I need to check on Dad."

Mimi and Rosie made room for her to pass. "Let me know if you need anything. More soup, or whatever," Mimi said.

Abby assured her she would and trotted across the grass to the safety of her own kitchen. Once inside she leaned against the back door and waited for her heart rate to slow and her cheeks to cool. Stupid. What had she been thinking snooping around the Jackson's property? She was turning into her mother, becoming paranoid.

Her father's reputation was more important to her than her own. She'd do anything to clear his name, but she needed to hang onto reason. She felt she was treading a tightrope. On one end of her balance pole was delusion, on the other Sylla's reality. Tipping too far in either direction would mean disaster.

3.4.7

ABBY SAW Carlos through the kitchen window as she washed the breakfast dishes. He grabbed his tools from the back of his truck and walked through Mimi Jackson's side gate into her backyard. A moment later, he returned and began unloading plants and carrying them to the garden two at a time. On his third trip to the truck, Abby dried her hands and ran out the kitchen door onto the porch.

He glanced up when the screen door smacked against the house. He set down the plants he'd just picked up and moved toward her. "I called you earlier. What happened?

"I couldn't take the call." She pushed her bangs across her forehead, not that it would help. Her eyes were bloodshot and had dark circles around them. Bangs couldn't hide her lack of sleep.

He crossed the yard in a few long strides. "What did Sylla say to you?"

"It was brutal. Can you come in for a coffee? I'll tell you all about it, but I need to sit down. I'm so tired."

Carlos followed her into the house, put his hands on her shoulders, and pressed her into a chair. Then, he crossed the kitchen to the coffee pot. "Not sleeping?"

"I spent half the night working on my manuscript so I could bring it to Sylla this morning. Convince her the anchorhold thing was my idea, not my father's." Carlos stiffened for a brief moment; carafe poised over the coffee pot. "I spent the other half of the night fighting nightmares." Abby leaned her cheek on her hand.

Carlos poured the water, then flipped the brew switch on the pot. "You need a nap more than you need coffee."

"Caffeine isn't going to keep me awake, trust me. I'm going straight to bed after we talk."

"Where's your dad?"

"He's sleeping in his chair."

Carlos turned toward her, backed up to the counter and crossed his arms. "So tell me what happened."

"It wasn't good." Abby lowered her voice. "Sylla seems to think my father was holding the girl prisoner. That he's some kind of psycho."

"What?" Carlos's arms dropped to his sides.

"I know. I tried to tell her I was the one in the anchorhold. The whole thing was my idea. I told her about the book. I told her everything."

"What did she say?"

"She made a big deal out of the fact that I didn't leave until my father was in the hospital, out of the way. That you rushed to my rescue as soon as you found out where I was. That you were the one who helped me get out."

"How could he hold anyone prisoner in a place like that? There are people around all day long. What would stop you or the girl from yelling for help?"

"A strange upbringing and misplaced loyalty for me. Stockholm Syndrome for the girl."

Carlos's brow furrowed as if he'd never heard of Stockholm Syndrome.

"The ME believed the dead girl had been held captive for some time," Abby said, her voice sounding weary even to her own ears. "Dad built a cell with no exit. He admitted to cementing his daughter inside, bringing her food and water, and not telling anyone where she was. It looks damning."

"And then, you told her about the anchorite thing," Carlos said.

"I had to," Abby snapped. "She needs to see it was all my idea."

He waved away her words. "Your dad is a religious man. Enclosing people in anchorholds is a strange religious practice. When you gave Sylla those pages, you might have given her a motive for your father's crime. A motive the police would never have thought of on their own."

Abby groaned. "She couldn't think that."

Carlos poured two cups of coffee and carried them to the table, but didn't respond. Obviously, he didn't agree with her.

"I have to find that boy, the one I saw at the mission that night. I feel like it's my only hope."

Carlos shook his head. "How're you going to do that? There are thousands of kids in Orange County who look like him. I got six cousins who fit the description."

"Thousands of people don't know my father was the one who went to the police as a witness."

"No one should know about that. The police were supposed to be keeping it quiet."

"I forgot to tell you. Sylla's accusations drove everything else from my mind. The man who found the girl's body, the garden volunteer, was at the station the morning my dad went in to make his statement. When he heard a Mission employee had come forward as a witness, he assumed it was Dad."

"Did he say anything to anybody?"

"He said he doesn't remember, but he might have said something to Tallulah and a couple of the other volunteers. Mimi is a garden volunteer."

Carlos's jaw tightened. "You're not going to start in on the Jacksons again."

"I went over there this morning," Abby admitted.

"Why? You didn't confront her?"

"No. No one was home. Not at first. I was looking for a place, a room."

"Somewhere someone could, say, lock up a sick Middle Eastern teenager?" His voice was laced with sarcasm. "Abby, that's nuts. Mimi is my client. She's a nice lady. She has a family."

"Her son is the right age and height to be one of the men I saw. His cheekbones are high and his eyes the right shape. That's what I noticed that night. Her husband has the right build to be the other man. And he makes business trips to the Middle East regularly. He even has an accent."

Carlos was quiet for a long moment, then he asked, "Did you?"

"Did I what?"

"Find a room?"

"No. Mimi came home before I got a chance to look through the garage windows. I was going to peek in after she went into the house, but her decorator showed up. Then you called and my cell phone went off."

"That's why you declined my call."

"Right. Didn't do any good though. They found me."

"Great. How did you explain why you were lurking around on their property?"

Abby ran a finger around the rim of her mug. "I said I saw a coyote."

"In broad daylight?"

"It happens."

"If we're going to start suspecting people, how about Tallulah?" He locked eyes with her. "Tallulah has a son the right age. She has a husband who's probably stockier than the average college student. She's exotic looking. Why not suspect her family?"

"I've thought about it," Abby said.

Carlos stood abruptly and walked to the sink.

"I don't think their family has any connection to the Middle East, though," she said. "Of course, just because the girl is from the Middle East doesn't mean the people who left her at the mission are or have connections there. We have no idea who she was, or why someone would let her die that way."

He turned to face her. "Abby, can't you see how nuts this is? I have three clients who are from the Middle East, all within a ten-mile radius of the mission. Two of them have teenage sons. One of them is always late with their payments, so they're probably bad people. Should we suspect them? This smacks of profiling, Abby."

"We never know who people are, or what motivates them, not really." Abby's eyes closed. "They change when bad things happen. I thought I knew my mother." A yawn split her face. "Just because I've known Tallulah for years, and just because Mimi shares your love of gardening doesn't make them faultless people."

They were fighting again. Fighting less than twenty-four hours after she made a vow to try to make peace. She yawned again.

"You need to get some sleep, and I need to get back to work," Carlos said. "We'll talk about this later."

Her eyes opened. "Look around for me while you're over there, would you?"

"Right." The word was uttered with such sarcasm, she was sure he wouldn't. "Now go to bed." He held out a hand, pulled her up and gave her a little push toward the bedroom.

Abby went a few steps, then turned. "I forgot to ask you. What are you doing Saturday?"

"I don't know. Why?"

"My dad wants me to stand in for him at the mission festival booth. I have to be there around eight. Want to come and help?"

"Sure. I have to stop by South Coast Nursery's booth anyway. We're doing a cross-promotion thing. I'll meet you there."

"Thanks." The word was interrupted by another yawn.

"Let me know how your dad is doing when he wakes up," he said. She nodded and shuffled toward her bedroom.

3.4.8

IT WAS hot but overcast when Abby woke from her nap. Carlos's truck was still in the driveway, but he was nowhere in sight. Abby walked around her neighbor's house in search of him. He wasn't in the garden, so she headed left, to the far side of the garage. She didn't see him there either. Maybe he'd returned to his truck while she was looking for him. She decided to continue her circle of the property.

There was no cement walkway along the far side of the garage, and weeds grew between the stones someone had placed there. She stumbled on a rock and balanced herself on the old wood siding. Flecks of paint peeled off on her hand.

She walked along the length of the building until she reached a small window. She stared at it. Carlos was right. The chances of Mimi and Bradley being the perpetrators of the crimes were infinitesimal, but what would it hurt to look into the garage?

The window was coated with grime. She shaded her eyes with cupped hands and moved closer. Boxes. That was all she could see.

She moved to the left and peered through the filthy glass toward the front of the garage. The boxes filled the space all the way to the single plank garage door. She took a big step to the right and looked in the other direction. The boxes stopped about four feet from the back wall.

Four feet by the width of the garage was a big enough area to hide someone, but it wasn't secure. There was nothing to stop them from leaving. From what she could tell, anyone could've walked to the front, pushed the door open and escaped. That was that. The Jackson's weren't her criminals.

She was about to head to the yard when the sun came out from behind a cloud. It shone on the window and lit the inside of the garage. That was when she saw a thin line running up the back wall. Her heart skipped a beat.

She breathed on the window and rubbed it with her arm. The line became a rectangle. Could it be the outline of a door? It looked like the outer wall of the garage was several feet farther out than the wall the door was set in, so it couldn't be an exit.

She walked to the end of the garage and turned the corner. There was no door, or window, or anything in the back wall. The door inside must lead to a storage room, or maybe a laundry room. A room that ran the width of the building.

She stood, hands on hips, for a long time. She'd been locked in a space smaller than this, but this would be so much worse. It was so secluded. There were no people. Nothing to watch and no window to watch it through. Could Mimi and Bradley be that cruel?

She turned and headed back to the garden. Was she losing touch with reality? The police didn't know if the girl had been held prisoner, not for sure. She was sick and starved, but that was all they knew. The rest was guesswork. No one knew what had really happened except the people who brought her to the mission.

Abby was panicking because of her dad. She wasn't thinking clearly. What she needed to do was convince Sylla that her father wasn't a religious maniac. If she was going to do that, Abby had to act normal. Breaking into other people's garages wasn't normal.

When Abby reached the garden again, she saw Carlos standing by a plot of dirt, leaning on a shovel. When he saw her, he pulled a water bottle from his tool bag and sat on a big rock. He guzzled half the bottle and wiped his mouth. He didn't ask her what she'd been doing. Most likely, he didn't want to know.

Should she tell him about the room? Before she could decide, she heard the squeaky screen door. They both looked up. Mimi came down the kitchen steps with two glasses. "You two look like you could use some iced tea."

"Sounds great." Carlos stood.

She handed them each a glass, then examined the plot he'd just planted. "What do you think, Abby? The garden is going to be amazing, isn't it?"

"Yes." Abby agreed wholeheartedly. It was nice to be sure about something.

"I have more ideas. Follow me." Carlos led them to another corner of the yard and explained his plans for the spot. Then he took them to the old garden shed and told them his idea to use hollyhocks to hide it. Abby listened as he and Mimi brainstormed their way through the garden and ended up back at the rock where they'd started.

"I love it, Carlos. I really do. I'm thinking about pitching it to the Home and Garden Tour committee for next spring. If they accept it, I want to make sure we're here together. That everyone knows this was your handiwork."

His cheeks grew pink, and Abby knew it wasn't from the sun or the work. She suddenly knew the answer to her prior question. She wouldn't tell Carlos about the room in the garage, not until—or unless—she got more evidence. This job was too important to lose because of her unfounded suspicions.

"Refill?" Mimi reached for their glasses.

"No. I'm good. I have to get to the office. This is the fun part of my job," Carlos said.

Abby shook her head. "I have to get back to Dad."

Mimi turned to go into the house but stopped. "I hope you don't mind me asking what's happening with Paul? I'm concerned about the amnesia."

Carlos blinked and glanced at Abby. She'd never mentioned the amnesia ruse to him.

She kept her eyes trained on Mimi. "Yeah. It's not bad. Just lost a couple of days."

Mimi's mouth tightened into a thin line. "I'm worried. For him, but also for the community. If he's the only one who saw anything the night the girl died, it would be a shame if he didn't have any recollection now."

Carlos narrowed his eyes at Abby. He understood. She wanted to make sure no one was worried about her father fingering them. She was trying to protect him.

"You know, I like Paul, I really do, but . . . "

"But?" Defensiveness rose in Abby's chest.

Mimi pursed her lips. "Well, he seemed to have an unhealthy interest in the area where the girl was found, and that was before his accident."

Carlos looked at his boots. What should Abby say to that? She'd wanted to defend her father. Make sure Mimi knew she didn't have to be afraid of him, but like everything she'd tried to do lately, she'd just made things worse.

She searched for something to say, but Carlos spoke first. "You know the Swallows Nest exhibit at the Mission?"

Mimi looked confused, but she nodded.

"Paul built that. Well, he didn't build the whole thing, but he added another wall and a roof to what was there. The police think someone was living in it."

Her eyes grew wide. "Who? Him?"

Abby's mouth went dry. Why was Carlos telling her this? She tried to signal him to stop talking with her eyes, but he didn't notice.

"No," he said. "Probably a homeless person. So, I think he feels a little responsible for what happened to the girl. You know . . ."

Where was he going with this? Carlos was a terrible liar.

"Do they think this homeless person killed the girl?" Mimi asked in a hushed voice.

"No. I mean, I don't know." Carlos began picking up his tools. "Maybe... Who knows?"

He hurried out of the garden, and Abby heard tools clatter into the bed of his truck. When he returned, Mimi still stood exactly where he'd left her, holding her iced tea glasses so tight her fingers had turned white.

MOLLY: Thank you, Carlos. Abby is right. He's a terrible liar.

Anyway, the plot definitely thickened in this episode. Now Detective Sylla seems to think Paul Travers is deranged. Not a good development. Add to that, Abby mentioned he had amnesia or brain damage to Mimi, and the lie backfired on her. She can't seem to do anything right.

Not to beat my supernatural horse to death, but could this be part of the circle closing around Abby and her father? Could there be such a miasma of evil in the air that it impacts their clarity of thought? Leads them to make poor decisions?

That esoteric question is not the question of the week, though. But before I tell you what it is, let's hear from The Wife. They're making some bad choices at her house too.

the wife

MY SON WAS in his room again. He spends most of his time there these days. It worried me. I was afraid for him. Afraid he'd been traumatized by the events of the past week. I thought about taking him to a counselor, but we couldn't tell anyone what he did. I know all about patient confidentiality, but I don't think that extends to a criminal case.

I checked the clock for the hundredth time. It was getting dangerously close to 5:00, the time people returned home from their offices, but my husband hadn't returned. I'd been frozen in my chair at the kitchen table with the same cup of tea—now as cold as my fingers—for one hour and forty-seven minutes.

I'd calculated the time. At three in the afternoon, when my husband left, it should have taken him only seven minutes to reach Seb Skandalis's home. It would take longer for him to get home with rush hour beginning—say fifteen minutes. If he walked in the door within thirty seconds, he'd have spent an hour and twenty-five minutes at Seb's. That was too long.

Every moment he spent on that man's property the risk of being seen by a neighbor, a mailman, or Seb himself increased. I'd wanted him to go in the morning, but Seb wasn't in the office. He hadn't been expected in until after lunch. The secretary had said he was at a client's, but we didn't want to take chances. We took turns calling and changing the timbre of our voices beginning at 1:30. He wasn't at his desk until 2:45.

My husband had now been gone for one hour and forty-nine minutes. I began my calculations again. It was the only thing that kept me from leaping from my chair and driving to Seb's house. If my husband walked in the door in the next twenty-two seconds, he'd have been at Seb's house for— I heard the front door open and close.

I did leap from my chair now, and I ran for the entryway. My husband strode toward me with a broad grin on his face. Relief cascaded over me, weakening my thighs.

"Here and here." He pulled two green booklets from his jacket pocket and thrust them at me. "Not one, but two. And—" He snatched them away from me, opened one, closed it, opened the other and waved it under my nose. "It's Hannah. Look."

I darted a glance over my shoulder, worried our son might have come out of his room when he heard the door. The hall was empty. "Come into the kitchen. I don't want to talk about this here."

He fairly danced into that room. He was as buoyant as a soap bubble. As soon as I closed the door behind us, I took the passport from him. It was Hannah. She looked younger and healthier, but I recognized her. The name printed near the picture wasn't Hannah's, but it was her face.

"Isn't this wonderful? I'd hoped I'd find the passport I'd seen before. Which I did, of course." He brandished that one like a weapon. "But I never dreamed I'd find one with Hannah's picture. This is proof. Absolute proof." He jigged across the kitchen. "Let's celebrate."

It was good news, of course. Having a passport with her picture was much better than having one with a girl who looked like her. I hoped it could be traced to its forger and provide a link from there to Seb. If not, it might not pose much of a threat. Of course there were always fingerprints. My enthusiastic husband had most likely destroyed them all, but Seb didn't need to know that. Either way this was a gamble, and it seemed too soon to celebrate.

"It only took me maybe ten minutes, to break into his house." He disappeared into the pantry. "I went around . . . window open . . . Jammed but . . ." His voice was muffled, and his words cut in and out.

He returned with a bottle in hand. ". . . slid open as easy as could be," he said with a flourish.

"That's wonderful, but don't you think—"

"This was the perfect solution. Skandalis won't dare throw his weight around when he finds out what we have." He rummaged through a kitchen drawer, dumping its contents onto the counter. "I'm just thankful we thought of it when we did."

We. Interesting choice of words. I moved to another drawer, opened it, removed the corkscrew and handed it to him. He barked a laugh. "You and I, we are on the same wavelength."

I poured my cold tea into the sink before I took my seat at the table again.

"I wasn't sure where to look once I got inside. So, I said to myself, if I was a dishonest, immoral, conniving son-of-a—" The cork popped from the bottle sounding more like champagne than wine. He placed it on the counter and began opening cupboards. It only took three tries before he found the wine glasses. "Where would I hide the evidence?" He poured two glasses to the rim. You'd think we were drinking soda.

"In my sock drawer." He handed me a glass and held it up for a toast. "Here's to sock drawers." I clinked glasses and took a sip. I wanted a drink as much as he did, if for a different reason.

"There they were. Not one, but two passports." He downed a third of his glass and burped.

"If you found them so quickly, what took you so long?" My voice was subdued. I felt at least one of us should keep our head clear.

"Ah, now that's the exciting part." He threw himself into the chair across from me and began a tale of suburban espionage involving stray dogs, neighbor children, and a nosy old lady. My mind wandered to our next steps.

Seb was certain to discover the missing passports sooner or later, and when he did, we would be the first people he would question. We should act swiftly. Finding the documents missing would be sure to both anger and scare him. He'd feel violated, threatened.

The man was horrible enough in a placid state. I didn't want to meet him when he was on a rampage. We needed to contact him and let him know what we had in our possession. Reassure him we had no intention of using them unless he forced us to.

"You're not listening to me." My husband's face was drawn into a pout.

"I'm a little distracted."

"By what?"

"We must call Seb tonight."

He set his half-drunk glass down with a thump. "Why would we do that? Then he'd know we were the ones who'd taken them."

"But that was the whole point."

He blinked at me. "The whole point?"

"Yes. We wanted them to use as leverage. Remember? He has something on us, but now we have something on him."

"Well, yes... I know... But..." He sputtered.

"If he doesn't know we have the passports, he'll keep pushing you to," I paused, "take care of things."

My husband slumped in his chair. "I guess I thought we wouldn't mention them unless he asked me about Paul Travers again."

"He will, you know." I took a small sip of my wine.

"Maybe not. He was upset. He's probably calmed down by now. Forgot he'd even asked me to do it."

I looked at him over the rim of my glass. Indecision and inaction were my husband's greatest weaknesses. He often slid down the path of least resistance to the swamp at its end. Look where he'd gotten us this time.

I was sure buying Hannah wasn't his idea. My husband didn't have a diabolical bone in his body. I was sure he'd been complaining about the price of cleaning services, and Seb had offered a solution. Most likely, my husband hadn't wanted to offend. It had seemed easier to accept the offer than reject it and risk upsetting Seb. He didn't like to upset people. Thankfully, he didn't like to upset me either.

We would handle this my way. I'd allow him his evening of celebration. His moment of glory. But soon, we'd call Seb Skandalis and explain our new position.

MOLLY: The husband is such an egotistical boob I almost feel sorry for him. He has no idea his wife is running the show. He was so proud of himself for breaking into Skandalis's house and getting the passports, like it was his idea. But then he doesn't understand the point behind the theft. They're useless if Seb doesn't know he and his wife have them. Sigh. I was going to say it's a good thing he married someone with some brains, but maybe not. Smart and evil isn't a great combination.

Anyway, question of the week. Let's get personal. What would you do if you were the wife? To protect your kid, I mean. She says she's only done what any mother would. Is that true?

I know you wouldn't have someone killed. At least, I hope not. But would you try to maintain your life as it is? Stay married, stay put, and stay quiet? Or would you leave the country? Take your kid and run? Or maybe go to the police? Turn your husband in and plead innocence on your son's part? Let me know on the Facebook page.

Join me next time for more *Murders Under the Sun*.

(cue music)

VO: This episode is brought to you by Oasis Air, your wings to paradise. *Murders Under the Sun* is edited by Jim Wilbourne, theme music is by Eclectic Blends, and I'm your host, Molly Shure.

part six

MURDERS UNDER THE SUN
SEASON THREE; EPISODE FIVE

MOLLY: Welcome back to *Murders Under the Sun*. I'm Molly Shure, your host. Things are about to heat up for Abby and her father in this episode—literally. You'll see what I mean, shortly.

However, before we begin Abby's narrative, I just want to say how much I appreciate the diversity of opinion in the group this week. There was some attitude going on. I had to delete a couple of comments that crossed over the nasty line, but only a couple.

Most of you said you'd have gone to the police immediately if you were The Wife. However, some of you noticed that her relationship with her husband wasn't an equitable one. She placated and manipulated him, two signs that there was an imbalance of power in their marriage. Because of this, she might have been intimidated into silence in the beginning.

Others disagreed. They believed that was giving her too much grace. They pointed out, she can be tough when she wants. She came up with the plan to steal the passports from Seb, told her husband to do it, and he did.

There was also debate over her identity. This was a question I didn't ask, but the conversation went there anyway. Some believe she is Mimi. Some think she's Tallulah. Some think she might be Rosie the interior designer. And some think she's a character we haven't met yet. Well, you're about to find out.

In fact, we're breaking from our usual format today. Because of the big reveal, we'll hear from

The Wife part way through this episode instead of waiting until the end, then we'll return to Abby's narrative.

We have a lot of ground to cover. So, let's jump in.

3.5.2

THE NEXT EVENING Abby watched the red Rojo landscaping truck disappear at the end of the driveway. Abby hadn't had a chance to talk to Carlos about their conversation with Mimi. He'd been busy with work, and tending to her father had consumed her time.

She entered the kitchen, walked across the hall and stuck her head into the living room. "I'm going to run to the store. We're almost out of coffee. You okay?"

"I'm fine." Her father's eyes were heavy with sleep. She might have lied about his having a memory lapse, but she was beginning to worry if there might be more brain damage than the doctors had thought. He'd been sleeping a lot. Even more than when she'd first brought him home. She was going to make an appointment for him Monday morning, first thing.

"Can I get you anything else?"

"Maybe some of those ginger snaps. You know the ones?"

"With the crystallized ginger bits?"

He yawned before he answered. "Right. Those."

"Have you eaten all the chocolate chip and all the molasses cookies already?"

He turned up the volume on the TV instead of answering her.

Abby walked out into the evening. The sky glowed red and orange in the dying light. She'd only been up from her nap for two hours. According to her internal clock it should be close to noon, not sunset. She was all out of sync with the world.

By the time she reached the grocery store, the sun was all the way down. She parked under a streetlamp, an automatic safety precaution instilled in her by her father, and entered the store. She hurried through the brightly lit aisles to the shelves of coffee. From there, she walked two rows over to get the cookies. She also planned to pick up cheese, a bottle of wine, and something to throw on the grill.

While she was drifting off to sleep earlier that day, it popped into her mind she ought to invite Carlos for dinner after the parade. It would be a peace offering. She was beginning to understand, maybe even share, some of his feelings about her book. Locking herself in the anchorhold to write it had caused a world of problems. But despite his feelings, he'd risked arrest by going to the Mission for her. She'd never thanked him.

As she rounded the corner to the dairy section, she caught a whiff of perfume. It was a strong, spicy scent, not unpleasant, but it aroused a vaguely unpleasant association. For a moment, she was in her anchorhold, but that was where the memory ended.

Abby looked down the row of milk, eggs, and cheeses. The aisle was empty except for a forty-something man with a gallon of milk in his hand. She chose a triangle of Brie and a square of Irish cheddar and continued to the cracker display at the end of the aisle. She should get some of the multi-grain crackers with the poppy seeds on top that Carlos liked so much.

She saw wheat crisps, soda crackers, baked pita chips, but no multi-grain. Oh, well. There were crackers at the house. She turned toward the checkout and heard a crash. A split second later the wall of cracker boxes erupted. She threw her arms over her face as cardboard cartons rained down on her. They bounced off her head and shoulders, piled up on the floor around her, and filled her cart.

"I'm sorry. I'm so sorry." A woman swam through the flotsam to Abby's side. "Are you all right? It was so silly of me. I was in a hurry, not looking where I was going."

"I'm okay. No harm done," Abby said, although she would be

surprised if she didn't end up with a bruise or two. The corners of some of those boxes had made contact with tender flesh.

The woman sprang into action, stooping to retrieve crackers, standing to re-shelve them.

"Here. Let me help." Abby began stacking the crackers from her cart onto the display.

"No, no. It was my clumsiness."

"I don't mind." The familiar perfume floated in the air around the woman. Abby slid a glance at her. Her dark hair was pulled into a knot at the back of her head, but a section in front had come loose and hung in her face, obscuring it.

A tall man in a red vest with the store logo on it joined the effort and seven minutes later, the crackers were on their shelves again. Abby plastered a smile on her face and turned to reassure the woman that all was well. But she was already halfway up the dairy aisle, beating a hasty retreat to the rear of the store. The wheels of her grocery cart protested with loud squeaks.

"Well," Abby said.

"I guess she was embarrassed," the man in the red vest said. "At least she helped pick everything up. You'd be surprised how often people don't. They don't even tell us when there's broken glass, or spilled milk, or whatever. Not if they're the one who did it anyway."

He walked Abby to a closed checkout stand, flipped the "open" light on, and began putting her groceries on the moving counter. "I'm not going to make you wait in line after that."

By the time Abby left the market, forty-five minutes had passed. She hadn't meant to leave her dad alone that long. She tossed her bags into the trunk and drove home.

When she turned onto the driveway, she was struck by how bright the kitchen lights were. She must have left them all on. Generally, if she wasn't cooking, she turned the overhead lights off and navigated by the glow of the softer counter lamp.

She also noticed the lights were flickering. Her first thought was there was something wrong with the electricity, or maybe the bulbs in the recessed sockets needed to be switched out. Then realization slapped her like a cold wave of water. It wasn't the electricity or the bulbs; it was fire.

3.5.3

ABBY PULLED her cell from her purse, hit 911, screamed fire, her father's address, and dropped her bag and phone on the grass as she ran. She threw herself at the front door. It flew open. Smoke rolled out and over her. "Dad," she yelled, but there was no answer.

The living room. She had to get to the living room. Harsh fumes bit her throat and seared her lungs as soon as she crossed the threshold. She pulled off her sweater and held it over her mouth and nose.

She pressed her other hand to the wall on her right. Thank God, it was cool. The fire seemed to be contained in the kitchen. For now. Two more steps and stinging tears sprang to her eyes. She closed them, and moved forward blindly, feeling her way along the hall.

When the wall dropped away, she opened her eyes. The living room was clearer, the air a hazy gray. She could see her father. He was still in his chair, a table lamp glowing next to him. The peaceful scene belied the danger.

"Dad." Abby choked out the word. Her father didn't move. "Dad." She ran to him and shook him. His head lolled from side to side. "Dad, wake up." She shook him harder. His eyes opened, but only for a second. At least he was alive.

A coughing fit struck Abby, beating at her ribs, tearing at her throat. Through streaming eyes, she saw a poisonous black cloud inching along toward them. She had to get him out of there. She looked in the direction she'd come. The wall of smoke in the hallway was impenetrable now. But even if it had been clear, she couldn't carry her father all the way to the front door. He wasn't a big man, but he was too heavy for her.

The picture window was her only hope. She grabbed the end table next to her father's chair. The lamp hit the floor, sparked, and went out. She slammed the table into the window. It bounced off. She struck again, and again, sobbing in her frustration with each failed attempt.

Finally, she held the tabletop against her chest, its legs extended like spears, and ran at the window. Crack. Fine lines appeared where the legs had hit. She lunged again and more of the window shattered. One more time and most of the glass lay in the yard outside.

She gulped in fresh air, but within seconds she was enveloped by pitch-black smoke as it rushed to the opening. She blinked back tears. Large shards of glass stuck up from the windowsill like fangs. She tugged at them, trying to clear the opening for her father. Her hand came away bloody.

It was dangerously dark in the living room now. Not dark like the absence of light. But a dark that had form and substance. A dark that was a deadly presence.

Abby wrapped her arms around her father, hugged him to her, and lifted. He rose a foot or so from his chair, then fell into it again. She adjusted her hold, and this time threw all her body weight into the effort. He lifted again, teetered for a second, then fell against her.

It was all she could do to stand upright and not collapse under him. When she got her footing, she began to drag him toward the window. It was only feet away, but their progress was slow. So slow. Right foot, step. Drag. Right foot, step. Drag. She feared the smoke would overcome them both before they reached the opening. Right foot, step. Drag.

She was so focused on the job at hand, the emergency vehicles were almost to the house before she heard the sirens. Relief washed over her with such intensity, her legs almost buckled. One more step. One more drag. And strong arms were reaching through the window taking her father from her, then lifting her across the sill into the unbelievably clean night air.

3.5.4

ABBY OPENED her eyes and closed them again. They burned. Her mouth was dry, her skin brittle. She felt like she'd been lost in the Mojave for a week. She coughed, rolled onto her side, and tried to return to sleep. But all the burned and frayed pieces of her new reality circled through her mind.

Her eyes fluttered open. Flowered curtains framed a small window set in a white wall. Two or three feet to the right of the window, a Shakira poster was stuck up with thumbtacks. Underneath that was a dresser covered with a crocheted lace doily. A statue of the Virgin Mary gazed mildly at Shakira from its top. This room was a memorial to the early years of Miranda Rojo, Carlos's sister. Abby's own childhood bedroom was uninhabitable.

Carlos had picked Abby up from the hospital last night after she'd been run through a battery of tests and was cleared to go. Her father hadn't been as lucky. He'd inhaled more of the noxious gases than she had and was still on oxygen. They'd be keeping him under observation for the next forty-eight hours.

The only good thing about that was it gave her a few days to figure out where and how they were going to live while the house was being cleaned, deodorized, and secured. Abby had a perfectly good apartment to go home to, but she couldn't bring her dad there. It was much too small. Besides, Sharona would have a fit.

Carlos's mother, Connie, wanted them to stay with her. Which would be a good solution except Abby didn't want to make things more awkward for Carlos than they already were. He'd been wonderful through all of this, but he'd done enough. They weren't married. They weren't engaged. And she was fairly certain he didn't want to be, not after everything that had happened.

It was time to establish boundaries, for his sake. To let him back away from his proposal gracefully. He shouldn't feel obligated to take care of her because of their past.

She put a hand on the bedside table and pawed around for her phone. One of the EMTs had found it and her purse on the grass and brought them to her before the ambulance drove away. Thank God for small favors.

She checked the time, rolled onto her back and groaned. She wanted to pull the covers over her head and sink into oblivion, but she couldn't. She had too much to do.

She sat up and groaned again. Pain shot through her back. She'd injured herself on a skiing trip in Big Bear City two years ago. Her back had never been the same. Lifting her father had pushed its limits.

A chair in the corner of the room held a pair of jeans and a pale blue T-shirt with "Sarcasm Is an Art" printed on it. Her own clothes were gone, maybe forever. She doubted any amount of washing would get the stink out. She'd shampooed her hair three times last night, and it still smelled faintly of smoke.

Miranda's old jeans were tight, low and boot cut. The T-shirt was tight and low too. But everything fit. Abby wandered downstairs. Mariachi music and delicious aromas flowed from the kitchen.

Connie turned away from the stove as Abby entered. She was a petite, bird-like woman, with bright eyes and closely cropped graying hair. "You look like a teenager in Randy's old clothes."

Abby eased herself into a chair. "I don't feel like one."

"It was a very brave thing you did last night." Connie cracked two eggs into a frying pan.

"I don't know. You'd have done the same."

Connie gave her a quick nod, acknowledging the truth of the words. Family was everything to Connie. "I'm making you *huevos rancheros*. You need to eat."

Abby's stomach rumbled. "Sounds great." She glanced at the clock on the wall; it was 7:15. Carlos must be at work already. "I'm not the only one eating, am I?"

"Carlos left a long time ago, and I already had breakfast. So, yes, you are the only one eating."

"You shouldn't—"

Connie waved a spatula at her. "Stop. Stop. I love to cook. You know that. You're doing me a favor when you eat my food."

"Thank you," Abby said.

"For what?"

"For everything. For taking me in last night. For the clothes. For breakfast."

"*Corazon*, you are family." That's what Carlos had said—that she and her father were family. But they weren't. Not really. "So, tell me, what is your father's favorite meal? I want to make something special for him his first night here."

Connie assumed her dad would stay with her. Abby wanted to protest, but honestly, she couldn't think of any place else for him to go. Connie placed a steaming plate in front of her and took a seat across the table. "I can make American food as good as I make Mexican."

Abby pierced a fried egg with her fork and watched the golden yolk flow over a mass of pinto beans. "You don't mind putting him up? It will only be until we can get the house in livable condition."

"How many times do I have to tell you? I want your father to come and stay. It will be nice to have someone to talk to, someone to cook for. Carlos is so busy, and Randy only comes once a week since she had the baby. I'm lonely."

Connie was an intelligent, educated woman, but she came from a generation and a culture in which women were expected to stay home and care for the family. Abby was sure her life was full and busy when Carlos and Miranda were growing up and when Manuel was still alive.

But things had changed. Maybe it would be a blessing for Connie to have Abby's dad there for a while.

"He likes just about everything. I guess barbecued ribs are his favorite," Abby said. Connie rose, took a pad and pencil from a drawer, and began making a grocery list. She hummed along with the music coming from the radio, stopping every so often to ask Abby's opinion about side dishes and snack options.

When Abby had eaten half the food on her plate, which was twice as much as she usually ate, she pushed away from the table. "I have to go," she said. "I promised Dad I'd stop by the mission booth at the fair and help set up since he can't."

Connie frowned and eyed her critically. "Doesn't the mission have someone else who can do that? Someone whose house didn't just burn up?"

Abby gave her a wan smile. "Honestly, it seems like more work to find someone else, than it does to go myself. Besides I can't face the house yet."

Carlos's family home was walking distance from the Mercado Street Faire. As Abby trudged up the street, she pulled her sweatshirt—actually Miranda's sweatshirt—tighter around her. The morning was chilly. Carlos was supposed to meet her at the mission booth around 8:30. As soon as things quieted down and she could leave, he was going to drive her to her father's house. Thinking about what she would find there made her feel sick. Last night all she'd cared about was her father's safety. But now that she knew he'd recover, the full weight of what they'd lost was heavy.

She couldn't imagine how the fire had started. She knew she hadn't left the stove on. It was possible one of the appliances had a short and started an electrical fire, but it seemed unlikely. The appliances were all fairly new.

A thought, one she kept shoving away, niggled at her. What if her father had put something on the stove, returned to his chair and fallen asleep? He'd been so drowsy and disoriented since the accident. What if forgetfulness and narcolepsy were the new normal? She'd have to keep a close eye on him. Maybe move in with him permanently.

Either way, she'd find out soon enough. Arson investigators were combing through the debris this morning. Whatever their findings, she'd deal with it. Meanwhile, a job that didn't require thinking was just what Abby needed. There would be a mountain of decisions to climb in the weeks ahead. She wasn't up to the task this morning.

3.5.5

ALL OUTDOOR EVENTS smelled and sounded the same, kettle corn and hotdogs set to the tune of inflating bounce houses. The Mercado Street Faire was no different. Abby pulled one of the boxes a staff member had just dropped off and opened it. Inside were decorative rosary beads in plastic bags and a stand to display them on.

As she arranged the items, she glanced down the aisle of booths, looking for Carlos. It was only 8:15, but she was feeling anxious.

She'd decided when he arrived, she'd tell him her father would be staying with him and his mother, but Abby would go to her apartment. She'd tell him she was thankful for his help last night and for all the other things he'd done for them. And, although he was driving her to the house and her car this morning, that was it. She was going to start managing things on her own. It was time to wean herself off him.

She loved him, and she'd miss him. But if he was having trouble accepting her for who she was before all this happened, she couldn't imagine he still wanted to marry her. Not now. Not after all this.

She bent, stowed the box she'd emptied under the table and grabbed another. When she stood, she saw Detective Sylla striding up the row of kiosks toward her. Abby's pulse quickened. What now?

"Ms. Travers," Sylla said when she got close enough to be heard.

"How did you know I was here?"

The detective looked surprised by the question. "Carlos Rojo picked you up last night. I assumed he took you home with him under the circumstances. I stopped by there, and Mrs. Rojo told me you were here."

"That's a lot of effort. It must be important."

Sylla's face softened, and she looked almost human for a moment. "Sorry about the fire. Glad you and your dad made it out okay."

"Thank you," Abby said. "But that's not why you're here."

"No. Just wanted to make sure your father wasn't planning to recuperate in Switzerland, or someplace. We'll need to talk to him when he's well enough."

"I don't get it." Abby's temper flared. Her fuse was shortened by fatigue and trauma. Sylla here, so soon after what had happened, burned right through it. "He's told you; I've told you, everything. We've implicated ourselves in a crime, a small one, but vagrancy is a crime. I don't know what more we can say."

"There's a bit of new information," Sylla said.

"What kind of new information?" Abby was too exhausted and too angry to feel nervous.

"A witness."

"A witness to what?"

"Afraid I can't say more now, but I wanted to let you know." Sylla smiled, it almost seemed sympathetic. "One more thing. It's not official yet, but it appears the fire may have been arson. Looks like someone started a pile of combustibles in the middle of the kitchen floor."

Abby's raspy throat constricted. Panic boomeranged through her chest. Arson? "Someone tried to kill Dad?"

Sylla tapped a finger on the table. "Too soon to say. But I thought you'd want to stay alert." She turned from the booth.

"Wait." Abby almost screamed the word. "Wait. Aren't you going to do anything? Aren't you going to protect him? Someone has tried to kill him twice now."

"He's safely tucked up in hospital. We'll know more by the time he's released. If he needs watching, we'll watch him."

"This must make you see he's innocent."

The detective stared at her shoes for a long moment. "He's not the only person of interest in the case."

"Thank God for that. I'm telling you, whoever left the girl at the mission thinks my father saw them do it. They're trying to get rid of him so he can't I.D. them."

"That's one theory."

"One theory?" Abby's voice rose. "It's the only theory that fits the facts."

"I can think of at least one more."

"What? Why else would someone want him dead?"

Sylla shrugged. "Revenge?" Abby couldn't speak. "I came by to let you know about the arson just in case theory number one is correct. Be careful."

She watched Sylla walk away in disbelief. The woman was a pit bull. Once she got her teeth into something, she didn't let go.

She wasn't sure how long she'd stood like that, staring at the detective's retreating back and then at the space it had occupied. But at some point, she became aware of Tallulah rushing toward her. Colorful fabric fluttered around her like the wings of an exotic bird.

"Honey, what are you doing here? You've got enough on your plate. I've got this." She picked up a box, set it on a table, and began unpacking it.

"I need the distraction," Abby said.

"Lord knows, I love your father, but he isn't the easiest man in the world," Tallulah said, without acknowledging Abby's words. "Not even when he's in the pink. I can imagine what he's like when he's recuperating." She bustled around the booth, straightening things Abby had already arranged.

"You haven't heard then," Abby said.

"Heard what, honey?"

"Dad is in the hospital."

Tallulah stopped her work, her hands mid-flutter, and pivoted to face Abby. "What are you talking about?" She seemed genuinely shocked.

"Someone tried to burn down our house last night."

"Is he okay?"

"He will be."

"Who would do a thing like that?"

"It's a long story."

Tallulah folded her slender arms and leaned against a table. "I got nothing but time."

Abby hesitated. Could she trust Tallulah? She was one of the people who knew her father was a witness to the events of the mission that night. She had a son the right age.

"Honey." Tallulah's voice was tender. "Let me help."

Something broke inside Abby. The wall of wariness she'd so carefully constructed around herself, and her father, cracked. She needed help. She needed comfort. She had to trust someone besides Carlos, or she'd never be able to let go of him.

She told Tallulah everything, about the attempts on her father's life, her book, the anchorhold, her father going to the police when it should have been her, and Sylla's insinuations that her father had held the girl and possibly even Abby captive.

Tallulah didn't say anything for several long moments. When she finally did, her voice was low. "Honey, that is the strangest story I've heard in a long time. Whatever put it in your precious head to do such a crazy thing?"

"I... I wanted to understand those women. To feel what they must have felt. Be closer to the Divine." Abby heard the words as if someone else had spoken them.

Tallulah snorted. "I don't think locking yourself up, away from other people is what the Divine had in mind when He made us. It might be less messy, but living is a messy business."

The truth of those words struck Abby like a blow. Locking herself up had caused her to become dependent, not independent. A curse, not a blessing. Because of her, her selfishness, her father was in the hospital, his home in ruins, and a person of interest in a police case. Tears welled up in her eyes.

Tallulah's face filled with compassion. "Oh, honey, I'm sorry. I don't mean to judge you." She opened her arms, and Abby walked into them. Tallulah murmured comforting words and smoothed Abby's hair while she cried.

"Everything okay?" It was Carlos's voice.

Abby pulled away from Tallulah and wiped her eyes with the back of her hand. "Sylla came by. They think the fire was arson."

"You're kidding?"

Abby shook her head.

"Of course you're not kidding. Sorry." He gave her a hug. "This must convince her your father's not guilty of all the stuff she accused him of. Right?"

"Wrong," Abby said. "She thinks the attempts could be motivated by revenge."

"Revenge for what?"

"Holding the girl captive, I guess. I don't know what she's thinking. She said she has new information, but she wouldn't say what it was."

Tallulah said, "I think it's time to get your father the best lawyer you can find, and I'm gonna pray. It will work out, you'll see. Your father is a good man. The best. They're not going to be able to prove any of this."

Abby wanted to believe her, but she was afraid. She reached for another box, too spent to talk anymore. The three of them worked together in silence until all the merchandise was on display.

Tallulah pushed the last empty box under a table with the toe of her shoe. "I heard something funny last week. It might not be anything."

"The police are really good at turning nothing into something," Carlos said.

"What is it?" Abby said.

"Steven and an Asian lady were working on the roses. I was sitting on that bench in the central courtyard, the one under the bougainvillea."

Abby nodded. She knew the one.

"I don't think they saw me. Anyway, Steven had heard someone having a big old conversation with himself, and it scared him. He thought, at first, the man was mentally disturbed. Dangerous maybe."

"Did he say who the man was?" Carlos said.

"No. But the woman said she thought the guy was talking to the swallows. The swallows. That's what made me think about your dad, Abby. Could they have seen you two talking through your little window?"

Abby's mind flooded with the memory of Steven and Mimi's concerned faces as they stood on the path near her squint. "Yes. Yes, they did. We had a rule. Dad never came to the anchorhold when the Mission was open, only after dark. But he was very upset that day. We were arguing."

"So, you think this guy is the new witness?" Carlos said.

"It could be," Abby said. "It was awkward. Dad told them he was practicing for a talk he had to give to the Swallows Day committee. But I wondered at the time if they'd bought it."

"But why come forward now? Why not when it happened?" Tallulah turned her palms up, as if hoping the answer would drop into them. "If I didn't know the police were looking at your father for that crime, surely volunteers wouldn't know."

"Maybe it was Mimi. Maybe she's seen the cops coming and going from Dad's house, and it put ideas into her head," Abby said.

"Mimi?" Carlos narrowed his eyes.

"She was the Asian woman with Steven," Abby said. "It was the first time I saw her, but Dad knew her. Mentioned they were neighbors."

Carlos looked like he was going to be ill.

"What?" Abby said.

"Maybe I shouldn't have told her your dad built the room." Abby tensed. She'd forgotten about that conversation with everything that had happened since. "It wasn't a secret. Everybody at the Mission knew that." He shot a pleading gaze at Abby. "I think she jumped to the conclusion it had something to do with the dead girl."

Abby's stomach knotted. "She must have gone to the police. She must be the witness."

"I was trying to support your amnesia story, but I wish you'd have warned me. I'm not that good at thinking on my feet," Carlos said.

"If she thought your father was guilty of something having to do with that girl, you can't blame her," Tallulah said.

Abby turned away from Carlos. Maybe it wasn't fair, but she was angry. She'd told him her suspicions about the Jacksons. He'd ignored her. Thought she was paranoid. Well, this proved she was right. Didn't it? Why would Mimi assume her father's conversation with a wall, and the dead girl were connected? Nobody told her they thought the girl had been kept in the anchorhold. The answer seemed obvious to Abby. Mimi wanted to build a case against her father to distract the police from looking too closely at her own family.

"Mimi knew where the hide-a-key was," Abby said. "She lives right next door."

"What are you saying?" Carlos said.

"She or her husband probably set that fire last night."

"You're not making any sense. Why would she go to the police, tell them her suspicions about Paul, then go burn his house down?"

"I don't know. I don't know anything anymore." Abby heard the edge of hysteria in her own voice.

"Abby," Carlos touched her arm. She jerked away from him. "I'm sorry I said what I said, but I still think you're jumping to conclusions."

She felt his eyes on her but refused to meet them. After a long, painful silence, Carlos said, "I'd better check in at the nursery booth." He disappeared down the aisle of kiosks.

"Honey, I don't want to intrude but I think you're being hard on that man," Tallulah said.

Before Abby could answer her, a fit looking woman in yoga pants accompanied by a pony-tailed girl, wandered up to the booth. "Mom, look at the necklaces. They're so pretty," the girl said.

"They're not necklaces. They're rosary beads," her mother said.

"What're rosary beads?"

Abby didn't hear the answer. The questions in her mind screamed too loudly. Was she being too hard on Carlos?

If he had taken her seriously, he might have unearthed some evidence by now. Evidence that would shift Sylla's attention off her father and onto the Jacksons. And he wouldn't have given Mimi any ammunition. It was possible the knowledge that someone had been in the anchorhold had scared the Jacksons enough to push them into making another attempt on her father's life. An attempt that almost succeeded.

A couple stepped up to the candle display on the other side of the booth and forced her attention onto the task she'd signed up for. Abby assisted them, then a single woman, then two teenage girls, and on it went. For the next two hours, she and Tallulah were so busy, she had no time to think.

The first lull came at 10:25. Tallulah looked at her watch. "The parade starts in a half hour. It should be a little quieter for a while. If you want to go for a coffee or something, I can handle things on my own."

Abby wandered away. She passed kiosks selling tie-dyed skirts and retro sandals, homemade jewelry, kitschy pet paraphernalia and one offering chiropractic adjustments on her way to the porta-potties. When she was done, she made a right instead of returning to the mission kiosk. She was pretty sure she'd seen a booth selling coffee and Greek pastries in that direction.

"He's such a dweeb." A young male voice caught her attention.

"Math nerd," another voice agreed.

"He wants to play basketball. On the team. But I said, 'Dude, you know you play it with a real ball, right?'"

Abby spun around. Two teenage boys—one tall, lean, and dark-haired, the other short, stocky, and fair—walked in the opposite direction. They must have gone right by her, but she hadn't noticed. Not until she heard the voice.

She hurried after them. The stocky boy laughed and adopted a falsetto. "I'm, like, a Wii pro. Check out my score." Abby didn't care about his voice. It was the dark-haired kid she wanted to hear speak again.

"So stupid," the taller boy said.

Stupid. That's what she'd heard that night. The young man at the Mission had said, "This is stupid." The voice, the inflection, even the way he held his "s" a little longer than most people did, it all sounded the same. She was close behind them now. Close enough to smell their cheap aftershave. Her heart thudded in her throat.

"Excuse me." She put a hand on the taller boy's bony shoulder. He stopped and snapped his head around. Eyes, exotic. Cheekbones, high. It was him.

3.5.6

WHAT SHOULD SHE DO? Before Abby could decide, the boy turned and began striding away from her. She looked around herself as if she might find an idea. That's when she saw Carlos. Their eyes met through the crowd.

He wove between parade goers, to reach her. She raced toward him. "Carlos." She was breathless. "Carlos, look." She pointed over his shoulder. "See those boys?"

It took him a minute to figure out who she was talking about. "The teenagers? Mutt and Jeff?"

"Right." She took his arm and pulled him along with her. "The tall one, he's the one I saw at the mission that night."

Carlos stopped walking. "Are you sure?"

"Yes. I'm sure. Come on." She urged him forward. "I heard his voice, and I ran after him. It's him."

"Did you talk to him?"

"Yes, for a second. I said I thought he was someone else. But I got a good look at his face. And it's him."

"You thought Chad, Mimi's son, was. . ." Doubt crawled across his face.

"I know. I know. There's a resemblance, but as soon as I saw this kid, I knew."

They were headed toward an intersection. Carlos stopped short. "See that lamppost?" He pointed a half block up. Abby nodded. "I'm going to get there before the boys do and take some pictures. I'll make sure I'm zoomed in on the kid. Then we have something we can show Sylla."

He didn't wait for Abby to answer but jogged left when they hit the crosswalk. She saw him cut past a row of kiosks, then disappear across a greenbelt.

Abby stayed as close to the boys as possible. She didn't need to worry about them noticing her. They never turned. They were in their own teen world, oblivious to everything around them. Including her.

The stream of people headed to the parade route had picked up its pace. The boys were getting close to the lamppost, but Carlos wasn't there yet. Anxiety tripped up her spine. If he didn't get there in time, what should she do? Keep following the boys? Shouldn't one of them keep the kids in sight? Carlos could find another opportunity to get a picture. Maybe at the parade route.

Just as she resigned herself to plan "B," Carlos appeared. She stopped. People separated behind her and came together in front like a stream parting for a rock. They jostled and nudged, but she held her ground. She didn't want Sylla to see her in the picture, to know she'd been following the boys.

She watched as Carlos raised his phone. He stood, as still as she, waiting. For a split second there was nothing between him and the boys. *Take it. Take the shot.*

But he didn't.

His arm dropped to his side. Why? Why hadn't he taken the photo?

Carlos searched the sea of people until he found her and swam through the throng to meet her. His face was troubled.

"What happened?" she said when he was close enough to hear. He didn't answer. He took her arm and dragged her out of the flow of traffic.

"I didn't need to."

"I thought you said—"

"I know him." Abby let those words sink in. Know him? That was amazing. So much better than a picture. It meant they had a name. Possibly an address. Excitement, hope, thrummed through her. "Who is he?"

"He's the son of one of my clients. They live in Nellie Gail. Leena and Tarik Basara."

"We need to talk to Sylla. Tell her we know who was responsible for the girl's death. The people who tried to kill Dad." She turned in the direction of the parking lot, anxious for the first time to talk to the police.

"Wait. We need to think about this for a minute." He drew her to a table on the empty patio of a coffee shop.

Abby perched on the edge of a chair, impatience not allowing her to sit. "We need to tell Sylla."

"Why would she believe us? You'll have to admit you and your father lied to her."

"She already knows I was in the anchorhold."

"But you didn't tell her you were the one who saw the men, not your dad."

Abby felt her face grow hot. Lies. Lies and secrets. Well-intentioned, seemingly insignificant falsehoods. They had a way of crawling out of the dark, scorpions under a black light, shining with flourescence, stingers poised. "So, what do we do? We know who did this terrible thing. Do we just let them get away with it?"

"No. Of course not. But we need more evidence. More than just your word, which," an apologetic look filled his eyes, "doesn't carry a lot of weight with the police right now."

"How do we do that?"

"Maybe the same way you were trying to gather evidence against Mimi's family." Abby's lips thinned. He didn't say it, but she heard the "I told you so" in his voice. "Let's go to the house. They owe me money. I've been trying to collect from them for two weeks. I'll knock on the door and see if I can get inside. You take a quick look around outside. There's only a house and a garage. No shed. No outbuildings. Maybe we'll see something."

"Like what?"

"I don't know." He threw his hands up. "You've been after me to snoop around the Jacksons' place. Look for who knows what. I'm just saying let's do the same thing. We know they're guilty."

"Okay. Sorry." She put a hand on his leg. "You're right. We might not see anything, but we might. Even talking to them could give us information that would help."

"Right. I've never even asked them what country they're from, or how long they've been in the States. I'm sure they're from the Middle East somewhere, and that's where authorities think that girl was from. We need more to give Sylla if she's going to take us seriously."

"When do you want to go?"

"Let's do it now."

"They might be here. At the parade."

"If they are, we'll walk around. Look for evidence that they started the fire, a place they could have held the girl. I can go back tonight or tomorrow and talk to them."

They took off for the parking lot. Abby heard the sounds of the parade in the distance. A high school marching band blaring the *Star Wars* theme, the jangle of horse harnesses. This was the first year in her memory she wasn't there on the route, cheering on the participants. It was also the first year in her memory her father wasn't there. That thought stiffened her resolve. They knew who had left the girl, who they suspected had hurt her father. Now they had to prove it.

MOLLY: So, there you have it. We knew from the beginning of the story that The Wife was Carlos's client. He came to the door to collect payment while Hannah was still locked in the laundry room.

He also mentioned to Abby that he had clients who never paid on time. Turns out Leena and Tarik Basara were those clients, but not paying their bills is certainly the least of their crimes.

From here on, I'll read the emails with the family's names included as they were originally written.

the wife

REALLY, Tarik was as vain as a woman. More vain than most. I was forever waiting for the man while he shaved, patted lotion on his skin, and styled his hair. He was proud of his hair. It was the only thing that remained of the stunningly handsome man I married. The physique had gone to pot. "Are you ready? The parade started ten minutes ago."

"Yes, yes." He scurried into the front hall where I stood, sweater on, purse over my shoulder. "I can't find my keys."

"I've got them." I struggled to keep the irritation from my voice. I didn't want to go to the parade. Not today. I wanted to contact Seb Skandalis before Seb Skandalis contacted us. It had been two days since Tarik had taken the passports. I'd asked him to call yesterday, but he'd resisted me. He wanted to wait until the fire had been set and Paul Travers was dead, so he'd have good news to soften the bad. It hadn't worked.

We sat on the street near Paul Travers's house every night for almost a week. Except for Thursday of course. Thursday Tarik had been celebrating the stolen passports and was in no condition.

We'd found a spot where we could see the house through the trees, and any car leaving the property would have to drive right past us. Finally, on Friday night our patience was rewarded. We saw the daughter get into her car and drive away, leaving her father home alone.

I did my part, just as planned. I followed Abby Travers to the market and kept her there as long as possible. Very cleverly, I might add. Tarik was the one who hadn't followed the directives.

He'd made his way through the trees to the house. Then, the way he told the story, he'd become such a professional at breaking into houses, he'd jimmied the back door with a credit card in no time at all. I thought it was more likely Abby had forgotten to lock it. However he did it, he got in. But unfortunately, that was all he did correctly.

I'd told him to plant the rags and papers in the center of the house, in the hallway or the living room, but he heard movement and got nervous. Why an old, sick man would make him nervous is beyond me, but that's what happened. He set the fire in the kitchen and ran back to the road. Abby and the fire department rescued Paul Travers, and now he was in the hospital where we couldn't reach him.

"Sunglasses?" Tarik said.

"In my purse."

"Mine?"

"Yes. Both of ours. If we're going to go, let's do it."

"You will be glad when you find out the reason for our little trip."

"What's that?" My nerves thrummed. I don't like it when Tarik concocts plans of his own. They rarely turn out well.

"Michael has seen the daughter." His face broke into a delighted grin.

"Abby?"

He nodded.

"How would Michael even know what Abby Travers looks like?"

Tarik looked at me like I was an imbecile. "Social media, of course."

"That's not what I'm asking. What reason would he have to know what she looks like?"

"Well." He checked his perfectly clean fingernails. "We will need to know where Paul Travers goes after he leaves the hospital, correct?"

I gave him a brief nod.

"I paid Michael a little extra in his allowance to look for Abby Travers, knowing she would lead us to her father."

Rage erupted inside me, choking my words. "You did what?"

He looked at me with wide eyes. "You heard me."

"Why would you do that? We agreed Michael would not be involved in anything else. What happened with Hannah was terrible enough."

"Relax. He was perfectly safe. He enjoyed it. He researched her on the computer, just like a real detective. He is very smart, our son. Simo helped him."

I wanted to ask him what this had to do with the parade this morning, but I couldn't speak. I couldn't believe he'd gotten both our sons involved in his crimes.

"Michael is at the fair with Gilbert, and he has a brilliant idea. He decides to go to the mission's booth to see if he hears anyone talking about the fire, or Paul Travers.

"But before he even gets to there, while he's on his way, a woman stops him. Put a hand on his shoulder. You'll never guess who it was?"

"Abby?" The word edged past my tight lips.

"Exactly." He looked triumphant. "Michael was so surprised, he lost her. But he is looking for her now, and when we meet him, we can take over surveillance."

"Why would Abby stop him? What interest would she have in Michael?" Dread whispered in my heart. Something wasn't right.

"Nothing," he shrugged. "She said she thought he was someone else."

Suddenly I wanted to get to the parade, find my son, make sure everything was okay. I moved toward the door, but Tarik jostled past me. He always has to get to the car first. It's his childish way of proving he hasn't kept me waiting.

He crossed the threshold in one long stride and stopped short. A moment later, he backed into the house as if pushed by a bulldozer. Seb Skandalis, gun in his extended hand, followed.

Seb is a small man, with a wiry frame, eyes that bulge, and cigarette-stained fingers. I'd only seen him in person on three or four occasions, and each time I was surprised again by his stature. He was much larger in my imagination. The menace hovering around him must give him the illusion of size.

He kicked the door shut, raised the gun to my husband's face and said, "Where are they?" His voice was soft, high and nasal, almost comical. But laughing at him would be a mistake.

"I don't know what you're talking about," Tarik said.

"The passports." My guess had been correct then. The passports must provide a link between him and the girls he'd smuggled into the country.

"Passports? I'm not sure what—"

"We have them." I interrupted my husband who was making a bad situation worse. We'd planned to tell Seb about the passports all along. Why lie to him now? It would only make him more angry. Make no mistake, despite the low volume of his tone, he was as enraged and unpredictable as a cock in a fight ring.

His eyes left Tarik's face for the first time since he'd entered and locked on me. "Where?"

"They're safe," I said.

"I want them."

"I'm afraid that's not possible." It took all my inner strength to return his coal black gaze with a cool calm one of my own. "But, as I said, they are safe."

He shoved Tarik aside and moved toward me. The smell of stale tobacco made my lips curl. "Where are they?"

"Why don't we conduct this conversation in a civilized fashion? Please come into the living room and sit down," I said.

He brought his face only inches from mine. "I don't want to sit. I want my property."

I concentrated on maintaining the mask of calm on my face. "I understand that. We want nothing more than to accommodate your needs. But, Mr. Skandalis, we have needs as well."

He barked a laugh, pivoted and faced my husband. "She stole your pair, Tarik. I should have been doing business with her all along."

My husband puffed up his chest. "Well, I stole your pair."

Seb poked the gun into Tarik's chest like it was a finger. "I know you did. You see, I've made very good friends with my busybody neighbor. She keeps an eye on things for me. She's a member of the neighborhood watch committee and takes her job very seriously. She described you and your car perfectly. So either you get the passports for me, or I begin breaking your wife's lovely bones."

"Mr. Skandalis." I heard a quiver in my voice and cleared my throat before I continued. "We placed the passports in an envelope with a letter explaining who they belonged to and what they were used for. We then mailed them to our lawyer. We've asked him not to open the envelope, but to bring it to the police in the event of our untimely deaths. So, as you can see, we can't get them for you."

This, of course, was a lie. I'd buried the passports in a new box of laundry soap in the garage, then resealed it. It wasn't a perfect solution, but it was the best I could do at eleven at night.

"You leave us alone, and the passports stay in my lawyer's safe. That's the deal," Tarik said. I didn't like the tough guy tone he used. It was dangerous.

Seb's hand shot out and struck him across the face. "Call your lawyer." I bit my lip to keep from crying out. Tarik's eye began to swell.

"Listen to me, Mr. Skandalis," I said before he hit Tarik again. "We have made another attempt on Paul Travers's life. Unfortunately, it wasn't successful. But neither was yours, if you remember. Our goal is to protect our family, not to compete with you or harm you in any way."

He pondered this for a moment. "Why would you take my passports then?"

"Only as an insurance policy. If the police never learn of our connection to Hannah, they will never learn of yours." I realized my miscalculation as soon as the words left my lips.

"So let me get this straight." He looked at me, but kept his gun trained on Tarik. "You and hubby are threatening to tell the police about my side business if I don't cooperate. That sounds like a threat to me. Let me explain something to you, Mrs. Basara. You have much more to lose than I do."

There was such evil in his voice I felt suddenly lightheaded. My thinking muddled. "You don't want to kill us, not in the suburbs."

He laughed the thin piping laugh of a naughty, young boy. "Should I take you out to the country? Downtown LA? You want to go for a ride?"

"Don't be unreasonable." Tarik's voice was an authoritative growl. It was the tone he used when the children misbehaved.

The children. My panic escalated. If Skandalis killed us, he had to kill them. Michael knew all about Hannah. I opened my mouth to soothe him, tell him we'd give him the passports. Tell him I'd kill Paul Travers for him. Next time, I'd get the job done. But Skandalis cut me off.

"Unreasonable?" His eyes narrowed. "You mean like this?" He raised his gun hand as if to slap me the same way he'd slapped Tarik. I squeezed my eyes shut and retreated a step. A second later, a shot rang out.

My eyes flew open. Grief and fear mingled into one unnamed emotion. Tarik, my indecisive blowhard of a husband, had picked this moment to become a hero. He must have lunged for the gun, because he now lay at my feet. A river of crimson seeped from under him and separated into rivulets as it spread out on the cold marble floor.

MOLLY: What just happened, people? Leena might not be as smart as we've been giving her credit for. She got her husband shot. But we can debate this later. Let's get back into Abby's story.

3.5.7

"SOMEONE'S HOME," Carlos said as he drove past the large house with the white SUV parked in the driveway.

"So how do we do this?" Abby didn't like it. The house was one of those tract homes that posed as a custom build with the addition of unusual architectural details. Floor to ceiling windows fronted it, and ran down the sides as far as she could see. Even if Carlos kept them inside, talking, how would she stay out of sight?

"I'm going to drop you off down the block, turn around and park out front. You walk up and sneak around the side of the garage while I keep them busy inside."

"How are you going to keep them away from the windows?"

"Just stay close to the bushes. If you're right under the windows, they won't be able to see you."

"How am I going to get to the bushes?"

He pulled up to the curb and stopped the truck. "Most people aren't sitting by their windows waiting for something to happen."

Abby flushed. That's what she'd done in the anchorhold.

She jumped out of the truck and Carlos sped off. As she trudged up the hill, she thought about what he'd said. It was true. By enclosing herself, she'd become more in tune with the outside world than she'd ever been.

Shut-ins live outside their windows. They imagine what the people they see are thinking, saying, and feeling. Most people on the outside live inwardly focused lives. They imagine what others are thinking and saying about them.

Abby crested the hill and saw the red Rojo Landscaping truck parked at the curb. Carlos was halfway to the front door. She decided to leave the sidewalk and cut across the neighbor's grass, where she might not be seen.

Despite her circuitous route, she felt exposed. The windows seemed trained on her like telescope lenses. Her instincts told her to crouch and run from bush to bush, but logic told her she'd call attention to herself if she did. She straightened and forced herself to walk normally.

She only had to cross a small side yard to reach the attached garage at the rear of the house. If someone saw her, she could say she was looking for her cat.

Carlos stepped onto the front stoop. After he rang the bell, she'd wait a few seconds, then make a dash for the garage. He raised his hand. Abby froze.

A blast cracked through the air. A firecracker? A car backfiring? A gun?

Carlos dropped to his hands and knees and searched for her with his eyes. He found her and waved her down. She fell to the grass.

He rose to a crouch and, hugging the wall, ran around the corner of the house. He reached the first set of windows, lifted his head above the sill and peered in. He must not have seen anything, because he dodged to the next bank of windows.

Feeling vulnerable in the open yard, Abby came to her hands and knees and began to crawl toward the house, toward Carlos. He beckoned to her. She hurried forward.

When she reached him, he pressed her against the stucco with a sweaty arm. "Stay here," he said. He made his way to the last set of windows. His head bobbed up, down, then rose more slowly. A long moment passed as he stared through the panes. He slid to the ground beneath the window and gazed out at the property.

Abby crab walked to him. "What's happening?"

"A man is holding a gun on Leena. I can't see Tarik."

"God. Do you think he's been shot?"

"I don't know. Do you have your phone?"

But Abby was already pulling it from her pocket. She pushed 911 with trembling fingers. While she alerted the emergency dispatcher, she watched in alarm as Carlos rose to peer in the window again. She tugged on his shirt, and mimed "Get down." But he ignored her.

"Are you in danger?" the dispatcher asked.

"No. No, I'm outside. The gunman doesn't know I'm here." As she said the words, Carlos ducked and ran to the garage.

"I'll stay on the line with you until you move away from the house."

"I need to get off the phone." Fear crawled across her skin. What was Carlos doing?

"Please leave the property, ma'am. You need to get to safety."

"I've got to go." Abby said and ended the call. She paused. Everything in her screamed for her to obey the woman on the other end of the line. To retreat. Get to safety, away from the staring windows. But she couldn't leave Carlos.

She forced reluctant limbs to follow the path he'd taken. Heart pounding in her throat, she rounded the far side of the garage and stopped. Carlos had positioned himself near a side door. He held a shovel like a baseball bat.

His eyes widened when he saw her, and he shook his head. He wanted her to leave. It wasn't going to happen. She strode toward him, ducking under the one small garage window.

"Go. Wait for the police out front." His voice was a harsh whisper.

"I won't leave you." She searched the ground for another weapon. She spotted a rock the size of a tennis ball and picked it up. "Are they in the garage?"

He nodded. She moved only as far as the window and peeked through the glass. "Go away. I've got this," he hissed. She ignored him.

It took a moment for her eyes to adjust to the dim interior. The first things she saw were the white outlines of a washer and dryer. She was looking into a small laundry room. It appeared to be empty.

Movement to the right caught her eye. The door from the laundry room to the garage was open. It gave her a limited view of the garage interior. She pressed herself against the outer wall and the view expanded by two or three feet. It was enough.

She saw a dark-haired, dark-complected woman standing before a short, thin man. Something about the woman was familiar. Abby could only see her profile, however, and couldn't be sure. The man pointed a gun in her direction. His face was fully visible and unfamiliar. When his mouth moved, she read, "Where are they?" on his lips.

They? Did he mean people? Was someone hidden here? Abby's eyes scanned the laundry room again. Could there be more girls? Girls like the one left at the mission?

Movement. Her attention was drawn to the woman. She was speaking quickly, gesturing with her hands. Abby felt she was pleading with him, arguing her case.

He raised his gun hand and slapped her. The woman's head snapped back. She lifted it again in a defiant gesture. When she spoke this time, Abby knew intuitively this was a mother defending her children, fierce and protective.

The man shrugged. Abby read murder in the movement of his shoulders.

She turned to Carlos. "He's going to kill her." Carlos raised the shovel higher, and she realized he intended to barge into the garage. A shovel was no match for a gun. He'd be shot before he was close enough to strike.

An idea sprang to her mind. For once, she didn't stop to evaluate it. Abby threw open the garage door, ran to the shelter of a camellia bush that was several yards away, and screamed wordlessly. A second later, the short man appeared in the doorway. "Here, I'm here." She stepped out of the leaves and waved her hands.

Before the man could take aim, Carlos moved from the shadow of the open door. The shovel came down with a crack of bone. The man fell to the ground.

Stillness settled on the scene replacing the frenetic action of the past ten minutes. Abby heard only her own ragged breath, and the soft sobs of the woman in the garage. Then the quiet filled with the sound of sirens.

3.5.8

TWO AMBULANCES PULLED AWAY from the curb, sirens keening. Tarik Basara was in one; the short, thin man in the other.

Abby sat on the front stoop of the house while a uniformed officer took a statement from Carlos. She'd already given her side of the story to the same policeman. She was numb. The day had taken on an unreal quality. She felt as if she was living someone else's life, that at any moment she might wake up in her anchorhold and be Abby again.

Intellectually, she understood her father was in the hospital. That someone had tried to kill him—probably multiple times. That he was being suspected of a horrible crime. But she no longer had the same sense of urgency to prove his innocence. It was there somewhere, looming just outside her consciousness, but she'd lost contact with it.

It would return, she was sure. But at the moment, she couldn't get worked up about anything. Leena Basara had told the police she had no idea who the thin man was. He'd broken in. He'd tried to rob them. Abby knew it was a lie but couldn't prove otherwise.

A pair of shoes appeared in the section of concrete she'd been staring at. She looked up at a long expanse of khaki covered legs, and past a white shirt to find Sylla's sharp eyes focused on her. "You're everywhere these days, aren't you?" Abby didn't answer. "After I have a look round, let's talk, yeah?" Abby nodded.

Maybe fifteen minutes later, maybe longer—Abby's sense of time had stopped functioning along with her emotions—Sylla returned. Carlos was with her. "I think we'd all be more comfortable at the station," she said. "I'll give you a cup of our wonderful coffee."

Abby climbed into Carlos's truck alongside him. Neither said anything for two and a half miles. "That was really stupid." Carlos finally broke the silence. Abby raised her eyebrows in question. She'd done so many stupid things lately, she wondered which one he was referring to. "Using yourself as bait for that guy."

"If I hadn't, you would have charged in there with your shovel and gotten shot." He didn't deny it. They finished the drive in silence.

As they crossed the parking lot to the police station, Carlos said, "Are you going to tell Sylla about the son?"

"I think so. I'm not sure it will do any good, but I feel like I should. Withholding the truth hasn't worked well for me." He nodded and opened the heavy glass entry door.

Minutes later, Abby was seated in the same interview room she'd been in only three days earlier. Sylla set a cup of murky coffee in front of her, and Abby wrapped her hands around it. She didn't plan to drink it, but she was grateful for the warmth.

"So, the obvious question first: What were you and your boyfriend doing at the Basara house?"

Abby sniffed the coffee and took a tentative sip to give herself time to think through her answer. The coffee tasted bitter and burned. She set it down but kept her hands on the mug. It was time to tell Sylla the whole truth, even though it meant admitting her father had lied to the police. "I saw a boy at the parade," she began.

Sylla didn't ask many questions while Abby told her narrative. She only stopped her twice, once to affirm that her father had never, in fact, seen any men, hadn't been at the mission that night at all. That he had, in fact, lied at Abby's request. The second time, she asked if Abby had ever seen either Leena Basara or the thin man with the gun before.

"I've never seen the gunman, I'm sure about that," Abby said. "But I did see the woman when I was in the anchorhold." She'd remembered why Leena looked familiar while she was sitting on the stoop. "It was three days after that night. You know, the night the girl died. I remember it because it was so odd. She walked directly up to my window and stared inside."

Abby paused, lifted her mug but caught a whiff of its contents and set it down without drinking any. "It was like she was looking for something. I hid in the corner, in the shadows, but my shoes were out in the middle of the room. I was afraid she'd see them. See me. It was nerve wracking."

"Must have been." Sylla said dryly. "What happened then?"

"Security came by and yelled at her. Visitors aren't supposed to leave the paths."

"Good thing for you."

"I wrote it off at the time. People do weird things when they don't think anyone is watching them."

"You'd be the one to know." A sarcastic barb.

Abby ignored her and continued. "But it makes sense now. She must have been checking out the place her husband and son had been. Worried they could have been seen by someone else."

"You mean besides your father? Who, as it turns out, she needn't have been worried about." Abby pressed her lips together and stayed silent. "So, you're telling me Tarik and his son brought this sick girl to the mission and left her there, and Leena Basara was in on the whole thing?"

"Yes," Abby said.

"Wouldn't it have been better to come forward, then, at the time and let us know about it?"

"Of course. You have no idea how much I regret not doing that." Abby paused. "I saw Leena Basara one other time. At the market last night, before the fire. She crashed into a cracker display. I helped her clean them up. She must have been trying to stall me. Keep me in the store as long as possible, so her husband could start the fire."

"Did anyone else see her?"

Abby's eyes darted to Sylla. Her face was unreadable, but her shoulders had lifted a little. She'd straightened her spine just a millimeter. Was she beginning to believe Abby's story? "Yes. Yes, there was a store employee. I don't remember his name, but he was tall, had thinning hair, and fortyish. I'm sure the store could tell you who was on duty."

Sylla made a note on the pad in front of her, then switched gears. "What did you and Carlos hope to accomplish at the Basara house today?"

"We were looking for evidence. Something we could bring to you to show you that these were the people you should be investigating, not my father."

Sylla glanced at the ceiling, then returned her gaze to Abby's. "You seem frantic to absolve him from crimes you're not certain he's accused of."

"You insinuated..." The acrid smell of the coffee made Abby feel sick. She pushed the cup away.

"Insinuated what?"

"That he's some weirdo lunatic who likes to lock up girls."

"Is he?"

Abby stared at her without reacting for several long seconds. "No," she said. "I've already told you; I was the one who came up with the idea for the anchorhold. I talked him into helping me cloister myself so I could write my—"

"Right," Sylla interrupted. "Your book."

"Don't you think it's a bit odd that Tarik Basara was shot today?" Abby raised her voice in frustration. "Doesn't that make you suspicious at all?"

"It is. But it isn't nearly as odd as building a cell at the mission and imprisoning someone in it." They stared at each other for a long moment. When Sylla spoke again, her voice was devoid of emotion. "It's very possible you were at the Basara house for another purpose, happened upon a robbery in progress, and decided to take advantage of the circumstances to spin a story. It's also possible your father and the Basaras both had culpability in the girl's death."

"That's crazy," Abby said.

"I don't know, the ME seems to think the dead girl was most likely imprisoned somewhere for a time. She was unnaturally pale, malnourished, dehydrated, and ill with tuberculosis, a treatable disease. Then I found a cell where someone was imprisoned. I also know the man who built the cell, and he admits he tended someone who was locked inside it."

Abby rose from her seat. "But I was the one in the cell."

Sylla relaxed her shoulders. "No proof. Not even a fingerprint." She paused to let her words sink in.

Abby lowered her eyes and her voice. "I wiped the cell clean."

Silence filled the interview room. Sylla sighed. "Your efforts to protect yourself from us continually backfire, don't they?"

It was pointless arguing. She was right. "Can I go now?"

"Please," Sylla said.

Carlos was sitting by the window when Abby entered the lobby. He looked up, a question in his brown eyes. But she didn't say a word as she sank down next to him.

"How'd it go?"

"It's a mess." Abby spun toward him. "She doesn't believe me. Not that I can blame her. She still thinks it's possible my father locked that girl up in the anchorhold. That's why he built it."

"But what about the Basaras? What about the fact Tarik was shot?"

"She said it could have been a robbery, like Leena said. That we're trying to capitalize on their trouble for our own benefit. Or maybe the Basaras were in on the whole thing with Dad. Who knows." Abby took a deep breath before continuing.

"When she came by the mission booth this morning, she seemed sympathetic for the first time. I thought she was beginning to believe us. But going to the Basara house, being there when the husband was shot, made her more suspicious of us, not less."

Carlos massaged his forehead. "She doesn't have any proof your dad ever set eyes on that girl. All she has is suspicion."

He was right. Sylla had nothing on her father. Not only that, she had a real murder to investigate now. This terrible saga had to come to an end. Hopefully, Abby and her father could now focus on rebuilding their home and their lives.

MOLLY: What do you think? Are Abby's hopes realistic? Will Sylla concentrate on Tarik's murder instead of trying to dig up dirt on Paul Travers? Is this the end of the story? The bad guys are caught. One is dead, the others are in custody. Is this the happy ending for Abby, Paul, and Carlos? Let me know what you think on Facebook.

Join me next time for more *Murders Under the Sun*.

(cue music)

VO: If you enjoyed this episode, please leave us a five-star review on your favorite podcast service—it really helps. *Murders Under the Sun* is edited by Jim Wilbourne, theme music is by Eclectic Blends, and I'm your host, Molly Shure.

part seven

MURDERS UNDER THE SUN
   SEASON THREE; EPISODE SIX

MOLLY: Welcome back to *Murders Under the Sun*. I'm Molly Shure, your host.

I've titled this season *The Hiding Place* because—as you know if you've been with me from the beginning—Abby started her narrative locked in a small cell at the San Juan Capistrano Mission. Today, we're going to hear about another hiding place. One she doesn't willingly enter.

This week you were divided into optimists and pessimists on the Facebook page. The optimists stood by Abby's final statement in the last episode. They hoped and believed along with her that the story was over. That she was moving into a time of recovery and rebuilding for herself and her father.

The pessimists disagreed. They weren't sure what would happen next, but they didn't think it was going to be good.

Normally, I'm an optimist, a glass half full kind of person. But people, I hate to say it, this time the pessimists are right. Things are about to get much, much worse for Abby.

Before we hear from her, we've got an email from Leena to read. It's pretty revealing. All the excuses she made for herself, the ways she tried to justify her behavior, they're out the window today.

But don't take my word for it. Listen to hers.

the wife

A NURSE PUT a hand on my shoulder. "We need to take him."

It hit me then, Tarik was dead. He *is* dead, and I am a widow. But I will mourn him later. At that moment, I was angry. Angry he'd left me alone to deal with the aftermath of his poor decisions.

I don't know how long I'd sat there by his body. The nurses believed I was in shock, grieving. But my mind was racing. It was up to me now to protect my son.

I stood. "Yes, of course."

I stumbled into the cold hallway. The lights were brighter there, and it took a moment for my eyes to adjust. While they did, I steeled my resolve. I had no time to be a weak widow, an emotional wreck. Ever since I had Michael, I was a mother first, a wife second.

I strode to the elevators fueled by primal, protective instincts. I descended to the ground floor and exited the building through the emergency room. The brisk walk up the sidewalk and through the parking lot to the main lobby cleared my mind. Fear and rage are powerful motivators.

"Seb Skandalis's room, please," I said. The gray-haired woman at the information desk typed the name into her computer and gave me a room number. So, he had been brought to the same hospital as Tarik. The ambulances had looked the same, but I hadn't been sure.

There was a uniformed officer in the hallway outside his room. He was young. He didn't look any older than Michael, but of course he must have been. I picked up my pace. "How is he?" I said breathlessly, as if I'd been rushing.

The officer shrugged. "I'm not a doctor."

"Can I see him?"

"No visitors. Sorry."

"I'm his lawyer," I lied.

The officer turned a bland face toward me, and cocked his head to one side as if to say, *so what?*

"You can't keep his lawyer out." I spoke softly but used the maternal tone of authority my children obeyed. I hoped he wouldn't ask me for I.D.

His eyes slid right, then left, and he gave me a short nod. "A few minutes."

I entered the room. Sun warmed the pale walls and Skandalis's pale skin. His bed was partially inclined. A white bandage adorned his head like a cap. His eyes were open. They widened when he saw me.

"I don't have much time," I said. "Listen to me. Tarik is dead. I told the police it was a home invasion. That you shot him when you were trying to rob us." He watched me through bloodshot eyes as I approached his bed. "I assume you haven't spoken to them yet."

"My lawyer is on his way," Skandalis said. Just as I thought. A man with a side business as lucrative and as illegal as his would know his way through the legal system.

"Tarik's death means you'll be charged with felony murder."

"So it would seem."

"That's a life sentence or a death sentence."

His eyes moved to the ceiling. He inhaled loudly. "Why are you here? To gloat?" The words came in a torrent of breath.

"I need your help."

He laughed, a sound like the rattle of dead leaves, then winced as if it had pained him. "Mine? How can I help you from a prison cell?"

"Maybe I can help you avoid that cell." He stared at me. "We have a mutual problem—Abby Travers. She's the only one who can identify my son as one of the people involved with Hannah's death. The police will have no problem tracing Hannah to you through him thanks to your idiotic decision to shoot Tarik."

"The daughter, eh? How do you know?"

"I had my suspicions. Detective Sylla confirmed them. She asked me why I was snooping around the mission the day after Hannah was found, although I'm sure no one I knew saw me that day. She also asked if I was at a certain market the night of the fire. The only one who knew I was there was Abby. And I heard the way Abby spoke to the police after Tarik was shot. She's our problem. Trust me."

"A shame I bent my fender on her father."

The simmering rage in my stomach boiled over and threatened my calculated calm. I crossed to the window, looked out on the parking lot, and swallowed the bile rising in my throat. Skandalis is an odious man.

Michael. I had to focus on Michael. I couldn't let my hatred of the man destroy the only hope I saw for my son. I willed my pulse to slow and turned. "Abby *cannot* be allowed to testify in court," I said.

"How do you propose we avoid that?"

I took two long strides and brought my face close to his. His jaw tensed, but that was the only indication my proximity alarmed him. "She needs to disappear."

"You want me to kill her?" Humor lit his face.

"I don't care what happens to her, but I want it to appear that she's run. Left town. The police already suspect her and her father; let them think she's disappeared because she's guilty and afraid."

"I don't see how this helps me if I'm charged with murdering your husband. Forgive me, but avoiding a second life sentence is an empty threat."

"If you shot Tarik in self-defense, or in defense of another, you could get off with a good lawyer."

"Who is it I was supposed to be defending? Just so I know."

"Me."

"Did I hear a domestic battle raging as I walked by on the street then rush to your rescue?"

I thought about that for a long moment. "No. I think you and I are lovers."

He snorted.

"I don't find the idea any more palatable than you do, but I think it's the best explanation."

"So Tarik discovers our affair and decides if he can't have you no one can?"

"Yes. I told him I was leaving. I was going away with you. He flew into a rage." I paced the small room as I thought through the scenario. "I locked myself in the bedroom, fearful of what he would do and called you.

"The story has legs." He looked thoughtful. "I show up with my gun, because I know how dangerous he can be."

"Yes," I said between tight lips. "But you didn't intend to use it. Only to scare him. Control him."

"Of course. I'm a wonderful man, but, unfortunately, he attacked me."

"In the fight, the gun went off. It was an accident." I finished the story, and we locked eyes. "Can your lawyer get you out on bail with that?"

"If he can't, I'll find a new lawyer."

I sank into the chair by his bed. The energy I'd felt earlier was beginning to wane. Working with this man, aiding him, allowing people to think he was my lover made my stomach rebel, but it had to be done.

"There is one problem," he said. "You already told the police you didn't know me, that I was a robber."

I waved a hand. "Abused wives say what their husbands want them to say. I'll tell the police I was afraid to tell the truth. But now that Tarik is dead, I have nothing more to fear."

The young officer stuck his head in the door. "I thought you said you were his lawyer?" A bald man in a black suit pushed past him.

"I'm amassing a team," Skandalis said.

He is evil, but he's smart. He instantly realized the ploy I used to enter his room and played along. I found some small comfort in that. "I'm leaving anyway," I said, and did.

I still believe, I am—if not innocent—certainly not guilty. I was thrust into an impossible situation by two men, Tarik and Seb Skandalis. None of this was my doing.

MOLLY: Leena and Skandalis joining forces bodes badly for Abby. They're out to get her. And possibly even more alarming is Leena's denial of her culpability in these crimes. It's staggering. If she can justify everything she's done already, what kind of terrible acts are in her future?

Let's get into Abby's narrative and find out.

3.6.2

IT TOOK two days for Abby to get up the courage to drive to her childhood home. She stood in the front yard, fists on hips, and surveyed the destruction. Everything to the right of the central hallway was intact. It smelled like smoke, but it stood. The left side of the house, which had included the kitchen and her father's office, was a charred skeleton.

She pushed open the front door and took a tentative step inside. The floor held her weight. Her father was being released from the hospital later today. He'd need some things to tide him over until he could move home again.

She entered his bedroom, pulled a suitcase from the shelf in his closet, sniffed it and put it back. She planned to take his clothes to the laundromat. But if she put them into that suitcase after washing them, she might as well save her quarters.

They kept garbage bags in the broom closet near the kitchen. She wondered if they were a melted mess. They weren't. They weren't there at all. The rear wall of the closet had burned. When she opened its door, instead of seeing brooms, mops, and cleaning supplies, she saw the burned-out hull of the kitchen.

A black refrigerator sat across from a black dishwasher. The sink lay on its side in a pile of rubble. But the sight that wrenched a sob from her was the old pine table. The table where her family had eaten countless meals, where they'd celebrated birthdays and holidays, where she'd played Monopoly with Scottie on rainy days. It was now a rectangle of ash.

And buried in the ash was a bit of soot-covered metal. Her laptop.

She'd never done what writers are told to do. She'd never backed up her work in the cloud or on a hard drive. She'd planned to, but things hadn't gone the way she'd expected. She'd been distracted. Never got around to it. Her research notes, her journal, everything she'd done was gone. All that was left of her work were the printed pages in Sylla's possession.

She'd entered the anchorhold to be alone, to experience the solitary life of the anchorite. She'd never lived by herself. She'd moved from her parent's home to the apartment with Sharona. Even though she'd dragged her feet, she'd assumed she'd move from there into a place with Carlos one day. The idea of cloistering herself for forty days had seemed so adventurous, so exciting. She'd thought herself so independent.

What a laugh.

Independence had been a complete illusion. Or maybe delusion was a better word. Except for in infancy, she'd never been more reliant on another person.

She bristled when her father or Carlos tried to influence her. But it was obvious now all her years of waffling, hesitation, procrastination, and indecision had only been possible because of them. Her one original idea, to hide in the anchorhold, had been a hypothetical until her father made it reality.

She'd never become an anchorite. She'd never actually separated herself from society. The conversations of staff and visitors rang around her during the day, but she hadn't been of service to them. Her father had come every night. Why? To take care of her. She'd been like a little girl playing at being an adult.

Tallulah's words came ringing back, *Life is a messy business.* Abby had been scared of the mess as long as she could remember. She'd retreated and watched others instead of taking part. Why? She didn't want to make a mistake. It wasn't hard to keep your hands clean when you weren't participating, weren't taking any risks.

At least that's what she'd thought. But here she was, the ashes of everything that had meant anything scattered around her. She may not have lit the match, but she hadn't doused the fire either. Sins of omission could wreak as much havoc as those of commission. Here was the evidence.

Abby heard a car pull up the long drive and wandered to the doorway. Maybe Carlos had decided to stop by and see how she was doing. But no, it was the newspaper delivery man. She fought off a feeling of disappointment. It was good it wasn't Carlos. She was glad. She wouldn't let herself cling to him anymore.

The car window opened, a hand shot out, and a paper fell onto the lawn. Abby laughed out loud. Her father had *The Orange County Register* delivered to the house every day as far back as she could remember. The mundane circumstances of day-to-day life went on despite their personal devastation. Ironic, wasn't it?

She walked out into the warm sunshine, picked up the paper, and took it to the outside trash cans at the rear of the house. They were still there, unchanged except for a layer of soot on the lids.

She returned to the front yard and stood for a long time allowing the sun to warm her. She was about to go in again when another car turned up the drive.

She shaded her eyes with a hand. It wasn't Carlos's truck, nor did it belong to the Jacksons. It was an unfamiliar white SUV. She watched it pull up to the house and stop.

A dark-haired woman emerged from the driver's side. She was dressed simply in gray trousers, a blouse, and white sneakers, but Abby could tell the clothes were expensive. It was a moment before she could see the woman's face clearly because of the sun's glare. When she did, her pulse quickened. It was the Basara woman. What was she doing here? Hadn't her husband just died?

She walked toward Abby with a tentative smile on her face. "Abby Travers?" Her accent, a cross between British and something unfamiliar, was cultured.

"What do you want?" The harshness of Abby's tone rang in stark contrast to the woman's smooth one.

Leena Basara stopped. "We are not enemies." Abby didn't respond.

Of course, they were. This woman had tried to kill her father. "I think we can help each other."

"Really?" Abby said. "The only way I see that you could help me is if you went to the police and confessed everything you and your husband did. Including this." She gestured to the house behind her.

"I had nothing to do with the fire," Leena said.

Abby barked a laugh. This day was turning out to be a humorous one. "You assaulted me with cracker boxes for fun?"

Leena's lips became a thin line. "My husband did tell me to distract you, to keep you away from home as long as I could." Her voice broke. "But I swear to you, I had no idea what he had planned. He told me he was only going to talk to your father. To find out what he'd seen the night the girl died at the mission."

"But then my dad would've seen him, known who he was."

"Tarik told me he planned to wear a ski mask."

"A ski mask?" Abby laughed. It sounded like a bad movie. "Why should I believe you?"

"Because I have information that will help you clear your father."

Abby crossed her arms over her chest and examined Leena. Her eyes were wide, her face open. She appeared to be genuinely distressed. "What kind of information."

"I have papers that prove Hannah was brought into the country illegally, and I know who brought her here."

"Hannah?"

"The girl from the mission."

"The girl your husband and son left to die? Alone? At night? In the cold?"

The woman gave a curt nod. "That was an unfortunate decision. However, Tarik, my husband, believed she would get help. The girl was a Christian. He left her at a place he believed Christians would find her."

"They did," Abby said dryly. "A little too late. He must have been upset to hear my father saw him."

"My husband was a weak man. He did the things he did out of fear. The man who caused that fear is your real enemy. The man who shot my husband, Seb Skandalis. He brings poor, young Egyptian girls into the country and sells them. Hannah wasn't his first victim, and she won't be his last if we don't stop him."

"If he didn't have a market, he'd stop bringing them."

An impatient look passed over the woman's features. "Another unfortunate decision. My husband, Tarik, had many fine qualities, but he wasn't an intelligent man. He was fooled into believing he was doing the girl's family a favor by taking her." She shrugged. "Maybe in some ways, he was."

"Imprisoning a young woman, withholding food, water, medical care, in what way would that be doing her or her family a favor?"

"We never withheld food or water. I cared for her as if she were one of my own children." The woman's eyes narrowed, and she leaned forward. "We only had Hannah in our home for one day. Her family was very poor. They couldn't afford medical care. She'd probably stopped eating due to her illness."

"Why are you telling me this? Why haven't you told the police?"

"If I tell the police my son will be arrested. I will be arrested. I don't care about myself, but I can't allow my son's life to be ruined because his father was an idiot." She spat the last word. "You must understand. My son's only crime was to obey his father. He's not a bad young man."

"What do you want from me?" Abby said.

"I will give you evidence. Papers that prove Hannah was brought into the country illegally. Papers that can be traced to Seb Skandalis. You can take them to the police. Tell them you were mistaken about Michael. It was my husband and Seb Skandalis you saw that night."

"Don't you think they'll be suspicious? Me changing my story like that?"

"Don't you think they'd be happier to catch a man who has trafficked dozens of young girls than they would a high school boy? A boy whose greatest crime before that night was not doing his homework?"

She had a point. If the police had enough evidence to go after a man like Leena Basara described, they'd forget all about her son.

"Besides, I plan to take my children home to Egypt. This country has not been as good to us as I'd hoped. The police won't follow us there for such a small thing. Not when they have the real criminal in custody."

Abby softened, just a little. Leena seemed to be telling the truth, and what she said made sense. She'd been thrust into a terrible situation by the foolish acts of her husband, just as Abby's father had been thrust into a terrible situation by Abby's foolish actions. "Where are the papers?"

"They're hidden. I can give them to you if you come to my home."

A chill passed over Abby's skin. Did she trust this woman enough to go with her? The last time she'd been to Leena's house she'd almost been shot. "Can't you bring them to me?"

Leena shook her head. "No. I don't want those papers on my person. If I'm caught with them, I'll be arrested. I'm having Tarik's body shipped to Cairo Thursday morning. The children and I will accompany his remains. You can tell the police I gave them to you after I leave the country. If they extradite me for a trial. . ." She shrugged. "At least my son will be in Egypt."

Abby hated to wait. Forty-eight hours of withholding this evidence was forty-eight hours more her father's life would be in jeopardy. But if she didn't agree she would never see the papers. "Okay. I'll follow you." Foolish, maybe, but driving her own vehicle made her feel safer.

3.6.3

ABBY PUNCHED Carlos's number into her cell at a stop light. She wasn't trying to involve him in her mess again, but someone needed to know where she was going, in case. . . It rang six times and went to his voice mail. "Carlos, you don't have to call me back. I just wanted you to know I'm following Leena Basara to her house. She said she has evidence that will clear Dad. I know what you're going to say. I shouldn't do this without you. We should go together, but I don't know how she'd feel about that. It might spook her if you were there. And I'm desperate. I can't sit home and do nothing. I'll call you later." Her finger hovered over the disconnect button. "I love you," she added. Then hung up.

She dropped her phone into her lap. She did love him. Even if she'd lost him, she loved him. She'd also lost Leena's car several miles ago, but she remembered where the house was. Maybe it was better she arrive a few minutes after the woman anyway. It would give her a chance to get the lay of the land before she had to follow her into the house.

A ripple of nervousness rolled over her. The last time she was here a man was shot. Even if Leena wasn't, the people she associated with were dangerous. What if one of Skandalis's cronies was there, waiting for Leena, looking for the evidence?

Should she call Sylla? But Leena had said if Sylla found the paper-work at the Basara house, she'd arrest her and her son. Abby was under no illusions that Leena had given her the entire truth. And she didn't blame her. She'd become pretty adept at bending the truth herself. People circled the wagons when they got scared. They did what they had to do to protect themselves and their loved ones.

Abby couldn't help comparing their situations. Leena wanted to save her son, just as Abby wanted to save her father. Both Michael Basara and her father had committed small infractions, but Michael, unlike her father, would be held accountable for a much larger crime if he were found out.

No, she wouldn't call Sylla. She'd given her word. She'd agreed to Leena's proposal.

Her front tire jogged onto the sidewalk as she parked in front of the Basara home. Despite all her inner arguments, she was jittery.

She exited her car and walked toward the front door. The house, although large and luxurious, held an air of decay. The flower beds were filled with the brittle corpses of impatiens, Icelandic poppies, and salvia. Small patches of green dotted the brown grass like mold.

She'd only gone a short way up the walk when she heard her name. Turning, she saw Leena standing on the far side of the garage. "Here," she said and tipped her head toward the building. Abby hesitated. The last time she'd walked across this yard, she'd ended up with a gun pointed at her. But if she wanted what Leena had, she had no choice but to follow.

When she reached the side door into the garage, she hesitated again. Leena, already inside, looked at her over her shoulder. "Are you coming?"

Abby's hands tingled, and she realized she'd been clenching her fists, digging her fingernails into her palms. A line from *Macbeth* came unbidden to her mind, "By the pricking of my thumbs, something wicked this way comes." Wouldn't it be wonderful if it was that easy to detect danger? She shook the tension from her hands and crossed the threshold.

Leena made a left. She headed to the small laundry room Abby had seen through the window four days ago. That made sense. Abby relaxed a little. She'd thought at the time it was probably where the girl had been kept.

Abby followed Leena into the laundry room. The scent of lavender detergent made her nose pinch. There were cupboards above an expensive looking washer and dryer, and cupboards lining the wall under the window—plenty of places to hide papers. Leena pivoted and looked at something over Abby's right shoulder.

At that moment, Abby knew she'd made a terrible mistake. A fraction of a second later a strong arm wrapped around her neck.

Crushing pain.

No air.

Color faded from Leena's face, from the room around her. In the black and white seconds before the curtain dropped and everything went dark, Abby saw Leena's blank expression transform into a satisfied smile.

3.6.4

THE TINY DOT of white light grew in diameter. It was as if Abby was drawn upward from the bottom of a deep well. A murmur of voices, like lapping water, splashed on the edges of her consciousness. She floated in torpor. When the bright circle overwhelmed all darkness, she opened her eyes.

It took a moment for her to remember where she was. When she did, fear crashed over her. Her limbs convulsed but were trapped by bonds.

The laundry room.

She was in the laundry room where the mission girl had once been held. Someone had choked her until she passed out. Now she sat, propped up in the corner between the washer and the wall, wrists and ankles bound, mouth taped shut.

She recognized the voices. Leena's was no surprise, but Skandalis. What was he doing here? Abby tried to control the pulses of liquid panic that rushed through her veins and roared in her ears. She needed to hear what they said. She needed to understand. She inhaled and exhaled deeply through her nose, convincing herself there was enough air. *Breathe. Breathe. You're okay. Breathe.*

Several long minutes passed before she was able to comprehend the conversation in the other room.

"...the car," Skandalis said.

"Why should I?" That was Leena.

"Would you rather I go? I assumed you'd prefer to avoid my associates. They'll be here after 2:00."

Leena took a long moment to respond. "You're right," she said, but her voice sounded grudging. "I don't want to be here when they come."

"That's what I thought. So, as I was saying, take her car to the train station."

Her car? He must mean Abby's.

"I expect a cut of the proceeds whether I'm here or not."

Skandalis laughed, a high-pitched whistle that made Abby's skin crawl. "Is this the same woman who was appalled by her husband's purchase? You've certainly embraced your inner villain."

"I have to think of my children." Her words were bitter. "Tarik did not leave us with much."

"Your children are a convenient excuse."

"Fifty percent?"

He laughed again. "Fifty percent is a bit steep, but you'll get some-thing. I may not be a just man, but I'm fair."

"I wouldn't have thought you were either."

"The feeling is mutual. Now, back to business?"

Leena murmured something unintelligible, and Skandalis said, "Take your time with the car. Get lunch or something. That way she'll be gone by the time you get back."

Gone? Gone where? Where were they taking her? Wherever it was, it sounded like there was profit in it for them. That thought terrified her. Abby heard the sound of footsteps, and the opening and closing of a door. A moment later a shape passed by the window.

She'd been left alone with Skandalis. His heavier footsteps moved through the garage toward the laundry room. Her heart thudded, and panic threatened to flood over her again. The steps halted. She held her breath and listened. They changed course and left the same way Leena had. She exhaled.

Who was coming? That was the question. Whoever it was, Leena was afraid to meet them. With a sinking feeling in her gut, Abby knew she didn't want to meet them either. But they were coming for her. Skandalis had said she wouldn't be here when Leena returned.

Abby thrashed frantically at her ties. The movement threw her off her balance. She wobbled and, unable to catch herself without the use of her hands, toppled onto her side. Her cheek slapped the cold, cement floor. The skin on her wrists burned. She roared through the tape on her mouth in pain and frustration.

Seb Skandalis trafficked in misery. The people he did business with bought and sold human beings. She could only believe that some version of that fate was what he intended for her. A tear slid down her cheek.

The irony of her position struck her. She had willingly shut herself into a room with much the same dimensions as this one. It had only one small window, like this one. It had no door, however. But even without a door, she'd had freedom.

The anchorites of old willingly consigned themselves to a cell which would eventually become their grave. They had a funeral service before they entered. Yet, they were freer than Abby was now, because it was their choice.

Would this room become her grave? She didn't know if Seb and Leena's plan was to kill her or to sell her, but either would mean the death of Abby Travers. Autonomy. She'd never realized before how beautiful that word was. When one was stripped of the ability to rule themselves, to determine their own fate, didn't they cease to exist in some way?

Sunlight streaked the gray floor with gold. By its slant, she guessed it was at least 1:30. Skandalis had said his associates would be here by 2:30. She still had one hour of freedom, one hour to be Abby. She wanted to experience every moment she had left. When the sun reached her and warmed her skin, that would signal the end of her time in this new anchorhold. But she couldn't bear to watch the minutes move across the floor. She closed her eyes.

Carlos.

His face appeared in her mind. She'd left a phone message for him. He knew where she was. He was her only hope. If he heard her message, he'd call her back. If he couldn't get through on the phone, he'd come looking for her. If he could get away from work, of course. There were so many ifs. Even if he didn't get there before 2:30, he'd tell the police about the call. They'd find her. Wouldn't they? She might not like Sylla, but she was a good cop.

Two images vied for primary viewing time in Abby's mind. The first: Carlos striding across the grass, throwing open the garage door and scooping her up in his arms. The second: A dark, locked room, empty but for a stained mattress and the strange men at the door. She forced her mind to the first, just as she'd trained her mind to focus on her prayers in the anchorhold.

But no amount of concentration could hold back the sunlight that moved inch by inch across the floor. Time crept toward her like a rising tide. Dread came with it. A half hour had passed.

A long finger of light stretched to the dryer. So close. Soon it would touch her ankle.

A flash.

Abby blinked.

Metal, copper or gold, flashed again. The sun played across an object partway under the dryer.

She squirmed along the floor. Was it jewelry? A lost necklace? The sun moved a fraction of an inch more, as if answering her question. It was a cross. A large, ornate cross. One jagged edge thrust out from under the machine.

Fueled by a surge of adrenaline, she pushed herself onto an elbow, then rocked to a seated position. Time, her constant companion in the anchorhold, had brought her hope. She backed up to the dryer and thrust her hands underneath. Blindly, she pawed through dust and lint.

Endless moments later, cold metal met her hands. She ran a fingertip along the object's edge. It felt like the serrated line of a key. She positioned her wrists against it and rubbed. Tentatively at first, afraid the object would shoot out of its crevasse and end up so far beneath the dryer she'd never find it again. But it held.

Encouraged, she applied more pressure and sawed at the duct tape. It caught on the metal, popped free and caught again. She worked at it for several minutes, sweat trickling down her sides. A cramp in her shoulder forced her to stop and rest.

When it passed, she began again. This second time, the work went more smoothly. Within seconds the tape snagged on one of the cross's teeth. Abby pulled. The sound of a rip, so loud in the quiet room, brought tears to her eyes.

Five more attempts, and the tape was ripped almost in two. One small yank, and her wrists separated.

She covered her face with her hands and sobbed. "Thank you. Thank you. Thank you." She whispered the words to the sun, to time, and to the God who made them both. Warmth crept over her bare ankle, reminding her of her need to hurry.

She tore at the duct tape wrapped around her shins and pulled her legs free. In one step she was at the door. She turned the knob and yanked. It held fast.

She spun and ran to the window. Her fingers scrabbled at the sill. She thrust up. No movement. Nailed shut.

Abby gripped her hair with her hands; her gaze roved around the space. If she couldn't get out, she needed a weapon. She had no idea how many men would be coming for her, maybe arming herself was a hopeless gesture, but she couldn't do nothing.

A shadow cut across the golden glow on the laundry room floor. Someone was coming. They'd just passed by the window. Abby bent and dug the cross from its crevasse beneath the dryer, but it felt small and feeble in her grip. Then her gaze landed on a box of laundry detergent, perched on a shelf above the washer. She reached for it, tore off its top, and positioned herself near the door.

Footsteps crossed the garage, growing louder, coming toward her. A man's footsteps, but only one. Abby widened her stance and braced herself, both hands gripping the large cardboard box.

A key scraped in the keyhole. She watched as the knob turned. The door swung open, and Seb Skandalis stood on the other side. A look of surprise flashed across his face. Abby launched the laundry soap into his wide eyes.

He screamed and covered his face with his hands. Abby dropped the box, and as she did a plastic bag tumbled to the floor. Through white soap film, she saw the dark green of a passport booklet.

She bent, grabbed it, and bolted around Skandalis all in one movement. She had one foot across the threshold when a vise closed around her left arm. She jerked to a stop, like a dog snapped by its leash. Seb's eyes, slits streaming with tears, glared at her from a powdered face.

Abby's pulse thundered in her ears. A clean, chilly breeze blew through the open door. She could feel freedom. The cross burned against her thigh. She'd put it into her front pocket without thinking when she picked up the box of laundry soap. It was a small weapon, but if she was close enough. . . She allowed Skandalis to draw her toward him. "You're going to pay for that girl."

She kept her eyes locked on his and slipped the cross from her pocket. "I wasn't going to take a turn with you. Just going to let the boys have you," he said. Abby anchored the crossbar of the talisman into the palm of her hand and slid the longer end between two fingers, so it protruded from her fist. "You're kind of old for me, but hell. I think I just changed my mind." His voice was filled not with lust, but rage. She shivered. He pulled her closer.

She was so close now the lavender scented detergent bit into her nostrils. Each piece of stubble on his chin stood out in powdered relief. He opened his mouth to speak again, its interior unnaturally red against the paleness of his soapy skin. She didn't want to hear what he had to say.

A breath of wind, of freedom, beckoned her from outside the open garage door. Her arm arced through space. The cross hit something solid, stopped for a split second, then sank into softness.

He didn't scream. His mouth opened wide, but no sound emerged. He loosened the grip on her arm. She yanked the cross free, bringing blood and tissue with it. Seb sank to his knees, hands pressed to his injured eye, or what had once been an eye. Abby ran from the garage, leaving drops of blood behind her like breadcrumbs.

3.6.5

IT WAS BEAUTIFUL OUTSIDE. One of those sunny Southern California days responsible for its inflated property prices. Not a good day to die. Abby tried to jog across the lawn, but a pain in her hip slowed her. Skandalis had handled her roughly, and she'd returned the favor.

But she had to get away before he recovered enough to come after her or call for help. Her phone was gone, and her car wasn't where she'd left it. She stood in front of the Basara family's house staring dumbly at the black tire track she'd made on the curb. Skandalis had told Leena to get rid of it, and she had.

His associates would be there soon, and this thought made her blood race. She scanned the street, expecting to see a group of thugs loping toward her with guns drawn. She needed help.

There were only a couple of cars on the street. Either no one was home, or their vehicles were parked in their large, three-car garages. An old Cadillac sat in the driveway of the house directly across the wide cul-de-sac.

Abby hurried across and knocked. The door remained closed for several horrible moments. Then she heard muffled footsteps and the click of a lock. The door opened only as far as a safety chain would allow. An elderly woman with a pink scalp covered here and there by wisps of gray hair narrowed pale blue eyes at Abby. "Yes?" Her voice wasn't friendly.

"I need your help. Please, can I use your phone? I have to call the police." The woman looked down the length of Abby, her eyes widened, and the door slammed shut. "Wait." Abby leaped forward to hold it open, but she was too late. "Please." She slapped the wood with her palm.

"Go away, or I'll call the police." The woman's voice was faint through the heavy oak.

"Call the police, please. Call them, but don't leave me out here. I'm in danger. There's a man. . ."

"What man?"

"A man, at the Basara house. He kidnapped me."

"A man at the Basaras." She sounded worried.

"Yes. Please let me in. He might come out at any moment."

"Could it be the same man who shot poor Tarik on Saturday?"

"Yes, yes, that's exactly who it is. He shot Tarik, and he wants to shoot me." This wasn't exactly true, but the truth seemed too difficult to explain at the moment.

"I'm calling the police." Abby heard the woman's footsteps fade as she moved deeper into the house.

"No," Abby screamed. "Let me in first. There isn't time." She beat on the door with her fists. The cross dug into her palm with each blow. She threw her shoulder into the door, but she bounced off.

Hopelessness filled her. She dropped her hands to her sides. When she did, she noticed them for the first time. They were splattered with blood. Glancing down at herself, she saw her blouse was a gory Rorschach test. No wonder the woman wouldn't let her in.

She turned to face the street. Maybe she could wait, sit here on the front porch until the police arrived. She wrapped her arms around her body, leaned against the door, and closed her eyes. She was weak, dizzy. Her head throbbed. Her breath rasped across her throat. Her lungs ached.

"Damn it." The curse struck her ears like a blow. Her eyes flew open. Skandalis stood across the street, staring in the direction she should have gone. The only way out of the cul-de-sac. He'd wrapped a cloth around his head and held it to his wounded eye with one hand. In the other was something black and metallic. A gun? She shrank into the shadow of the doorway. He didn't see her, but he could. If he looked her way. There was nothing blocking his view.

"Damn it, damn it, damn it." He pulled a phone from his pocket and dialed with his gun hand. As he spoke, he turned his back to her exposing the bandage on the crown of his head—a present from Carlos. He'd had a rough few days. The thought was comforting. A little comforting, anyway. She strained to hear what he was saying into the phone, but his voice was too low.

Abby slipped from her place to the shelter of a large camellia bush, and then darted to a stand of cypress trees. He walked onto Leena's front stoop and opened the door. *Go inside. Inside.* She held her breath and willed him to go. The yard to her left only held foundation plantings bordering a huge expanse of lawn. There was nothing to hide behind. Past that, was an oak, but it would take precious seconds to reach the tree.

She would make a run for it when he entered the house. Even if he planned to post up at a window, it would take time for him to close the door and walk to either of the rooms that fronted the house. She could make it to the tree. She was sure. Pretty sure. She stepped into a lunge, like a runner taking her place at the start of a race.

He walked across the threshold.

She shifted her weight to her front leg.

The door began to close.

She vaulted from behind the tree.

The door flew open. He reemerged.

Momentum drove Abby three steps forward before she was able to throw herself into reverse. She fell on her knees behind the cypress, heart hammering in her chest. Did he see her?

She peered between branches. He wasn't looking her way. His eyes were trained on something at the end of the walkway. When he reached the curb, he examined the tire track she'd left there. He rubbed at it with the toe of his shoe. "Damn it," he said again. Then he pivoted, returned to the house, and this time slammed the door behind himself.

Abby waited for several seconds before finding the courage to bolt for the oak again. Maybe she should wait for the police? She was safer here, behind the trees, than she'd been at the front door. But it was also possible the woman hadn't called for help. Perhaps it had only been a threat. A way to get rid of Abby.

If she had called, wouldn't they be here by now? Abby wasn't sure how many minutes had passed while she'd watched Skandalis walk back and forth across the street. It had seemed like a year's worth.

She also didn't know who he had called. Maybe it was his associates. Maybe they were on their way. Maybe they would arrive before the police, who might not be arriving at all. She sat and stared at the Basara house frozen by indecision. Then she saw it.

A trail of blood droplets decorated the asphalt between the properties. She might as well have painted an arrow in the middle of the street. *Escapee this way. Look here.* Skandalis must not have seen them because of his limited vision, but his associates certainly would. Abby wiped the cross on the thigh of her jeans and shoved it in her front pocket.

That made up her mind. She had to leave. To walk out of the neighborhood, find a public place, someone who wouldn't be afraid of her, and get help.

She bolted across the neighbor's grass to the oak tree ignoring the pain in her hip. When she reached it, she hugged the bark, caught her breath, and eyed the next yard, then the next. She made her way along the cul-de-sac hiding behind bushes, trees, and trash cans until she could no longer see the Basaras's windows.

At that point, she moved to the narrow sidewalk. She would make better time here. She was fairly certain if she made a right at the end of the block it would lead her to one of the larger Nellie Gail roads. And those roads led out of the neighborhood.

She crossed the street. Before she reached the other side a car, going much too fast, rocketed around the corner. She had to leap out of its way. She shot a glance after it, half expecting the driver to stop. To apologize. Hoping she could ask him for help. He didn't stop, but she wasn't surprised. It was a taxi.

MOLLY: Thank god, Abby got away. She's definitely developed a backbone through the course of this experience. When I interviewed her, this is the woman I met. A woman who could shove a cross into a man's eye if she had to. Honestly, I've had a hard time envisioning her the way she described herself at the beginning of the season. She's no wallflower today.

Anyway, while all this was happening to Abby, Leena took Abby's car to the train station and dropped it off. She actually wrote about it. It seems a pretty insignificant thing to write about, but the email does give us more of her backstory. I think it's worth reading because of that. It helps us understand her a little better. So, here's Leena.

the wife

I PARKED seven spaces from the box where one buys metered time. I counted the bills in my purse. I'd liquidated my checking account the day before. From now on I'll be using cash.

I bought a ticket for two hours and placed it on the dash. The longer it took for the police to find Abby's vehicle the better. I exited the car, locked it with the key fob, snapped off the latex gloves I'd been wearing and faced the ocean. A gentle breeze brushed my cheek, and the afternoon sun warmed my shoulders. It was a beautiful Southern California day. The kind of day I read about when Tarik and I were discussing the move to America.

To the right was the San Clemente train stop, to the left a walking path leading to the pier. I turned left, stopped at the third trash can I came to, threw away the gloves, then continued on. The path paralleled the beach and the train tracks. I'd come here many times with Tarik when we first arrived. We'd walk along the shore and talk about our plans, this new adventure we'd embarked on.

I'd been happy in Egypt for many years, but as I got older, the limitations placed on women began to chafe. I'd married Tarik willingly, although my parents had arranged the marriage. He was handsome, and I was young enough to be taken by a pretty face.

I was more intelligent than he was. I knew that immediately, but even that was part of his charm. It made him easier to control. Many of my friends' lives were greatly restricted by their husbands. I learned to twist Tarik around my little finger early in our relationship.

Then Tarik lost his business, and I was overlooked for a promotion to principal yet again. The time seemed right for a move. Tarik applied and was hired by the California division of a company he'd worked with in Cairo.

We never mentioned his disastrous business decisions, the ones that had preceded the move, or the teaching career I'd left behind, when we walked this path. We only discussed the wonderful advantages for ourselves and our sons that were ahead of us.

The sun sparkled on the water then, an ocean of diamonds just waiting to be plucked up. It looked the same today, but my perspective had changed. Today I saw it for what it was—a landscape of cheap imitations. California was the land of empty promises and fool's gold.

The clanging of a warning bell drowned out my thoughts. I stopped as the traffic barrier came down across the tracks, and the metro roared past.

I imagined Abby on that train—that's what I hoped the police would believe anyway. Abby, realizing she and her father were found out, had run. She had nothing left to lose, so she parked her car and headed south. Most likely she was in Mexico, maybe her boyfriend Carlos would join her in time.

It seemed believable enough. More believable than what was about to happen to her. She was close to thirty. Women weren't molded into prostitutes at her age. They were too opinionated, too hard to train, too old to look at. But Abby had a waif-like way about her, a passive, shy personality. She seemed much younger than she was.

Seb didn't normally traffic in that kind of product, he told me, preferring to bring in young girls for domestic purposes. It was more humane. But he knew people. And the people he knew weren't humane, nor were they all that particular. They believed they could get their money's worth from Abby, even if she wasn't in the business for long.

I didn't want to think about it. Especially not on such a beautiful day. Especially not on one of my last days in America. I've purchased tickets to Egypt for the children and myself. We leave in two days.

I hiked up a long footbridge. At its top the ocean unfurled before me like a map. I could see the pier jutting out into the blue. A child on a bike whizzed past, followed by a woman about Abby's age pushing a stroller. A pang of sympathy gripped me. Abby would never become a mother. Would never push a stroller along the beach on a lovely day.

But I tossed the thought away and let the wind take it wherever it would. It was a shame, but I had to think about my children. About Michael and Simo. I had no other choice.

The path wended its way down to the beach. There were more people here. Volleyball players punted and threw themselves on the sand reaching for the ball. Two surfers, sheathed in black wetsuits, carried boards on their shoulders. A lone man, baseball cap pulled low, sat in a beach chair reading.

When I reached the pier, I made a right into the more casual side of the Fisherman's restaurant. It wasn't crowded at this time of day. Too late for lunch and too early for dinner. There were several empty tables in the outdoor seating area. A young waitress with hair the color and texture of straw led me to one.

"My friend should be here soon, but I'll have a glass of Chardonnay while I wait," I said. She placed menus on the table and walked away. Wine—another bad habit acquired in America. I never drank in Egypt. My parents didn't approve of drinking. It wasn't until we'd come to California, and I attended Tarik's business parties that I'd started drinking. I planned to stop when I got home, but today I needed a glass of wine.

The server returned, stemware dripping with moisture and filled with pale gold liquid in her hand. "My friend is one of those people who'll be late to her own funeral." I plastered an expression of mock alarm on my face. "But don't tell her I said that when she gets here. Please."

The straw-haired girl laughed. "Sounds like most of my friends."

I wanted to establish a rapport with my waitress. Create a story she might remember, just in case the police were curious about how I spent my time the day Abby Travers disappeared. I sipped my wine and watched a seagull dive into the surf.

Fifteen minutes later, the server returned. "Still waiting?"

"I think she must have forgotten our date," I said in an irritated voice. "It wouldn't be the first time." I pulled my purse into my lap.

"Would you like the check?"

"Yes, please."

After the girl left, I took out my phone and typed in the number for the cab company I'd found before I left the house. They told me they had a driver close. He'd arrive within ten minutes.

I'd been hot and sweaty from the walk when I'd first sat but was cold now. The ocean wind blew through my damp clothes, fondling my skin with icy fingers. I pulled Abby's keys from my purse, leaned over the railing, and dropped them. As they disappeared into the foaming sea, I had a mild attack of vertigo. I looked away.

I gulped the rest of my wine. Its warmth steadied me. Maybe this one American habit would follow me home after all. My parents didn't need to know. I shook my head and laughed under my breath. There were many things about my time in this country they didn't need to know. Wine was the least of them. I am not as innocent as I believed.

MOLLY: How could she ever have thought of herself as innocent? It's beyond me.

As I mentioned earlier, Abby grew stronger through adversity. Leena, on the other hand, grew more evil. I'm glad she finally admitted it.

Anyway, I'm sorry to say, this is where we'll have to end for today. I hate to leave you on a cliffhanger, but we're out of time.

My question for you this week is a little more philosophical than usual. Do you believe that evil is a form of strength or of weakness? I mean, yes, Leena has been the one to come up with the plans and, yes, she seems to be able to coerce people into doing what she wants them to do. But is that strength? Or was all that motivated by fear? Or does it even matter what motivated her if her actions were bold ones? I'd love to hear what you think.

Join me next time for more *Murders Under the Sun*.

(cue music)

VO: This episode is sponsored by the Law Firm of Randall & Richter, specialists in family law. *Murders Under the Sun* is edited by Jim Wilbourne, theme music is by Eclectic Blends, and I'm your host, Molly Shure.

part eight

MURDERS UNDER THE SUN
  SEASON THREE; EPISODE SEVEN

MOLLY: Welcome back to *Murders Under the Sun*. I'm Molly Shure, your host.

Well, this is it people. The final episode of Season Three. It's been a wild ride, but it's not over yet.

Last week we left Abby on the run. She'd just escaped from Seb Skandalis by stabbing him in the eye with the cross that Hannah left in the laundry room. There is something fitting in that. I hope it gave Hannah some satisfaction if she was watching from the wings. We also left Leena racing home from the train station in a taxi.

Speaking of Leena, your thoughts on the origin of evil were deep. I think it was the most fascinating discussion we've had since the beginning of the season. And, as usual, you weren't all in agreement.

The majority seemed to feel that the kind of strength Abby developed through the course of this experience has probably served her well since. Whereas the strength—if we can call it that—that Leena acquired will most likely ruin her. Interesting analysis. I hadn't thought of it that way, but I think it's true.

Here's a follow-up to that thought. Can you call something that's destined to break you a strength? That sounds more like a liability to me.

But enough of that. I know you are all chomping at the bit to find out what is going to happen next.

We'll start with an email from Leena.

the wife

THE TAXI WAS GOING MUCH TOO FAST. I was focused on my phone—texting Michael—but I thought I saw someone jump out of our way in my peripheral vision. Normally, I'd reprimand the driver. This was a family neighborhood. Children played and pets strayed here. But I was in a hurry. I wanted to get home before the associates arrived. I was having second thoughts.

I know it sounds hard-hearted, but I believed the best plan was to kill Abby. Drop her off the end of the pier at night or throw her off a boat. Surely, Skandalis knew someone with a boat. He seemed to know everyone. If she washed up on a beach, the police would think she committed suicide.

The point was, leaving her alive made me nervous. What if she escaped? What if she found her way to safety? I was fairly sure the American government would extradite someone for kidnapping and selling another human being. I didn't want to be linked to an international trafficking ring.

No, it was best to silence her for good. I still had the passports, Hannah's passport and the other one. They were powerful inducements for Seb to cooperate. Besides, it was the most humane thing to do. I would rather die than be made the sex slave of violent men. We would be doing Abby a favor.

The driver pulled up in front of my house. I paid him in cash and stepped from the vehicle. He drove off and my heart skipped a beat. On the asphalt, where the taxi had been, was a splatter of brownish red dots. Blood?

I followed the trail with my eyes. It grew less and less as it crossed the street. I pivoted and followed it in the other direction. I tracked a shine of moisture across the lawn. The blood splashes became thicker and more pronounced on the concrete path on the other side of the garage.

What had happened here? Had Seb's associates already taken Abby? Had they beaten her? Brutalized her? Here? On my property? I strode into the garage, indignation growing with each step. This wasn't part of our agreement. The droplets ended in a pool outside the laundry room door.

I stepped over it, careful not to get any on my shoes, and entered the small room. Abby was gone. Detergent covered the floor like snow. My throat constricted with anxiety. The passports. I yanked up the cardboard box. It was empty but for a half cup or so of soap. Seb had found them then.

This destroyed any leverage I had over him. My plan had been to hand them over at the airport, right before boarding my flight to Egypt. Give them to him in a public place, swarming with security. Then walk away into the sunset.

I dropped the box to the floor and wiped my hand on my pants. What now? What did this mean? I thought fast. I would have to convince him to help me kill Abby. But how?

I planned my argument as I retraced my steps to the front walk and entered the house. Dead air greeted me. The house, once filled with the hum of family life, was now an empty shell. I had started taking down pictures, packing knickknacks, and covering furniture. The children were with Aunt Sara. I wanted them far away when Seb and his associates were here.

I walked into the living room. My footsteps echoed across the wood floor. "Leena?" It was Skandalis's voice.

He lay on my couch, one foot on the floor, hands on his chest, a maroon-stained bandage wrapped around his head. "Leena?" he said again.

"Yes." I choked out the word.

"Did you get rid of her car?" I couldn't believe he asked me that, so calmly, as if he wasn't as white as the sheet covering my sofa. As if his face wasn't painted with dried blood. "I put them off as long as I could, but my associates will be here soon. We have work to do."

"What do you mean?"

"Abby is gone. They're not going to be happy."

"How?"

"She got loose. There must have been a knife, scissors, something in the laundry room." His words were an accusation. Like somehow, I was responsible for her escape.

"And she attacked you?"

"Obviously. She stabbed me in the eye with something. She'll pay."

"How do you plan to make that happen?" I heard a tremor of rage in my voice. "She's gone."

"She can't be far. She's on foot." Did he expect me to go after her? In answer to my unspoken question, he said, "You'd better hurry. We need her here when my associates arrive. They're not. . . pleasant when they're disappointed."

His audacity rendered me speechless. Here he lay on my couch, in my living room, barking orders at me as if I were one of his slave girls.

"Take my gun, as an inducement for her cooperation." He gestured to the weapon on the floor, then draped his hand across his forehead like a maiden about to swoon.

I picked up the gun and looked at it. I had no idea how to use it. I'd go after her. No one else was going to do it. But I'd take care of things my own way. It seemed I was always cleaning up after inept men.

I left him and walked to the kitchen. I dropped the gun on the counter, opened a drawer and withdrew my favorite butcher knife—the one I cut onions with the night I thought Hannah was gone and all this was over. I returned to the living room.

Seb still lay in a pathetic heap, arm across his eyes. "I told you, you need to hurry," he said, his voice weak. I stepped closer to him. "My car keys are on the kitchen counter if you need my vehicle."

I held my knife with both hands, raised it high above my head.

"What are you waiting for?" He removed his arm and opened his one good eye. A look of horror crossed his face.

I brought down the blade and plunged it into his chest in one swift movement—a dagger into the heart of a vampire. He gasped. I pulled it free, and blood arced from the wound. I'd hit an artery. Forgive me, but I was glad. He would die soon. I wiped the blade on the sheet he lay on.

I walked to the hall, took my purse from the floor where I'd dropped it when I entered, and put the knife inside. Then I lengthened the strap so I could wear it across my chest. It seemed best to have my hands free.

I was about to check on Seb one last time but paused. Maybe it would be best to take the gun. It couldn't hurt. I stopped in the kitchen to retrieve it on my way to the living room.

Seb was still alive, but barely. His face had turned a pale gray. His mouth gaped like a strangling fish's; his lips were tinged with blue. I couldn't wait for him to die, though. He'd been right about one thing today anyway; I did need to hurry.

I only took the time to send you this one final email, because I'm afraid of the future. In light of current circumstances, it can't be good. If this is the last time you hear from me, please watch over Michael and Simo.

MOLLY: And this is the last email we have from Leena. I can't say I'm sorry. They were difficult to read aloud.

I'm sure you'd like to know why she doesn't write again, though. So, I'll get back to the story.

3.7.2

ABBY SLOWED. After the taxi almost mowed her down, she moved off the main street onto a horse path that ran in the same general direction. It felt safe, secluded. But she was walking in circles, she realized as she came on the same maintenance shed for a second time. The overdose of adrenaline that had been keeping her going was gone. It left exhaustion in its wake.

She looked at the shed. It didn't appear to be locked. The door was open a crack, and its cool, dim interior beckoned to her. She longed to enter, curl into a corner, and sleep. When threatened, some animals fought, some ran, a few hid. Abby was one of the latter. But she knew she needed to find help, and she needed it soon.

She could hear the occasional car hum by somewhere through the trees. Overcoming her ostrich instincts, she dragged herself in the direction of the sound. Eucalyptus trees, tall and close, surrounded the equestrian path. They'd been planted to create an illusion of riding in the countryside, she supposed. The deception was a bit too good. She listened for more cars but heard only the cawing of crows and crunch of dried leaves under her feet. She felt like a child lost in a dark, deep wood.

A small shape darted past her. She started and stumbled over a tree root. An excruciating jolt shot through her leg and injured hip into her low back. Abby cried out and fell against the tree the squirrel now clung to. Black spots formed behind her eyes, and she doubled over. When she could see again, she tried to straighten and gasped.

The pain was intense. Usually, when she felt the familiar tightening around her coccyx, she'd lie on an ice pack, take an anti-inflammatory, and rest. But everything had been so upside-down since the fire, she hadn't taken care of herself. She'd put up with the low-grade pain. And now, none of those things were possible.

She shuffled forward through the leaves stooped like an old woman, forcing herself to keep moving. In a short while, she was rewarded by the sound of an engine. She couldn't see the car through the stand of trees, but she could tell it was close.

She followed the sound. A carpet of black appeared between tree trunks. Asphalt. She moved as fast as her back would allow. When she reached the road, she propped herself against a streetlamp to get her bearings. Directly across from her were unfamiliar homes. She'd never been in this section of the neighborhood before.

Fighting the creeping feeling of vulnerability that rippled across her skin, she searched left, then right for a vehicle to flag down. The chance that she'd collapse here, where it could take people hours to find her, was greater than the chance Skandalis would drive by. He didn't know where she was. She didn't even know where she was. But there were no cars on the street.

Most of Nellie Gail Ranch was built on hilltops. The exit, therefore, was generally down. Abby decided to follow the descending slope of the street and turned left. She had to stop every ten or twelve steps to rest her back against the fence that separated the eucalyptus grove from the residential area. She continued this way for several minutes before she saw a car. It motored past on a perpendicular street only a half block or so in front of her. She wanted to run forward, yell, wave her hands, but she couldn't. Not in her condition. A sob of frustration rose in her chest.

By the time she reached the cross street, the car was long gone. She paused. Should she continue next to the split rail fence, or turn in the direction the car had gone? She chose to go straight. Not for any logical reason, she was past logic, only because she could rest against the fence, and the trees comforted her.

After another block, the downhill slope became more pronounced. Her muscles spasmed with every jarring footfall, and she was forced to slow her steps. She was starting to hate Nellie Gail Ranch.

The car behind her was close before the rumble of its engine broke into her consciousness. She spun toward it, hope soaring. It hadn't been much more than an hour since she'd escaped from Leena Basara's laundry room, but she felt like someone who'd been castaway on a deserted island for months.

A white Lexus SUV was coming down the hill toward her. Abby dropped off the curb onto the blacktop and raised both hands over her head. The car didn't slow. The driver must not have seen her. She stepped farther into the street and waved both arms. Still, it barreled on.

Anger flickered in her chest. What was wrong with these people? Did living in a gated community make you immune to need? Were their consciences barricaded up too? She took another big stride, raised her arms higher, and commanded the SUV to stop in a loud voice.

It didn't.

It accelerated.

Several things happened in the span of two heartbeats. Abby saw the face of the driver. Fear pumped like speed through her veins. She leaped away. The car skimmed by so close, she felt its wind on her face and smelled the tar the tires left behind.

Leena Basara's eyes, calm and determined, had been focused on her. Leena had seen her. Leena had tried to run her down.

3.7.3

ABBY ROLLED under the split rail fence and into the trees. Everything in her screamed *HIDE*. She crawled through the underbrush. The rattle of leaves only partially drowning out the screech of tires behind her.

Placing a hand on peeling bark, she stood. The new wave of adrenaline coursing through her acted like an analgesic. Her back was on fire, but the pain no longer seemed to belong to her. She limped through the small, wooded area, aiming for the horse trail. And the shed. It couldn't be more than a third of a mile behind her.

Maintenance sheds were usually locked. It was a liability to leave them open. Children could get stuck inside, be hurt by tools, or poisons. She told herself all this as she hurried toward it. She was drawn to that slender crack she'd seen between the door and the doorframe like a parched man to water.

Her breath and the crush of leaves under her feet were all she heard for a long time, but then another sound registered. A steady thump, growing louder. Someone was running behind her.

The shed came into view. Abby picked up her pace. Every muscle surrounding her lower spine protested. The gap between the door and the building was there, it hadn't been her imagination. And she could see a metal hasp hanging loose. When she got closer, she noted a padlock was threaded through its loop but wasn't clicked shut. The door had opened as far as the loose lock allowed. Abby said a prayer of thanks.

She removed the padlock and pushed the door open. The interior of the shed was crowded with tools, buckets, and bags. It smelled of mildew and chemical fertilizer.

She wedged herself inside and pulled the door shut behind her. As the light from the doorway faded, horizontal stripes of sunshine became visible on her right. There was no window in the shed, but there was an air vent near the floor.

Abby dropped to her knees and lowered her face. The view between the metal slats was minimal, a small section of dirt and the base of a large eucalyptus. She sat up on her haunches and surveyed her cell. If the runner she'd heard was Leena, Abby needed to be careful. She should wedge something against the door to keep it closed. Shovels of different sizes and shapes, a rake, pitchfork, and long shears—the kind used for tree branches—were attached to the left wall. Burlap bags and buckets spilled from the back wall into the center of the five-by-five room. On her right were stacks of plastic pots, the kind new plants come in.

She rose to her feet, grabbed the shortest shovel and wedged it between the door and a pile of fertilizer bags. She gave the door a gentle pull. It didn't open. She braced herself to pull harder but stopped. Foot-falls. They'd been muted by the closed door but were now loud enough to be heard through it.

She fell to the ground and peered through her tiny squint. Within seconds a pair of tennis shoes came into her circle of vision. A woman's feet, small and narrow in dirty white canvas. They were Leena's feet. Abby had noticed her bright, white shoes a million years ago, when they'd stood together by the ruins of her father's house. Leena had been busy since then. Flecks of red, like mismatched polka dots, were splattered on the now brown shoes.

Leena stepped toward the shed door, out of Abby's view. Abby wiggled left until she could see the shoes again. She caught her breath. The padlock glinted on the ground near the door. *Damn. Damn.* She should have taken it inside with her.

For a moment she was back in the anchorhold. A different white sneaker lay exposed in the sunlight. The fear that Leena Basara's searching gaze would spot her carelessness had paralyzed her then. She almost laughed out loud at the memory. At the time, she'd thought the worst thing in the world was public humiliation.

A tan hand reached down and picked up the lock. Abby's heart skittered inside her ribs like a caged animal. A knock. Her eyes jerked to the door. It came again. Wood on wood. The door rattled against the handle of the shovel.

Then it stopped. Everything was still. Was she giving up? Did she think the door was secured some other way? Abby's gaze leaped to the vent again. Leena's feet were still at the door. One foot shifted back, like she was bracing herself.

There was one loud thump this time, as the door slammed against the shovel. This was followed by the hiss of shifting sand. Leena was using her body weight against the door.

Would it hold?

The answer came a second later. The tip of the shovel blade disappeared under a bag of fertilizer. The door popped open. A thread of daylight shone on the concrete floor.

Abby thrust both hands around the shovel's handle, anchored her feet against the vent, and shoved back. The door's progress halted.

A moment later, the shovel jolted in her grip. A lightning bolt of pain shot through her. She bit her lip to keep from crying out. Leena had thrown herself against the door. Abby wrapped her hands more tightly around the wood pole and waited. Leena flung her weight at the door three more times. Each jarring movement was more excruciating than the last. Abby tasted blood.

Finally, it stopped, and there was silence. Abby, afraid to move, afraid to breathe, held tight until she heard Leena move away from the door. When she released the shovel handle, she collapsed, exhausted.

The concrete felt cool and solid under her sweaty back. She would wait here, hidden in this hole. She'd stay put until Leena gave up the search. She'd rest until darkness fell, then she'd creep out under cover of night and find help.

Abby turned her face to the air vent. Leena's feet were nowhere to be seen. Was she gone? Abby closed her eyes, straining to hear. A shuffling sound came from several directions at once. She couldn't tell if it was growing louder, or fainter. A voice broke through the confusion of noise. "Leena." Abby tensed. Carlos was loud and clear.

3.7.4

"WHAT ARE YOU DOING HERE?"

At the sound of Carlos's voice, tears sprang into Abby's eyes. He was here. He would rescue her.

"The same thing you are, I imagine," Leena said.

"Abby isn't. . ." His words petered off. He was probably about to say she wasn't there, or she wasn't a threat, but none of that was true. Abby was here, and she was very definitely a threat. She was the only eyewitness to Tarik and Michael's crime.

"This is unfortunate." Leena's tone was apologetic. "I hold no ill will toward you or your girlfriend."

"That's a comfort." Sarcasm put an edge to Carlos's words.

"I'm sorry about what I have to do."

Abby rolled onto her knees and began to rise. Her only thought to run from the shed, and into Carlos's arms, but his next words stopped her cold.

"You don't have to shoot me, Leena. You could leave. Take your kids. Run," Carlos said.

Shoot him? Leena had a gun. The immediacy of the situation hit Abby like a splash of ice water. Rage flared behind her eyes. That was it. She was done.

Done running. Done hiding. Done. She grabbed the closest tool—the long, pointed shears—and placed a hand on the door.

"Detective Sylla is at your house now," Carlos said, and Abby paused. "We found Skandalis. She knows you killed him. Abby and me, we're the least of your problems."

"Really?" Abby heard the disbelief in Leena's voice. "And how does she know that?"

She inched open the door to the shed. Carlos's eyes met hers when she emerged into the dappled sunlight. She shook her head to warn him to keep silent, but she didn't need to. He'd already returned his gaze to Leena.

"He's, ah, he's in your house, on your couch," he said in the same tone he'd been speaking in.

"When the police look into Seb Skandalis's affairs, which doubtless they've already begun doing, they'll find he wasn't a nice man," Leena continued. "His business associates are the kind of people who kill others like you, or I would swat an annoying fly. In fact, I'm fairly certain it was one of them who murdered my lover."

Leaves shuffled under Abby's feet. Carlos raised his voice to cover the noise. "How are you going to explain Abby's death?"

"I don't have to. I can guess, though. She saw something she shouldn't have; we all know that. Those same associates wanted all the loose ends cleaned up. I'm sure they were the ones who set fire to Paul Travers's house."

Carlos was doing his best to keep the conversation going, giving her a chance to get close enough to strike. "You might have some trouble selling that."

Leena's shoulders slumped a little. "Why is that?"

Abby was only feet away now. So close she could smell Leena's perfume. It was the same scent she smelled in the market. The same one she'd worn the day she came snooping around the anchorhold, but now it was fouled with blood and sweat.

"Abby called me when she was on the way to your house," Carlos said. "She told me you asked her to come, that you had evidence to clear her father. I played the voicemail to the cops already."

Leena stiffened. "I'm done talking about this." She put her other hand on the gun and widened her stance.

Abby held the shears like a sword and swung. They bounced off Leena's arm with a crack of bone. The gun skittered away into the leaves.

Carlos leaped forward, grabbed Leena's right arm, flipped her around and pulled it behind her back. She yelped in pain.

"You should have run while you had the chance." His voice was soft, but Abby could feel the rage coming off him in ripples. "Abby, my phone, in my pocket."

Abby reached into his back pocket and took hold of his cell. Before she could withdraw it, Carlos roared and exploded backward knocking her to the ground. A split second later, he landed on top of her.

The breath ejected from her lungs. She lay beneath him stunned. Then the need for air became desperate. She tried to shift him, pushing with one arm, but he was dead weight. If she could get her other hand out of his back pocket, maybe she could move him.

She needed oxygen more than she needed answers. But as she pulled her hand from Carlos's pocket, she felt the warm, wetness of his shirt. Whatever happened, it was bad. She pushed him off and, sucking in deep draughts of air, raised onto her elbows. A shuddering pain shot through her back. She collapsed onto the ground again.

In the short moment she'd been up, she'd seen Carlos's anguished face. One hand was pressed to his stomach and blood seeped between his fingers. Leena must have stabbed him, but with what? How many weapons did she have?

Abby lay panting, waiting for the muscle spasms to pass, trying to think. She saw movement in her peripheral vision and turned her head. Leena, a lethal-looking butcher knife dangling from her left hand, searched the ground. She must be looking for the gun.

If she was, she was looking in the wrong place. It wasn't where she'd dropped it. Abby had seen it bounce across the ground. It was buried in a pile of leaves about four feet away.

Knowing didn't do Abby any good. Her legs were tangled under Carlos's. Her back wasn't cooperating. If she made a move for the gun,

Leena would get there before her. Panic snaked through Abby's throat and into her mouth. She tasted bile.

Carlos would bleed out if she didn't do something. This gave her strength. Saving him couldn't be added to the long list of things she didn't do. Tears welled in her eyes, and she turned her head, searching the ground.

The shears. Thank you, God. They lay where she'd dropped them when she reached for Carlos's phone, only a foot away.

She placed a hand on his leg and began to slide hers out from under it. He moaned. Abby froze, but Leena didn't look their way.

When her legs were free, she inched her right hand toward the shears. If she could knock the knife away from Leena, it might buy her a few seconds to find the gun. She would have to move quickly, use momentum to push through the pain that was sure to come.

Her hand closed over the long handle of the shears. She drew her legs under her and stifled a yelp. She tightened her abdominal muscles to keep her back as still as possible. She could do this. Her legs were fine. They were good. She'd use their strength to propel herself.

She inhaled, coiled, and sprang.

Leena pivoted; shock widened her eyes.

Abby swiped at the knife with the shears, but Leena yanked her arm away. The shears whistled through empty air.

Abby's exhausted muscles twitched, about to give out. She sank into a crouch to ease her back, but her right arm began to quiver. The shears were heavy. Much heavier than Leena's knife. She repositioned them, using both hands to hold them spear-like in front of her.

Leena was tiring, too. Her movements were slow and uncoordinated, her right arm cradled against her ribs. She slashed at the air, but the knife didn't come near Abby.

So, this was the standoff? Two middle-class, suburban women, neither having any idea how to fight, waving kitchen and garden implements at each other. If she hadn't been so afraid, Abby would've laughed.

Who would fail first? That was the question. Abby had youth. She was thinner, probably stronger. But she'd been strangled, tied up, had run miles, and her back was sending distress signals down both thighs. Her money was on Leena.

They circled each other, eyes locked on one another's, for endless minutes. Leena's were brown, like coffee, or chocolate. Why was brown always associated with food? If Abby compared them to dirt, or something worse, it would be an insult. And Leena's eyes were beautiful. Beautiful eyes set in a face contorted by anger and resolve.

The trail was quiet, almost peaceful. If it wasn't for her anxiety over Carlos, Abby would consider dying here. It wasn't a bad place to go, under the trees in the dappled sunshine, and she was so tired.

The shears had drooped several inches. Gravity pulled them earthward like a water witch's fork. Soon they'd be pointing due south. Then it would be over.

Noises. A scratch of dirt. A gust of leaves. A gut-wrenching yell. All behind Abby. Leena's eyes left hers for just a second. It was long enough. Abby lifted her spear and charged.

She felt it penetrate soft tissue and, as they fell, pound into something much harder. The impact sent shock waves through her back.

Leena didn't scream. Air whistled from her in a high whine. She flailed beneath Abby for a moment, then lay still.

Strong hands rolled Abby away onto the ground. Carlos thrust something at her. "Phone," he said, and collapsed.

3.7.5

Two Months Later

MIMI PUSHED her chair away from the long picnic table and began stacking dishes. "It was a major success."

The last of the Home and Garden Tour attendees left an hour earlier. Abby was proud of Carlos. He and his team had worked hard to get everything ready, and it showed. They'd marked the plots of herbs with informational signs. Perennials and annuals bloomed between them. The old shrubs and trees had been pruned to best advantage. Even a stand of hollyhocks nodded in front of the old garden shed, which had been cleaned to shabby chic perfection. His creativity and eye for detail were visible everywhere.

Mimi had invited the Rojo staff and their families to stay for a "thank you" lunch. A long wooden picnic table covered with a red checked tablecloth and the remains of a Mexican feast sat near the ginkgo biloba tree in one corner of the yard.

Connie and Paul were seated across from Abby and Carlos. Mimi and Bradley were positioned at the heads of the table. They'd finished eating at least a half hour ago but were content to sit and chat in the warm sun. The others stood in the shade sipping beers and iced teas watching the kids play horseshoes and catch.

Bradley pulled a toothpick out of his mouth. "People raved about your work."

Abby watched Carlos as he digested the compliment. A hand rose to cover the grin he couldn't suppress, and color flushed his cheeks. "I think I'm going to be busy. I got a lot of requests for consultations."

"Does this mean you'll be doing more landscaping and less yard maintenance?" Paul said.

Abby knew that was what Carlos wanted, what he'd gone to school for. The maintenance work might be his bread and butter, but landscape design was what made the meal interesting.

He shrugged a shoulder. "That's what they said they wanted."

"Of course that's what they want. And it wouldn't surprise me if you get inundated with calls after *Beach Cities Magazine* comes out." Mimi pivoted in her chair to face Abby. "A journalist and a photographer went to each house on the tour, taking pictures and interviewing the hosts. They loved this place. The writer must have talked to Carlos for an hour."

Abby placed a hand on his thigh and squeezed. "That's wonderful."

Mimi stood and began clearing the table. Abby rose, picked up their empty dishes, kissed Carlos on top of his head, and followed Mimi into the house.

When they returned to the yard, Rosie and an athletic looking man stood near the table. She turned when she heard them coming. "Mimi, the place looks stunning. I was just telling Carlos; he outdid himself this time."

"Next year we can include the interior of the house in the tour and show off your work," Mimi said.

"At the rate we're going, it might just be ready."

Bradley, who'd been balancing his chair on its rear legs, brought the other two down with a thud. "I thought you two were done."

"Not even close." Mimi laughed.

"It never ends, trust me," the athletic man held out a hand to Bradley. "Eric," he said.

"This is my husband everyone." Rosie made introductions all around.

"What can I get you to drink? Beer, wine, iced tea?" Mimi scurried off to fill their order, and Rosie and Eric settled into chairs.

"Sorry we're so late. Eric had a meeting he couldn't get out of," Rosie said.

"Thought I was the only one who had to work weekends. What do you do?" Paul asked.

"I work for Pacific Financial, an investment company. Generally, I don't work Saturdays, but the company is in an upheaval. We recently lost a senior partner."

The sun still shone, but Abby felt a sudden chill. She rubbed her arms. Pacific Financial, hadn't that been the firm Seb Skandalis had worked for? She'd thought she'd read that in the paper.

Bradley looked at Mimi. "Was that the guy who. . . " His words trailed off.

"Seb Skandalis," Abby's voice sank to a monotone.

Eric nodded his head. "It was a shock."

"We had no idea what kind of person he was." Rosie stared at the glass of wine Mimi placed in front of her. "We couldn't believe what we read in the papers."

A minute ticked by while no one spoke. "It's been a nightmare, dealing with his clients. Doing damage control with the press," Eric finally said.

Abby felt Carlos tense next to her. "It was a nightmare for Abby and her dad too."

Eric's gaze darted to Abby, then Paul. She saw the light flicker behind his eyes. "Oh," he said. "Wow. Sorry. Didn't put two and two together."

"I told you." Rosie's lips thinned. She covered Abby's hand with one of her own. "We didn't mean to make light of your ordeal. Eric has been at the office seventy hours a week since that man was killed. He's tired, not thinking."

"You don't need to make excuses for me, Rose." His voice was tight. "Abby, Paul, I truly apologize. I didn't in any way mean to compare the two situations. Work is work. Your experience was life and death. I'm sure it was horrendous." His lips formed an empathetic smile. "I'm a dolt. Can you forgive me?"

A communal exhale circled the table. Abby could see why Rosie had married him. Eric had a winning way, a certain charm. "It's okay," she said.

"Forget about it," her father said rising. "I promised Connie a tour of our construction site. Abby, Carlos, do you want to come along?"

Abby said goodbye to everyone. But Carlos only nodded coolly to Rosie's husband. He'd been very protective of her since the day Leena had died. Which was ironic, since Abby was the one who'd saved them both. But she understood now. He wasn't trying to control her, as she'd thought before. It was how he showed love.

The new kitchen, bedroom, office, and bathroom were framed out. Clean planks stood where black ash had covered everything only two months before. Abby stepped through the doorframe onto the concrete slab. The smell of freshly cut pine boards now replaced the sickening odor of smoke that had hung over the place.

"This is bigger than the old kitchen isn't it?" Carlos asked.

"Yup," Paul said. "We decided as long as we were redoing things why not do them right? I got some insurance money to play with and had some put away." He gestured to the spot the old table had stood. "There'll be a bank of windows right here, and a built-in breakfast nook."

Abby's father showed Carlos and Connie around what had once been her childhood home. Even without the walls, she could tell nothing would be the same. Not only would it be more spacious, but it would also have more light, more air, more breathing room.

"So why the expansion?" Connie said. "Are you planning to start a new family?"

Paul grinned at her. They'd become good friends while he'd boarded at her home. He'd left three weeks ago, and now lived in the standing half of the house. A fire cleanup and damage repair company had made it livable, and Abby had set up a makeshift kitchen for him in the old living room. But he still went to Connie's for dinner two or three nights a week. "What can you make in a microwave?" she'd say, her voice filled with disdain, whenever he expressed worry that he was taking advantage.

"Increases the value of the house," Paul said. "Most young couples these days, they want at least three bedrooms. This will technically be four. My office could be converted into, say, a nursery." He didn't look at Abby as he said the words, but she flushed anyway.

"Are you going to have Rosie in once the rooms are built?" Connie asked.

"No. None of that fancy stuff for me. I have my own decorator." He put an arm around Abby's shoulders. "Besides, if I decide not to sell, she'll inherit. Might as well have things the way she likes them."

Abby had been enjoying the rebuilding project, consulting with the contractor, shopping flooring and fixtures, and it surprised her. She was making decisions, and she liked it. Granted choosing kitchen tile wasn't life changing, but it was the kind of thing she would have avoided only months ago.

"You ready?" Carlos stepped close and took her hand.

"Yeah," she said. She'd made other decisions recently, more significant ones, and it was time to see one of them through.

3.7.6

CARLOS STOOD and wiped the dirt from his hands. "It's beautiful," Abby said. The camellia bush already had one white bloom and several buds. The lone flower shone from the shade of the surrounding shrubbery like a full moon in the evening sky.

They stood only feet from Abby's anchorhold on the spot where she'd first seen Hannah. Very few people would understand the flower's significance. There was no plaque, only a small, copper Coptic cross set into a bit of cement near its base. She'd asked Grant Hawthorne for permission to pour the cement and plant the bush as a memorial to the girl who'd lost her life and changed Abby's forever. He'd given it.

He'd been wonderful, even after he learned about Abby's stay in the anchorhold. He'd agreed to keep her secret, as did the police. And he refused to accept her father's resignation. "I don't want this getting out any more than you do," he'd said. "Let's keep it quiet. That way we can both hold on to our jobs."

"I feel like we should say a prayer or something," Abby said.

Carlos took her hand. "That's your department."

Abby closed her eyes and searched for the right words.

"Very nice." A voice interrupted her thoughts. It was Sylla. "Grant Hawthorne told me what you were doing. I came to pay my respects."

Surprised, Abby moved closer to Carlos and made room for the detective to stand next to her. "We were about to say a few words." Sylla came alongside and clasped her hands behind her back.

No one spoke for a long moment, then Abby said, "Father of lights, we know no one is ever truly lost. Your eyes are on the sparrow. Receive Hannah into Your home, we pray. Amen." Carlos and Sylla repeated the amen.

"Hopefully, there's one less ghost at the Mission now." Sylla spoke in her usual brisk fashion, but Abby heard the sadness underlying her words.

Abby looked at the mound of dirt around the base of the new plant. "It's too bad we couldn't bury her ashes."

"We've got to hold her body for another year or so," Sylla said.

"Nobody has claimed her yet?" Carlos asked.

Sylla shook her head. "The picture was the only real thing about that passport. The rest was fabrication. We contacted the Cairo police. They've run the photo through their missing persons database, but they haven't found a match. Not yet. Maybe never will. It seems large numbers of Coptic girls go missing every year. Some end up in forced marriages, some as domestic slaves, some are trafficked to other countries. It's a big problem for the Egyptian government."

The weight of Sylla's words fell heavy in the quiet morning. "The weaker, the poorer, are always preyed upon by the greedy," Abby said.

Sylla met her gaze. "We're doing our best, but sometimes it feels we're trying to bail out the Titanic with a thimble."

"Not here?" Carlos's eyebrows arched. "I mean, that's why my parents immigrated. America, the land of the free and all that."

Sylla gave him a small smile. "Ever been to Beach Boulevard in Anaheim after dark?"

"That's where all the prostitutes hang out?"

"They're far from free."

"It's the oldest profession in the world. I figured it was their choice."

"That's not a profession many people go into willingly. Most are victims of one kind or another."

"How do these guys, like Seb, how do they get away with it?" Carlos said.

"They're smart. They cover their tracks. We know who many of them are, but their victims are too cowed to press charges. We'd had our eye on Seb Skandalis for years. He was slippery."

"I guess that's the one good thing Leena did—getting rid of him," Carlos said.

A shiver traveled up Abby's spine at the mention of Leena's name. "If you knew about Skandalis all along, why did you suspect my dad?"

"I never suspected your father of trafficking," Sylla said. "I thought he might have been a John with a religious mania, like the man who took Elizabeth Smart. We have to follow every lead. Speaking of religious manias." She reached into her jacket pocket and took out a roll of paper.

Abby recognized it at once. It was the pages from her book. The ones she'd given to Sylla. A flush of defensiveness rushed to her cheeks at the words "religious mania." But when she looked at the detective's face, she saw a smile.

"I thought you might want this back." She handed the roll to Abby. "You make some good points. It's interesting."

"Thanks," Abby said.

"It was persuasive, intelligent. Not the writing of a brainwashed proselyte. I was almost certain you and your father had nothing to do with Hannah's death—other than to be in the wrong place at the wrong time—after I read it. You should finish it."

Abby shook her head. She no longer believed her premise—that separating oneself from the world was what led to true objectivity. It wasn't until she'd left the anchorhold and engaged in the battle that she'd gained understanding. Although in some ways she was still recovering from her ordeal, she'd never had more clarity of mind.

She'd fought for her life, for Carlos's life, for her father's life, and in the fighting found strength. She'd looked death in the face and life had fallen into perspective. She no longer feared becoming like her mother. She no longer cared what others thought about her, at least not much. She no longer felt guilt for Scottie's accident. Life and death weren't in her hands, and it was pretty presumptuous for her to have thought they were.

"I have a new idea," she said.

Sylla arched an eyebrow. "I hope this one doesn't include lawbreaking."

Abby laughed. "No, officer. I'm reformed. Believe me." She'd been booked and held for Leena's death until bail was set. Then she'd had to wait almost a month for charges to be dropped while the DA examined the evidence. She'd had enough run-ins with the law to last her a lifetime.

"Good then. I guess I can leave you to it." Sylla saluted and disappeared around the bend of the path. Abby and Carlos cleaned up the garden tools and ran a hose on the new bush before heading toward the exit. "So, what's this new idea?" he said.

"Sailing across the Pacific. Alone. I thought I could record the journey and..."

"It's been done." Carlos's voice broke when he said the words. He sounded so horrified; Abby grinned.

"Kidding." She grasped his arm and leaned onto his shoulder. "Actually, I'm thinking of trying my hand at Middle Grade fiction."

"Kid stuff?"

"Yeah, kid stuff. Sarah Richards, the children's author, did a reading at St. Barnabas for an assembly a few weeks ago. It was wonderful. The kids were riveted. So was I."

"No more anchorites then?"

"Are you joking? Waste all that research?" Carlos furrowed his brow. "Here's the idea: The year is 1500ish. The place, Norwich, England. A young girl's father is cursed by an evil witch and falls into a coma. Colette, the girl, runs to Julian, the local anchorite, and begs for a solution. Julian tells her the only thing that will cure her father is holy water from Westminister Abby, then the Church of St. Peter in Westminster."

"How far away is London?"

"A hundred and seventeen miles. But Julian sends her to another anchorhold along the way, and that anchorite sends her to the next. The little girl travels across England going from anchorhold to anchorhold. She learns the story of each anchorite, and they give her relics and say special prayers to help her with her quest."

"Is that the way it was? Were the anchorholds laid out like the California missions? Each a day's ride from the next?"

"No, I got that from California history. But I plan to blend in stories from anchorites who lived at different times and in different countries. It's fantasy. A quest story with a bit of history thrown in. I might even have her meet a dragon. I like dragons."

Carlos took her hand. "I think it's a great idea."

"I thought you might."

"You're good with kids."

"I am." The new, reformed Abby was learning to accept praise.

"You'll be a good mother someday," Carlos said, playing with the ring on her left hand.

"I think I will be too," she said.

MOLLY: As sweet as that last scene was, I happen to know that Abby never wrote that book. She and Carlos did marry, and she's expecting their first child. However, instead of writing children's books, Abby has turned her attention to true crime.

She saw the same connection I saw between the stories we are covering in *Murders Under the Sun*. Which leads me to an announcement. After I interviewed her for this season, we decided to collaborate. We'll be sharing research material. The podcast has become so popular, thanks to you all, I need the help. And Abby is planning to write a book on the crimes after Season Seven is released.

She is also helping me look into the missing CSU-Fullerton student mystery. In fact, she actually came up with an interesting piece of information. Camilla Jimenez told Abby she received an insurance check about six months after her son went missing. She had no idea her son had a life insurance policy.

At the time, she didn't think much of it. She was in a state of shock and wasn't thinking clearly. She assumed it had something to do with the school. Kind of like a big "I'm sorry" from the state. In retrospect, however, it seemed odd. The state doesn't send money to people willy-nilly. And how many 20-year-olds are responsible enough to take out life insurance policies?

I agree with Camilla. This is strange. Really strange. Insurance companies don't cover missing people. In my experience, most insurance companies are in the business of taking your money, then trying to figure out how not to pay you when you try to collect.

We're not sure if this is relevant, but during the season break we'll poke around and see if we can come up with more.

On another topic, several of you emailed me this week to ask what comes next. Who, from this season's cast of characters, will be featured in Season Four?

Let me give you some background before I answer that question. Next season is entitled *The Tower*. This is the nickname for an intimidatingly large, stone house in Laguna Beach on Cliff Drive. If the name of the street rings a bell, that's because the Tower is only a block and a half away from the Cliff House, the setting of the Real Estate Killer's crimes in Season One.

In fact, this is how I first made the connection between the stories I'm reporting on. When news of what happened at the Tower came across my desk, the street name pinged in my memory. Could it be a coincidence that two such strange crimes took place on the same street? It seemed unlikely. The more I dug, the more connections I saw. It was as if a spider spooled out her silk from the Cliff House, and anyone who got too close was caught in the web.

Next season, you'll hear about an author with a uniquely terrible problem. You may already know his name. Jacob Rinehart is a popular horror writer, a household name. However, several years ago, a body was found in a park. The victim had been murdered and mutilated in the same manner as the victims in his latest book. The corpse was actually posed with a copy of *Pillory*—the book in question.

The publicity was overwhelming, and Jacob, being an introvert, needed to escape. So, he left his hometown of Seattle and secretly bought a house in Laguna Beach. It needed a remodel. Who do you think he hired?

If you guessed Rosie Ring, the interior designer who worked with Mimi this season, you'd be correct. The ever-increasing pond circles envelope Rosie next.

One more thing before I sign off, if you haven't picked up a free digital copy of *The Dark Room* yet, why not? As I mentioned in Episode Two, some believe that story is the genesis of every crime I'll be reporting on.

That's it for Season Three, *The Hiding Place*. Join me next season for more *Murders Under the Sun*.

(cue music)

VO: If you enjoyed this episode, please leave us a five-star review on your favorite podcast service—it really helps. *Murders Under the Sun* is edited by Jim Wilbourne, theme music is by Eclectic Blends, and I'm your host, Molly Shure.

Get your free digital copy of *The Dark Room* at
https://bookhip.com/ZQMTCLP

If you enjoyed this book, please do one or more of the following:

- Leave a review on your favorite book review site
- Tell a friend about the *An Almost True Crime Story* series
- Ask your local library to put Greta Boris's work on the shelf
- Recommend Fawkes Press books to your local bookstore

VISIT US ONLINE
www.FawkesPress.com
www.GretaBoris.com

FAWKES PRESS

also by greta boris

An Almost True Crime Story:

The Cliff House

The Garden

The Hiding Place

The Tower

The Keep

The Manor

The Cabin

The Mortician Mysteries:

To Dye For

Mortuary School

Hair Today, Gone Tomorrow

Bald-Headed Lies

A Permanent Solution

Buzz Cut

Splitting Hairs

www.ingramcontent.com/pod-product-compliance
Lightning Source LLC
Chambersburg PA
CBHW061639190726
48289CB00006B/1661